RANDOM ACTS OF MALICE

Holly Anna Paladin
Mysteries,
Book 3

by Christy Barritt

Random Acts of Malice: A Novel
Copyright 2015 by Christy Barritt

Published by River Heights Press

Cover design by The Killion Group

CHAPTER 1

"Holly, I have to go somewhere and do something."

I stared at Chase Dexter, my boyfriend of almost nine months, and the love of my life. He'd called me a couple of hours ago and asked if he could come over after he finished working a homicide.

As Ella Fitzgerald sang "Someone to Watch Over Me" in the background, I thought about the perfect evening I'd planned for Chase and me. After church today, I'd even baked two of Chase's favorite desserts: chocolate chip cookies and a toffee poke cake. I couldn't decide which, so I'd made them both.

I'd pictured Chase coming inside. I'd take his jacket and encourage him to relax for a few minutes. After coffee and dessert, we'd cuddle on the couch and maybe watch *An Affair to Remember* if I got to choose, *Dragnet* if Chase picked.

But something was wrong right now, and it caused all the plans I'd had for tonight to disappear faster than a rainbow on a cloudy day. I shifted, the motion causing my black-and-white skirt to flutter around my knees as I tried to pinpoint what exactly had made me feel uneasy. Maybe it was the uncertainty that had lingered in Chase's words—his very vague words.

Somewhere. Something.

What did that mean?

Right now, Chase's sleeves were rolled up and his tie dangled around his neck like a noose. He looked especially tired, and I wondered about his day. Maybe the homicide investigation hadn't been closed as he'd hoped. Or maybe another crime had occurred, one that had gotten to him in a bad way. Either way, his face looked grim with masked emotions.

But there was more to this than professional stress.

Usually the two of us were like giddy teenagers in love around each other. We were always holding hands, or poking each other in the ribs, or sitting close enough for our arms to brush.

Except at this very moment.

Chase's hands were at his sides as we stood across from each other in the formal living room of my mom's *Better Homes and Gardens* house. Darkness yawned outside, and the only light in the room was the soft glow of a table lamp. He was distancing himself from me, I realized.

"You have to go somewhere?" I finally asked, pushing a wide curl behind my ear. "You mean, like, the grocery store for some milk?"

I knew I was downplaying what he'd said, but I was the eternal optimist.

"No, not exactly." He paused, his stiff stance growing more pronounced by the moment. "I've taken two weeks' vacation from work."

I blinked in surprise, the best-case scenarios slowly disappearing from my thoughts as his aloofness remained. "Two weeks? Is there some kind of emergency?"

Chase hadn't held his position as detective for even a year, and he was conscientious about making a good impression as one of the new guys on the force. This just didn't seem like him, especially since he hadn't mentioned anything about it in our past conversations.

"I wish I could tell you more, Holly, but I can't." His eyes looked apologetic as the skin around them crinkled on the corners. He started to reach for me but abruptly dropped his hand.

My heart lurched. Something was seriously wrong, and no amount of lightheartedness could make this better. Not even a chocolate cake could fix whatever was going on, and usually chocolate cake could fix anything. Well, cake and prayer.

My thoughts quickly zoomed back to the present. "All you can say is, 'I wish I could tell you more, but I can't'? Don't I deserve a little more of an explanation than that?"

"You do." Chase's voice cracked as the agony in his eyes deepened. "I know this doesn't make sense."

That was an understatement. But I tried to give Chase and this situation the benefit of the doubt and keep a cool head. I had to focus on the facts and not my spinning emotions. My emotions told me that I should freak out and let worry consume me. The facts . . . well, I didn't have any of the facts right now.

Lord, give me a level head. I beg You to slather Your wisdom on every part of my being at the moment.

I licked my lips, trying not to seem like a control freak. "Where are you going? Can you tell me that?"

Chase looked away. The motion was subtle—I'd almost missed it. But he'd definitely averted his gaze. That was never a good sign.

Oh, what I would do at the moment not to know that averted gazes happened before deceit. To forget my training as a counselor. To pretend like I didn't know how to read people.

"I can't say, Holly."

Chase's cell phone began beeping on his belt. With each notification, his muscles seemed to tighten. He didn't bother to look at the screen or see who was calling.

I nodded slowly as I processed our conversation—both the verbal and the nonverbal. I wanted to respect Chase's boundaries, but I didn't want to be walked on. If he left and I had no answers for two weeks, I would go out of my mind.

Relationships ended all the time because of poor communication. That's why I needed to speak my mind—gently and respectfully, of course. "I'm going to be honest here, Chase. This is all leaving me uncomfortable. I didn't think we kept secrets from each other."

"We don't."

I let my head drop toward my shoulder. "Then what do you call this?"

His eyes pleaded with me. "You just have to trust me."

I crossed my arms, trying to separate myself from the hurt that seemed inevitable. "Is this a police thing?"

That would make sense, but not in conjunction with vacation time. Unless that was just a cover. But I just couldn't believe there were no other details Chase could give me if that was the case. He could at least *hint* that he was going undercover.

Chase's eyes implored me, losing some of the ambiguity for a moment. "You trust me, right? Tell me you trust me."

Up until this moment, I'd undoubtedly trusted him. But now a smidgen of uncertainty had crept in. The two of us had been through mountains and valleys since we'd been together, and Chase had only proven himself trustworthy. Most relationships wouldn't survive what we'd endured, and we'd only come out stronger.

"I feel like you're pushing me out," I finally told him. "Maybe I'm reading too much into things, but my gut is telling me something's seriously wrong."

He remained silent.

My gut dropped. All my fears—the ones I tried to tell myself were irrational—weren't actually that irrational. Whatever he was hiding, it was big. Serious. Maybe even life changing.

I pulled myself together, even though my insides were a tousled mess. My words sounded as stiff as my spine felt when I said, "When are you leaving?"

"Tonight."

I forced myself to nod, even though the fact he was leaving past eleven indicated this matter was urgent. "Okay."

He leaned down, and his lips lingered against mine. The action was subdued yet passionate. It made a statement without saying a word.

Almost like he was saying good-bye.

My heart lurched again.

"Good night, Holly." His hands slipped from my shoulders.

Somehow that moment seemed symbolic, like the bond that pulled us together had been ruptured. I hoped I was reading too much into things. I prayed I was.

"Good night, Chase."

As he walked away, I feared I might never see him again. His secret had forged a barrier between us. And the next two weeks would determine if that divide grew stronger or if it diminished.

***

Monday and most of Tuesday had passed, and my head had been in an entrenching fog. I'd somehow gotten through work. I'd volunteered at the local youth shelter. I'd gone to a task force meeting. I'd baked cakes for four different people—two coworkers, a neighbor, and a woman at church who'd just had surgery.

My thoughts always seemed preoccupied, though, no

matter how busy I kept myself. I couldn't stop thinking about Chase and his secret.

Something was wrong. Something in my relationship with Chase was on the cusp of change, at the edge of a turning point. Eleven more days felt like a long time to figure out what.

"You still haven't heard from Chase, have you?"

I snapped my focus back to my best friend, Jamie. She stared at me from across the table at our favorite pizza place. Actually, it was *her* favorite pizza place, but I came here because it was one of the few restaurants where my gluten-free, grain-free, sugar-free friend could eat. We met here almost every Tuesday.

Last time we'd been here, the waitress had actually brought Jamie a glass of water with apple-cider vinegar already spritzed inside. Jamie claimed it helped cleanse her system and keep her trim. I didn't question her. She had lost more than one hundred pounds and seemed healthier and more vibrant than ever.

During the forty minutes we'd been here, I hadn't said a word about Chase. Yet somehow Jamie had known what was wrong. Maybe she'd seen my preoccupation or sensed my heaviness. Best friends were good for things like that.

I pushed my plate of pizza across the booth, realizing my appetite was completely gone, and shook my head. "Not a word."

My friend leaned closer, her normally cheery face filled with the subtle signs of worry. "He said he'd be gone a couple of weeks. It's only been a couple of days."

I forced myself to nod, hating how melancholy I felt. I wanted to be strong and unaffected, but love often didn't work that way. As much as I tried to wrangle my emotions to the place where I wanted them, I failed.

"You're right," I said. "It has only been two days."

"It's probably nothing." Jamie's springy curls bounced out from around her face in a way that made her look ever cheerful.

She was trying to make me believe I was reading too much into things, I realized. But I knew my friend better than that. She rarely took things at face value, which made her a great reporter but, at times, a frustrating conversationalist.

"Things clothed in this much secrecy are hardly ever nothing." I wished the happy music playing on the overhead would go away. "Uptown Funk" clashed too much with my gloomy thoughts. "Otherwise, they wouldn't be a secret."

She twisted her lips, which were red rimmed with neglected lipstick. "True that. But Chase loves you. You can't deny he cares about you."

"What possible reason could Chase have for not being able to share even one little detail with me?"

"It's probably an undercover sting," Jamie offered.

"Then why did he have to take vacation time?"

She pressed her lips together. "Maybe that was just a cover."

"Maybe, but he should have been able to hint at that."

She shifted, still staring me in the eye. "You've got to think of it this way: he didn't want to lie to you. That's a good thing. He could have easily made up an excuse so you wouldn't be in this position right now. But honesty is important to him."

I hadn't considered that. It *would* have been easy to outright lie in order to stop me from asking questions.

"So you should just chill for a while," Jamie continued. "Trust Chase. Give him space to do whatever it is he has to do. Another eleven days and he'll be back, you'll have a good laugh, and this will go down as another memory of the time you stressed out more than you needed."

I shifted in my seat and leaned toward her, lowering my

voice so no one else would hear what I said next. I prefaced it with "I don't want to be one of those girlfriends. You know—the clingy, insecure ones. I like being strong and independent."

"You're not insecure. You're worried and rightfully so."

"I'm afraid he's in trouble, Jamie."

"Trouble?" She quirked an eyebrow.

"It's the only thing I can think of. It's the only reason I can imagine he would act like this."

"What kind of trouble?"

I pressed my lips together, hesitating to admit what I'd done. After all, I'd been trying to stay strong, to not be neurotic but to respect boundaries. I'd taught people to respect boundaries all the time in my former career as a social worker. It seemed like a shame if I couldn't follow my own advice.

Not to mention I would be showing a total lack of manners. *Pretty is as pretty does.* Being clingy, untrusting, and insecure was *not* pretty.

Finally, I sucked in a deep breath and plunged ahead. "So, after a few of the events of the last year, Chase and I thought it would be a good idea to install one of those apps on our phones, the ones where we can track each other. It was purely a safety thing, not like a weird we-want-to-stalk-each-other thing."

Half of her lip curled. "Sure it was. I know you guys can't keep your eyes off each other."

My cheeks heated. "Anyway, I may have checked my phone yesterday."

A full, satisfied smile replaced the lip curl, and Jamie angled her head as if impressed. "Really? Seems kind of devious for good-girl Holly Paladin."

I shrugged, feeling a little guilty at what I'd done, even if Chase knew I had the app on my phone. "What can I say? Even I have my moments."

Jamie's insatiable appetite for a good story ignited a fire in her eyes. She pulled one side of her lips back in a sassy urban manner. Sometimes she even broke out in the Z-shaped finger snap that ended with a hand on her hip. I called that move "the Diva." "So, spill it. What did you discover while stalking your boyfriend?"

I lowered my voice. "He was at a racetrack."

Jamie narrowed her eyes. "Like, he's doing a marathon?"

I shook my head, wishing it were that easy. "No, like he's near Louisville at a horse-racing facility. Wyndmyer Park, to be exact."

Jamie twisted her head again, this time with inquisitiveness. "You think he's into gambling?"

"I have no idea. I didn't think he gambled. It's never come up in conversation."

She leaned back, looking deep in thought with her hyperfocused gaze and her fingers laced together in front of her. "He used to have a drinking problem, right? Don't these things go hand in hand?"

My stomach clenched at the thought. Was Chase hiding a demon like that from me? Did he not realize that I'd be willing to help him? That I'd still be there for him? That thought hurt in a different way than his deception. "As addictions go, the two are related."

"I just can't see it, Holly." Jamie shook her head, her orange dangly earrings slapping her cheeks. "I don't see him betting his hard-earned cash. I thought he was saving up so he could buy you a ring. This doesn't fit."

I leaned back, trying to deny my conclusions. But I couldn't hold my thoughts back any longer. I needed feedback. "I knew this woman once, Jamie. We went to church together, and she

11

was married to the perfect man. I mean, seriously, he seemed like the ideal spouse. He was polite and funny and always said the right thing. Together, this couple was like Barbie and Ken."

"I'm assuming you're going somewhere with this?"

"It turns out the husband was producing pornography. Even more sadly, he'd been doing it for years without being discovered. No one had a clue."

Jamie gasped. "You think Chase is producing—"

I raised a hand to halt her thought.

"No, no, no." Each "no" had a different emotion behind it. Surprise. Embarrassment. Conviction. "No on so many levels. Maybe that was a bad illustration. The point is that no one really knew this man. He had this entirely different life that he hid, and he hid it well. No one saw through his perfectly crafted facades."

Jamie squinted and assumed her counselor position again— only this time she tilted her head analytically. "I thought you trusted Chase, Holly."

"Can you ever completely trust anyone?"

She glanced at her watch and then stood, tapping her foot. "Come on."

"Come on where?" I had no idea where she was going with this.

"There's only one way to solve this. We're going to Louisville. Admit it: you're chomping at the bit to get answers."

I groaned. "Chomping at the bit?"

"Smart money says we should check things out."

I didn't even bother to respond, lest she spout more racing expressions. I grabbed my purse and pushed aside my doubts.

And with that . . . we were off.

CHAPTER 2

We found a parking space in the massive lot outside the arena-like racetrack. Cars were neatly arranged in rows for as far as I could see. Bright lights illuminated the track beyond the stands, and I could hear an announcer speaking to the crowds.

Before we got out of the van, I reached behind me and pulled out a wide-brimmed hat I'd grabbed before I left home. I placed it on my head, even though it was almost too big to wear in the van. The edges hit the seat behind me and the window beside me and nearly took out Jamie's eyes.

"What are you doing? This isn't Churchill Downs or the Kentucky Derby." Jamie had that incredulous, diva-like look on her face.

I pulled the brim lower, hoping to make the hat sit even on my head. I wished I had a mirror to double-check. "Oh, come on. When else will I have a chance to wear this?"

She stared at my black hat and raised an eyebrow. "A funeral, maybe?"

I scowled, figuring if anyone would understand my dilemma, it would be Jamie. "This will help conceal my face. I don't want Chase to recognize me."

"And you think *that's* not going to draw attention?" She dropped her head, but her eyes remained on me in the sassy urban manner I loved her for.

She acted as if I was wearing a sombrero and flamingo feathers. I was halfway insulted, but I pushed past it. "Well . . .

13

it's the best I can do at the moment. What do you want me to do? Wear a baseball cap with this outfit?"

The black scoop-neck dress with the flared skirt was feminine. My oversized hat would match it perfectly.

"More power to you. These *are* your monkeys, and this *is* your circus." She wrapped a scarf around her head several times and subdued her curly semi-afro.

"My life is a three-ring show. What can I say?" I placed my sunglasses over my eyes.

"Sunglasses too? It's dark outside." Jamie gave me an exasperated half-Diva.

I shrugged, finally owning up to the fact that my outfit might be over the top. I hadn't had much time to plan, though. We'd swung by my house before we left, and I grabbed the first things I could think of. "Okay, I know it's a bit much. But a girl's gotta do what a girl's gotta do."

We climbed from the van, and as soon as my heels hit the asphalt, I shivered. It wasn't cold for the September night. My shiver came from somewhere internal. I really hoped this didn't all blow up. I hadn't had much luck with things not blowing up, however.

I'd learned the hard way that good intentions paved the path to . . . trouble. Lots of trouble.

My anticipation grew with each step. I glanced at the entryway to Wyndmyer and sucked in a breath as I tried to brace myself. A huge set of steps led to a third-floor entrance. "Wyndmyer Park" was displayed in large letters above the entryway, along with the silhouettes of two running horses.

Stone benches were located along the edges of the long walk toward the steps. Despite the grandiose entrance, the walls of the building appeared to be metal with the color fading. Landscaping looked to be neglected with weeds overgrowing the beds around saplings. It was almost as if the glory days of this place had passed.

As we stepped inside the building, I pulled my hat lower and scanned my surroundings for the first time. It reminded me a bit of a baseball stadium, only a little more upper class. TV screens graced various walls, broadcasting the race to those inside, an announcer blared from the overhead, and people chattered in the stands. Several machines where people could place their bets stood strategically along the walls.

Though it might initially seem similar to a baseball game, it smelled nothing like one. It smelled like animals and dirt. At the moment, it also smelled like sewage, thanks to the nearby restrooms.

There appeared to be three levels of seating—the nosebleed area on the dirt right next to the track, midlevel seats with narrow tables running across them, and another area that offered box seats and club seating.

Three levels? I mentally sighed. How was I ever going to find Chase? My app would only show me his general location. I was on my own from here out.

As we strolled along the deck, I kept my motions cautious and subtle. There was no need to draw any more attention to ourselves than my hat was already drawing. We paused and took a moment to gather our surroundings.

"There are a lot of people here, Jamie," I whispered, feeling a bit like a spy. "This will be like finding the proverbial needle in the haystack."

"If the Navy SEALs can smoke out bin Laden, we can find Chase."

I blinked, certain I hadn't heard her correctly. "The Navy SEALs? You know we're nothing like special ops, rights?"

"Oh, I'm special all right, and this is what I call an

opportunity like no other." She grabbed my arm and pulled me toward the stands. "Come on."

My heart pounded in my chest with each step. If Chase was here, I prayed that he didn't spot me. I didn't even have a good excuse. What would I tell him?

I was following you on my Friend Finder app.

Fancy running into you here. Who would have thought?

You forgot the cookies and cake I baked you on Sunday. I wanted to bring them to you before they went to waste.

I'd sound desperate. Maybe I *was* desperate, though.

Jamie and I found two empty seats midlevel. We'd apparently arrived just in time, because all around us, people cheered and drank and waved wagers in their hands. In the distance, horses, lean and muscular, sprinted around the track. Small, trim-looking jockeys perched atop them, appearing more like plastic figurines than real people.

"You see him yet?" Jamie whispered, leaning closer.

I scanned the people around me. Chase was hard to miss. I just had to look for Thor's clean-cut twin brother. "No, I don't see him yet. It's going to take a while, though."

"Besides, maybe he's . . . volunteering with underprivileged children at a charity event," Jamie continued, sounding dead serious.

"He'd have no reason not to tell me that."

"Oh . . . maybe one of the underprivileged kids is his!" She said it like she'd struck gold.

I cut a glance at her. "Is that supposed to make me feel better?"

She frowned, all signs of self-proclaimed brilliance gone. "I suppose not."

"Maybe we shouldn't be here," I finally muttered. "This seems so invasive."

"Just taking a look won't do any harm."

"That's what David said when he spotted Bathsheba on the rooftop."

Her lips formed an O. "True that. I say we stay here a few more minutes and then we can walk around again. We've got a lot of ground to cover."

"That sounds good to me." I didn't have any better ideas, so I didn't argue. This whole stalking thing was new to me.

The minutes passed slowly. I felt out of my element here. I wanted to leave. I wanted to stay. I wanted answers. I didn't want answers.

One thing was certain: from where I was sitting, there was no sign of Chase.

I nudged Jamie, and we stood. We walked to the back, where a deck surrounded the complex. My gaze continually roamed the area and searched faces.

I saw rich-looking businessmen. I saw people who looked—and smelled—drunk. I saw women laughing with fruity drinks in their hands.

Whom I didn't see was Chase.

Jamie and I walked each level. We walked from side to side across the back of the decks. We stood at the front of the stands and scanned the crowds.

Chase was nowhere to be seen.

It was getting late.

And this trip had been futile.

We paused near the entrance, and we both realized there was nothing else we could do here.

"I'd hoped we might find some answers and put your worries at ease," Jamie said. "I'm sorry."

"We tried. That's all we can do."

My fears hadn't been alleviated. But the good news was

that we hadn't discovered anything life-changingly bad either. Maybe God had been protecting me.

As we started back to Jamie's van, I braced myself for the ride back to Cincinnati. The trip here had taken a long time, but the journey home would seem even longer. My questions still mocked me. Despite that, I was going to have to pull myself together and move on. I supposed I'd find out in eleven days what was going on.

I hoped.

We'd parked out in the far end of the parking lot, near the stables adjacent to the track. There were several large RVs and trailers in this area. Maybe they belonged to workers or jockeys. I had no idea. Thankfully the lot was well lit.

We rounded one of those trailers when something caught my eye. I grabbed Jamie and pulled her behind the trailer.

"What are you—?"

I silenced her and pointed toward the distance. I could hardly believe my eyes. "Jamie, it's . . . Chase."

She followed my gaze. "Jackpot!"

Sure enough, Chase walked out of a back gate. He was dressed casually, wearing jeans and a henley. Not his typical work attire of dress slacks, a button-up shirt, and a tie.

There was one other thing: he wasn't alone.

"Who's that with him?" Jamie asked, squinting at the person beside him.

I stared at the stunning brunette and frowned. "That's his ex-wife."

CHAPTER 3

"*She's* his ex?" Jamie's eyes were fixed on the woman in the distance as if her favorite movie star had just stepped into the lot.

"Unfortunately." I frowned. Peyton was as beautiful as I'd imagined. The cheerleader. The girl every guy wanted to date. The head turner.

Not to mention she was the woman who'd stolen Chase's heart and crushed it into a million pieces when she left him behind like a limp horse at the meat factory.

The woman was gorgeous—had I mentioned that?—with glossy brown hair that cascaded around her shoulders. She was thin with just enough padding in the right places. Her face was flawless, the kind that made the front page of beauty magazines for its perfection.

Remaining behind the trailer, my hand pressed into the cold metal. I kept my eyes on the two of them. They strolled side by side, a hushed, seemingly pleasant conversation between them, before finally stopping by an oversized black truck.

"Whose truck is that?" Jamie leaned over me, trying to watch also.

"Peyton's, I guess. It's not Chase's." I continued to watch as Peyton leaned against the door, her hands shoved into the pockets of her second-skin jeans. Chase lingered in front of her, listening as she said something.

The conversation looked serious, based on the way they

leaned together and the manner in which Peyton continually glanced around. Chase's shoulders were tight, just as they'd been when I saw him on Sunday.

Based on their body language, I tried to form a conclusion about what was going on. I failed. All I could think was that they were getting back together. Then it would make perfect sense why Chase couldn't tell me any details.

"How do you know that's his ex?" Jamie backed up and gave me space to answer.

I continued to stare, just waiting for Chase to lean toward Peyton and plant a kiss on her lips. The thought made me want to hurl. Betrayal was an ugly beast. I'd never had to deal with it before. Not on this scale at least.

"I've seen pictures of her," I told Jamie.

"Chase showed you pictures of his ex-wife?" Her voice rose with agitated disbelief.

"No, of course not. I found her on Facebook."

"You looked her up on Facebook?" Jamie's voice rose even higher in pitch.

I shushed her before scowling. Honestly, I couldn't own up to it at the moment. It sounded desperate. I'd never been desperate. I'd been content in my singleness. In my poorness. Even in the face of death. But my boyfriend went off the grid and I lost it? I go all Navy SEAL and try to track him like a terrorist.

I needed serious help.

"I'm not really in the mood to have this conversation now," I finally said. "I just want to see what happens."

She raised her hands in surrender. "I'm not judging. Just surprised. What's Miss Manners say about Facebook stalking?"

"I'm not stalking. And Facebook, thankfully, wasn't around when those etiquette books were published. Besides, that doesn't matter right now. There are bigger issues at stake. Like: Why couldn't Chase tell me he was meeting her? There's only one reason that makes sense."

Nausea now roiled in my gut with more intensity. I hoped I didn't get sick. I had a tendency to hurl when I got stressed. And I felt stressed right now. Really stressed.

"Don't think the worst."

"Too late." I frowned, wishing Chase had just told me instead of sneaking around behind my back.

Life was simpler before the Internet, I decided. Before Facebook could connect ex-sweethearts. When friendships happened face-to-face. When relationships were formed on front porches and not on websites.

If it hadn't been for that stupid app, I would have never known where Chase was. I would have been left to wonder, been forced to be submissive to my patience.

Instead, technology had led me here, and I'd followed like a dog looking for a bone.

This wasn't the way relationships were supposed to work.

Forgive me, I silently prayed.

Holly Anna Paladin, the girl who yearned to be born in a different generation when ladies had been ladylike and men had been gentlemen. When life was slower and less complicated. I'd succumbed to everything I hated.

"Look, she's leaving!" Jamie nudged me.

I watched as Peyton climbed into her truck. I held my breath, waiting for confirmation they were back together. But Chase didn't lean in to kiss her good-bye. Instead, he shut her door and waved. He tapped the side of the truck as she backed out.

I sank farther into the shadows as Chase started away from the truck.

"Where's he going?" I whispered.

"To his Jeep. He's in."

I tried to formulate what to do next. Just leaving would be the simple thing. But my curiosity had taken me hostage. I wanted answers. I *needed* them.

"We don't have time to get back to your van and follow him," I muttered.

"We don't have to. We can use the app that led us here in the first place, Sherlock."

I smiled at Jamie's reminder. Hers seemed much better than my idea of madly dashing after him. Maybe technology did have a few advantages. At least for the moment, I wanted to put my old-fashioned manners behind me. "Good point. What are we waiting for?"

***

Twenty-three minutes later, Jamie and I pulled to a stop in front of an apartment complex. Chase's Jeep was there in a space between other cars. Chase must have gone inside one of the six oversized buildings.

But I had no idea which one.

I stared at one of the contemporary structures, which appeared well kept. Vinyl siding covered the outer walls, but the sturdy-looking balconies and neatly trimmed landscape probably came at a cost. The patches of grass around the buildings were so small they were practically accessories. There was even a pond at the center of the complex with a fountain in the middle. The only thing missing was a gated entrance.

Did Peyton live here? I didn't see her truck, but that didn't mean anything.

"There's not much else we can do here." Jamie sat in the

driver's seat, headlights dimmed and gaze fixed out the window. A certain melancholy had fallen over both of us.

I didn't know what I expected, but more than this, for sure.

I glanced at the clock. "It's already past ten. It's going to feel really early when I have to get up for work tomorrow."

"Tell me about it." She frowned, her expression barely visible except for the parking lot light overhead that scattered just enough brightness through the dark. "Are you sorry we came?"

I thought about it a moment, weighing my response and plunging into those gray areas of contemplation. "No. I want to know the truth . . . I think. It's confusing."

"Just remember that you still don't *have* the truth. You're operating under assumptions right now."

"And now I have to live with this knowledge until Chase returns home in a week and a half." I shook my head, beyond flabbergasted with myself. "I should have just let this go from the start. That's what normal people would do. I've propelled myself into the upper echelons of psychos and obsessive, clingy women."

"*I* know you don't belong there."

"No one thinks they belong there. That's what makes them unstable."

"Don't be ridiculous." Jamie brushed off my neurotic rant. "You're the most stable person I know."

"Then what am I doing here? This is the kind of thing that ends up on those *Forensic Files* type of shows. And this is precisely why it's a bad idea to be led by emotion. I'm everything I counsel people not to be."

"You're going overboard." She nudged me, her gaze fixated on something in the distance. "Check out that van."

I followed her gaze and saw a black van with tinted

windows creeping through the apartment lot. Something seemed off about the vehicle. I couldn't pinpoint what exactly.

Maybe it was the van's pace. Maybe it was the dents and dirt. Maybe it was the way it seemed out of place in the sea of foreign vehicles parked at the upper-class complex. Besides, wasn't there always something creepy about old panel vans with no windows in the back?

"It's stopping by Chase's Jeep." I sat up straighter and unable to believe my eyes. This whole situation was getting stranger by the moment.

I really should have kept my nose out of this. That was becoming staggeringly clear.

I gripped the seat as I waited for whatever might happen next.

A man hopped out of the passenger seat. He wore black, all the way from his feet to the knit hat on his head. The darkness prevented me from making out any of his features. I was 95 percent sure he was white and around six feet tall.

He squatted beside Chase's Jeep, just out of sight.

"What's he doing?" Jamie craned her neck, trying to get a better look.

"If I had to guess—something not good," I mumbled, my eyes glued to the scene.

A couple of moments later, the man rushed back to the van, hopped inside, and pulled away. Well, kind of pulled away.

The driver actually backed in at the rear of the lot, near the woods surrounding the complex. The van stayed there for several minutes. But nothing happened. No one opened the side doors.

Was the driver waiting to see something play out? The scenario didn't add up in my head.

"What in the world are they doing?" Jamie asked.

I shook my head. "It's almost like they want front-row seats for something."

Did it tie in with whatever they'd been doing by Chase's Jeep?

I couldn't see the van well. It was directly in front of me, so I really only had a view of the vehicle's front bumper. The tinted windows blocked whatever was happening inside from my sight.

Finally, a couple of minutes later, the van slowly pulled away.

I glanced at Jamie, unsure of exactly what had just happened. Her nose and forehead were scrunched, mirroring my own confusion.

"That was weird," she muttered. "Should we follow them?"

"It's unclear at the moment."

She tapped her fingers against the steering wheel, her forehead still wrinkled. "I'm more concerned with making sure that Chase doesn't get in his Jeep."

That Chase doesn't get in his Jeep? It took me a moment before I realized her implications and gasped. "You think it's a bomb?"

"I have no idea, but those guys were up to something no good."

In a *movie*, I could see a bomb being planted in a situation like this. But in real life that scenario seemed so dramatic and unlikely.

I pressed my lips together in contemplation. I had to take action here. "I should call Chase and admit everything."

"Only if you want him to think you're a crazy stalker. And that you have no manners."

Jamie knew how to hit me where it hurt. No manners? I had some pride left.

I scowled. "What's your idea, Ms. Smarty Pants?"

"We call the police. Anonymously. Then we wait here and make sure Chase doesn't try to get inside his Jeep before the cops get here."

That seemed so drastic. Maybe we were reading too much into things, and there was some kind of alternative here. A happy medium between the extremes.

"Maybe we should go check Chase's Jeep first," I said. "I mean, what if it's a . . . puppy or something."

"A puppy?" Jamie gave me the stupid stare. "Really?"

I threw my hands in the air, knowing good and well I was having a rose-colored-glasses moment. "I don't know. I'm just trying to look at all the possibilities. If it's a . . . puppy—"

Jamie gave me the stupid look again.

I ignored her. "We walk away. But if it's anything remotely dangerous, we call the police. Deal?"

Jamie nodded. "Deal."

My hands trembled as I pushed the door open. Puppies were much nicer to think about than bombs. The truth was whatever had been left was probably something in between a puppy and a bomb—something like a note or flyer.

Or maybe nothing had been left at all. Maybe the tires had been slashed or the man had messed with the brake line. The nefarious possibilities seemed endless.

Staying low, we hurried through the parking lot. My legs strained from rushing forward in a hunched position, but I couldn't risk being seen. As we neared Chase's Jeep, I glanced behind me in time to see Chase emerge from the building.

I gulped.

He was far enough away that he probably hadn't spotted us. But he was walking toward his Jeep. Toward us.

"Chase is coming out." I pointed to his figure in the distance before grabbing Jamie's hand. With more strength than I realized I possessed, I tugged her. Panic nearly engulfed me. "Come on!"

We rushed toward the woods just beyond the parking lot. I ducked low, desperate not to be seen. Jamie's van would have been a better choice for us to stay concealed, but it was too far away.

I was also desperate for Chase not to get into his Jeep, just in case those men had done something.

Puppy. Please let it be a puppy.

"What now?" Jamie asked. "He's going to his Jeep. *Tick tick tick tick.*"

"It's not a bomb." I said each word slowly, carefully, desperate to believe them myself.

"This is where some Navy SEAL training would help."

"What is it with you and Navy SEALs today?"

"I watched *American Sniper*, and I'm fascinated. What can I say?"

I needed a plan, and I needed it five minutes ago. I looked at the ground, careful to stay behind the tree. A rock caught my eye. Scooping it up, I threw it across the parking lot. I held my breath until I heard the stone *ding* against a hubcap in the distance.

Chase paused midstep and turned. He surveyed the dark parking lot a moment before starting to walk again. I found another rock and threw it also.

He stopped again.

"You're better at this spy thing than I thought," Jamie whispered.

"I had to distract him. What else am I supposed to do?"

Chase studied his surroundings, his stance stiff and on guard. "Who's there? Is it you, Larry?"

Larry? Who was Larry?

He started walking away from us, toward the sound, then paused. He turned in our direction.

He suspected someone was trying to redirect him! Of course. He wasn't a dummy.

Heat tinged my skin as panic rose in me. Thankfully, just at that moment, a car pulled to a stop near Chase. A single light was atop it, whirling silently.

An unmarked police cruiser, I presumed.

Chase gave one last look in our direction before turning toward the person who stepped out from the driver's seat. I could barely make out a man of medium build and height. He appeared to be mostly bald with pricks of shaved hair along the edge of his head. His plain clothes led me to believe he was a detective.

"Chase Dexter?" the man said. "It's been a long time."

Chase squinted. "Victor Rollins? No way. It has been a long time. I didn't think you were around here anymore."

"Well, I turned things around and got me a job here, not far from our old stomping grounds. I figured if you could do a 360, anyone could."

"I'm glad to hear it," Chase said. "Our mistakes are nothing if not an example for others of what not to do."

His words didn't sound full of guilt or regret. I didn't have time to analyze it at the moment, though.

"So what brings you out this way tonight?" Chase continued. "Everything okay?"

"Someone reported a weapon under a Jeep in this parking lot. It might be nothing, but I was in the area, so I told patrol I'd check it out."

Chase squinted. "A Jeep? I drive a Jeep."

Those men had planted a gun by Chase's Jeep and then

called in a tip to the police. Someone was trying to set Chase up. But why? I had so many questions.

The detective ducked before rising again. He dangled a gun on his index finger.

Something unseen caused tension to pinch at my spine. Something internal sent warning alarms through my system, and I had no idea why.

I had that feeling people got while watching horror movies when the heroine thought she was safe, not realizing the killer was hiding right behind her, just waiting to strike.

That was crazy. There was no killer here.

Right?

With a stiff neck, I glanced over my shoulder, just to make sure.

I sucked in a breath.

There *was* a man there.

Only he wasn't about to kill me.

He was already dead.

CHAPTER 4

I held back my scream and took a step back, nearly toppling as my knees turned to jelly.

"What—" Jamie started to scold when her gaze followed mine. She gasped and grabbed the tree beside her. "Oh my goodness."

That was what the men in the van had been doing. First they'd left the gun they used to kill this man by Chase's Jeep in order to implicate him. Then they'd dumped his body.

Nausea gurgled in me again, though I tried to hold it at bay. Something messed up was going on.

As I stared down at the man, shock set in. He wasn't that old—maybe in his midtwenties. He wore a flannel shirt, jeans, and cowboy boots. But a huge red blotch stained his shirt.

Dear Lord, please be with this man's family. Comfort them when they hear this news.

"We've got to get out of here," Jamie whispered, grabbing my forearm.

Her fingernails dug into my skin, snapping me out of my stupor. I swallowed hard, not knowing if that was the best plan or not. But I knew I had to get away from this corpse before I purged the contents of my stomach all over him.

I turned around and glanced at Chase. He still talked with the officer. Their conversation seemed calm, like they were two colleagues discussing that gun. Good. They seemed distracted enough that they probably wouldn't notice us. Still, we'd need to remain out of sight as much as possible.

"Do you think there are security cameras on those light poles?" I asked, nodding toward the lights in the parking lots as we carefully maneuvered through the woods.

"An apartment complex this nice? Probably."

"Then the police will see us on the feed."

"But they'll know we didn't drop this body off. They'll see the van."

I swallowed harder. "Do you think they'll see our faces?"

"We're concealed back here in the woods. The ground is hard, so we're not leaving any footprints. All I know is that we need to move. Stay at the edge of the woods and out of sight. We're only disturbing the crime scene here. We've got to get back to my van."

I nodded, still feeling numb. Slowly, I wove behind the trees. My hands trembled uncontrollably.

Another dead body. I'd seen my fair share in my lifetime. I'd be okay if I never saw another one.

What had happened to that poor man? He probably had a family, a life, people who cared about him. Soon they'd receive bad news. They'd mourn. The police would investigate.

Someone had decided to play God and determine when a person's time on earth should end. Life was unrelenting at times. I'd felt it before, too many times to count.

I took another step and heard a snap. The sound echoed. A stick. My foot had landed on a stick. I froze.

Jamie's eyes widened, and neither of us dared to move.

Chase and the detective went silent. They'd heard it too, hadn't they?

How would I explain this to Chase if he caught me here, hiding in the woods only a few feet from him? The hole I'd dug was getting deeper by the second.

Dear Lord, what am I going to do? I'm good at fixing things, but I'm also really good at making messes.

"Probably a squirrel," the detective said.

I released my breath.

That was right. A *squirrel* had made the sound. Not two women who should know better than to play spy.

Jamie and I exchanged another glance before continuing our escape. Something nagged at the back of my mind, telling me that this wasn't a great idea. Regardless of that, I kept moving. I'd arrived at fight or flight, and I'd made my choice.

I'd make this right. Somehow. Someway. But not by stepping into the limelight right now.

Finally we reached the edge of the woods. Jamie's van was only a few feet away.

Jamie put her finger to her lips, as if I needed to be reminded that we should stay quiet. Together, we darted toward the van, careful to remain concealed by the other cars. Quietly, we climbed inside.

I barely closed the door. I wasn't 100 percent sure it even latched. But I didn't care. I remained hunched, biding my time until we could get out of here.

We were far enough away now that I doubted either Chase or the detective could see us. The tricky part would be driving away without drawing attention to ourselves.

As a car pulled into the parking lot at the opposite end, Jamie started her van and slowly cruised away.

I didn't release the air from my lungs until I could no longer see the apartment complex behind us.

A few minutes later, Jamie stopped in front of an old grocery store and put the car in park. Neither of us looked at each other.

"I'm a terrible person," I whispered, staring out the

windshield.

"I should have never suggested that we come here. It was one of my worst ideas ever. Almost as bad as your idea to break into people's houses and clean them."

I couldn't argue with that. "We've got to call the police."

"And tell them who we are? They'll want us to come in."

"But it's the right thing to do."

"I have a better idea." Jamie reached into her glove compartment and pulled out a phone.

"You got a new cell?" I asked, not recognizing the plastic flip phone.

"No, this is a burner."

My eyebrows shot up. "A burner phone? Why in the world do you have a burner phone?"

"I thought one of them might come in handy sometime. They always do in the movies. And see? I was right."

I shook my head, at a loss for what to say. I should probably be giving her a high five. "So we call the police and leave an anonymous tip about the body?"

"Exactly. If we use one of our phones, the police might trace it. We can't let that happen because we look as guilty as a jockey with an electric shocker in his hands."

I had no better ideas. Besides, our identity wasn't as important as the information we could share.

Jamie thrust the phone into my hands. "You do it."

I didn't argue. This situation was my doing. Sure, Jamie had persuaded me to come, but it hadn't taken that much convincing. Actions had consequences. I preached that to my clients all the time as a social worker. I needed to remember that myself also.

I dialed 911 and an operator answered. I explained to her what happened—everything from the men with the van, to the gun, and the dead body. I basically told her everything except who I was.

As I spoke, I tried to speed the conversation along as much as I could. I wasn't an expert on these things, but I figured the longer I was on the line, the better the chance that police could find us.

As soon as I'd shared everything I knew, I hung up. Jamie took the phone from me and pulled the battery out.

"Just so they can't trace the pings." She put the van in drive. "We've done our civic duty. The police know the body is there, and that a panel van dropped it off, along with a gun. There's nothing else we can do. Now let's get out of here."

I didn't argue. I was ready to put all of this behind us.

CHAPTER 5

I couldn't concentrate at work the next morning. Instead, I stared at the pile of work on my desk while my thoughts remained elsewhere. Mainly on the dead body Jamie and I had discovered last night.

I'd been working for the past several months as a constituent aide for my brother, Ralph, who was a state senator. I liked my job. I did. I prayed I was making a difference in people's lives and bringing change to a political system that sometimes seemed stuck and unwilling to budge. But I still wasn't accustomed to being behind a desk instead of out in the field. I missed being hands-on in the community.

Sitting behind a desk also made it harder to keep my thoughts occupied. Like right now. Every time I let my thoughts wander, I saw the man in the woods. I pictured his lifeless face. I pictured the bullet wound in his chest.

I'd turned it all over in my head a million times. The men in that van—I assumed there were at least two: one driving and the passenger who'd hopped out—must have dumped the body when they backed up toward the edge of the lot. They'd been in the ideal position to do so. The back doors could have opened, and they could have placed the man in the woods and then driven off.

It had been the perfect setup on their part.

I was trying to reconcile what had happened last night with

Chase's secretive trip. But every conclusion I arrived at was flawed. If he'd gone to investigate, then it didn't appear to be in an official capacity. Plus, the crime had happened around him, but he didn't seem to be investigating it.

Then there was Peyton. What was the likelihood she was connected with the murder? Slim to nothing.

Turning the thoughts over in my head was making me crazy. I liked solutions, and right now I didn't even have any good theories.

At the moment, I closed my eyes, listening to Sinatra sing "Beyond the Sea" in my earbuds. I wanted to go to the place he sang about. I wanted to sail. I wanted golden sands. I wanted a lover waiting there on the shore for me.

Only if that lover was Chase. The Chase I'd known up until this week. The Chase who hadn't kept secrets.

With its carefree lyrics, I wanted the song to carry me away from my problems. Instead, I stared at my computer screen. I'd found a news article this morning from the *Louisville Courier* about the body. *Unidentified body. Died from gunshot wound to chest. Police are pursuing suspects. Any tips can be called in to . .*
.

I shivered. Earlier, my biggest problem had been whether or not Chase was cheating on me. I was still kind of worried about that. But this new worry consumed me in a different way.

I did a double take when I noticed a figure looming over my desk. I gasped, realizing I'd been caught up in my own little world. Quickly, I pulled my earbuds out.

"A bomb could explode in here, and you wouldn't know it when you're listening to your music," my brother, Ralph, said.

I let out a weak laugh. If he only knew. "Maybe."

"You're still on for our meeting in five minutes, right?"

Ralph wore his typical vest and bow tie, along with wire-framed glasses. He was tall, lanky, and what some described as nerdy cute. He was my big brother, and I adored him—usually, at least.

What had he asked? About the meeting. That was right. We were discussing a new tax initiative. "I'll be there."

He leaned against my desk, not appearing suspicious. "I meant to ask you earlier. I'm having some people over tomorrow night to play board games. I was wondering if you and Chase want to come? It will be low-key, but low-key is good, right?"

I opened my mouth to respond, but nothing came out. How would I justify Chase's unexplained absence? I wasn't a proponent of lying. Besides, Ralph would see through me.

Finally I attempted a smile. "Chase may be working, but I'll see what he says."

"Big case?"

My mind went back to last night. Would Peyton be considered a case? Case number 304: Operation Get Back with the Ex-Wife. Or Case 305: Pick Up Gambling. Case 306: Interact with Shady Characters with Killer Instincts. The possibilities were endless.

"Holly?"

I jerked my gaze toward Ralph. "Yes?"

"Is Chase working on a big case?" he repeated.

I let out a feeble laugh, glad my thoughts weren't public. "Oh, of course. There's always a big case, isn't there?"

"When's he going to give you that ring?"

My heart did more than sink. It plummeted. Like an elevator whose cables had snapped. I glanced at my empty ring finger. Everyone assumed that Chase and I would be engaged by Christmas. We'd already talked about possible honeymoon locations, where we'd want to get married, and how much we couldn't wait to spend the rest of our lives together.

"That's the big question."

"Well, it's great to see you so happy. You deserve it, Holly. You pour your life into other people. It's time for you to reap some of what you've sown."

I wasn't feeling like the saint my brother made me out to be. I'd practically stalked my boyfriend; I'd fled the scene of the crime; and I was thinking the worst about the man I was supposed to love. I wouldn't be getting any "Girlfriend of the Year" awards.

The conversation seemed to appease Ralph. But as soon as he walked away, I picked up my phone and pulled up my Friend Finder app.

It showed that Chase was at Wyndmyer Park again. At least he wasn't in jail.

Yet.

Out of curiosity, I did an Internet search on the track. The establishment wasn't even open right now. What did it mean that Chase was there? How did it tie in?

I'd already ruined my standing as Super Girlfriend. I couldn't turn back time and undo everything I'd seen and done. Chase's well-being was more important than our relationship. Finding a killer superseded keeping a good name. A clear conscience took priority over hiding bad choices.

I believed that being a part of a community meant speaking truth into the lives of others. My dad had told me a story once about when he was a teenager and he'd started to get involved with drugs and drinking. One of his friend's dads had pulled him aside and given him a stern talking-to. My dad had turned his life around after that—slowly but surely. I wanted to be bold enough to do the right thing, despite the risk.

That did it. I couldn't just sit back and do nothing. If Chase was going under, I needed to stop him. I needed the truth before this whole fiasco consumed me. I was his girlfriend, but I didn't want to be walked on or deceived.

With that settled in my mind, I called Jamie.

"What are you doing tonight?" I asked.

"I have a feeling I'm going back to Kentucky with you."

She knew me too well. "Meet you at five?"

"I'll see you then."

***

When Jamie and I arrived at the horse track that evening, Jamie seemed to instinctively head toward the area of the parking lot where we'd seen Chase and Peyton last night.

Sure enough, Chase's Jeep was there. Apparently he wasn't in jail after the gun had been planted by his Jeep. That was the good news.

The bad news was that Chase was here. I looked across the lot and spotted a familiar black truck. Peyton's truck. That was the even worse news.

"They're here again." Jamie put the van in park. "But why? That's what doesn't make sense."

"Agreed. Of all the places they could rendezvous, why at a racetrack?"

I couldn't deny that the facts all pointed to a possible reunion between Chase and Peyton. It made sense. It was the perfect reason for Chase not to tell me where he was going or why. But it didn't tell me if the dead body was somehow connected to his time here in Louisville or why someone wanted to frame him.

We settled back, deciding to stay in the parking lot and see if Chase appeared again.

"So, I researched Wyndmyer online today," I started. "It made sense, since Wyndmyer appears to be somehow linked to Chase, and Chase is linked to the dead body."

"What did you find out?"

"It opened back in the eighties, but almost closed its doors a decade ago because of declining attendance and poor management. A man named Winston Kensington purchased it around five years ago."

"Winston Kensington? He sounds rich."

"Apparently his parents made millions in the pharmaceutical industry," I continued. "Otherwise, the man seems rather private. I couldn't find much information or personal details about him. He did manage to turn the place around."

"Horse racing has been full of scandals throughout the years. Doping, under-the-table deals, stolen thoroughbreds. The list could go on and on. But I'm not sure what that has to do with all this." Jamie paused. "Do you think this somehow connects with Chase's time of living here? I mean, he was a detective here. Maybe a past case has opened again."

I nodded. "Maybe."

"Tell me again what happened between the time he left Cincinnati and the time he moved back to Cincinnati. I know he Mr. Football Superstar for the university and then he was drafted for Indianapolis. I also know an injury sidelined him and he became a cop."

"That's right. Of course, that was a huge pay cut. Peyton married him when he was still rich and affluent. The change was hard on her, but they were surviving. Then Chase's brother was killed."

"What happened?"

I shrugged. "He doesn't like to talk about it. He didn't even know his brother Hayden existed until the year before that. Apparently, his dad had fooled around and gotten another woman pregnant when Chase was only a toddler. Anyway, the case never closed, and it turned Chase's life upside down. He became obsessed."

"He started drinking?"

"Yes. And drinking ended up putting his job in jeopardy, as well as his marriage. Everything fell apart."

"How did he get it back together?"

"A friend of his was a chaplain with the police department. He intervened in Chase's life. He didn't give up on Chase. Eventually, Chase sobered. Peyton didn't want to make things right. In fact, I think she remarried fairly quickly. Chase was able to get a job in Cincinnati, and we reconnected. You know the rest of the story."

"From football star to star detective to fallen hero who hits rock bottom. Sounds like the stuff movies are made of." An overhead light from the parking lot illuminated half her face, showing her frown.

"Jamie, look!" I pointed in the distance.

Chase stood outside the stable area talking with a man. *Arguing* was more like it.

I could barely see them. The man with Chase was older, probably in his sixties. He was tall and lean with gray hair, and he had a look of distinction about him. Two other men lingered just behind the older man. Bodyguards? That was my first thought based on their suits and rigid stances.

Chase stood with his hands on his hips. As he spoke, his neck looked stiff and his movements terse. Angry. He clearly looked angry.

His hands slapped against each other, as if trying to drive home a point. Chase was usually very in control, and seeing him wound up and upset left me feeling unsettled.

"What do you think that's about?" Jamie whispered, as if someone else might hear us.

I shook my head. "I wish I knew. It doesn't look good, does it?"

The more I searched for answers, the more questions I discovered.

"Uh-oh. I don't believe this. We've got company." Jamie nodded toward the distance.

I craned my neck and spotted the same van from last night. It started through the parking lot on the opposite end, headed toward . . . us?

Alarms sounded in my head.

My gaze swerved back toward Chase. He continued to argue with the man in front of him. I wanted to see more. I wanted answers.

I jerked my head back toward the van as it crept toward us. What awful timing.

We were in plain sight right here. I didn't want to take any chances that the driver might spot us, but I had no reason to believe the men in the van knew who we were.

"I hate to do it, but I feel the urge to put distance between us and that van," Jamie said.

I cast one last glance at Chase. What was he doing?

I wouldn't be finding out right now. "Let's go."

As Jamie slowly pulled toward the parking lot exit, the van continued creeping behind us. My shoulders pinched. The van seemed to speed up, as if the driver didn't want to lose us.

"Is it following us?" I asked, certain I was being paranoid.

"Let's just say, I don't think this is a coincidence." Jamie pressed the accelerator harder before suddenly stomping on the brakes. A car backed out in front of us, effectively cutting us off.

My blood pressure rose as I waited for the car to slowly slink from its spot. I glanced behind me. The van hadn't stopped. The driver had turned down the same row where we waited, inching closer and closer by the moment.

Finally the car in front of us pulled away—traveling slower than a losing Triple Crown contestant through the parking lot. We stayed on its bumper, desperate to put distance between ourselves and the creepy van. The driver of the sedan obviously didn't sense our urgency, though, because his pace kept us barricaded between him and the killers behind us.

"Needless to say, the driver of that van is not looking for a parking space," Jamie said, her eyes fluttering to the rearview mirror. "They just drove right past the one just vacated by the snail in front of us."

"What are they planning?" I whispered, the tension between my shoulders growing by the moment. Visions of guns, car chases, and pain danced not-so-merrily in my head.

"Let's find out." As the car in front of us turned one way at the end of the row, Jamie swerved in the opposite direction. She was testing them, I realized.

And, sure enough, the van followed us, gaining speed with each second.

Guns, car chases, and pain were becoming more of a reality by the moment.

CHAPTER 6

"Jamie, watch out!" I screamed. "I think they're going to ram us!"

She floored it, going entirely too fast for a parking lot. But we had little other choice. Not with psycho killers chasing us.

When my equilibrium righted, I craned my neck. The van still headed toward us at an alarming rate. They weren't going to relent.

"Keep going!" I urged.

"I never took you as a backseat driver," Jamie mumbled.

"You just keep your eyes on the road!"

As the edge of the parking lot neared, Jamie jerked the wheel hard, and we somehow ended up perpendicular to the row. We skidded toward the fence where Chase had been.

I glanced over, holding my breath. We were definitely causing a scene. Our whole investigation could be blown.

The area where he'd been standing was now empty. Chase was gone, as was the man he'd been talking to.

Thank goodness.

As soon as the van slowed enough for Jamie to gain control, she pressed the accelerator and we headed for the exit.

I looked behind us again. A trailer backed out, effectively stopping the van from pursuing us anymore. At least for the moment.

Thank You, Jesus.

Jamie turned out of the parking lot and sped onto the

highway.

We'd lost them. At least for a moment. My shoulder muscles went limp. That had been close.

"How did they recognize us?" Jamie asked.

I shook my head, still shaken. "I don't know. But whoever dumped that body last night somehow knows that we saw them."

"It seems impossible. We were concealed."

"Something doesn't smell right. You know?"

"Do I ever."

I leaned back, trying to control my breathing. How had the men in that van discovered us? Had they seen us leave last night and realized we knew too much? Had they somehow followed us, trying to make sure we stayed quiet? It just didn't make sense.

But one thing was becoming clear: Jamie and I were way deeper in this than we ever intended. What started as making sure Chase wasn't gambling could turn out to be a fight for our survival.

The thought wasn't comforting.

Just then, my phone rang. I glanced at the screen, and all the air left my lungs when I saw the number. "Jamie, it's Chase! What if he saw us?"

"Well, what are you doing? Answer it!"

I looked behind us again, making sure the van wasn't on our tail. I didn't see any sign of it. With that worry receding, I could focus on this conversation and whatever it might bring.

My hands trembled as I put the phone to my ear. I tried to keep my voice casual, although I feared I sounded like a chattering mess. "Hey there."

I decided that in my haste to be relaxed, I sounded like one of those professional phone operators who used their voices for not-so-moral reasons. Not good.

"Holly." Chase's voice sounded warm yet strangely detached. "I had a free minute, so I wanted to check in, to say hello. How are you?"

"Me? Oh, I'm like . . . fine. Totally fine." My voice had gone from sultry to Valley Girl. I had to get a grip. "How are you?"

"I've been better. But that's a story for later. Did I catch you at a bad time?"

I rolled my eyes toward the ceiling in a silent prayer to God for forgiveness. "I'm just . . . hanging out with Jamie."

"I don't want to keep you from your girl time." He lowered his voice. "Thanks for being so understanding about me taking off suddenly like I did. I wanted to let you know that your trust in me means a lot."

Regret churned in my stomach. I was such a disappointment right now. Doing this was against everything I believed in. Yet here I was, and I couldn't seem to stop. I was in too deep.

It was time to call him out on what was going on. No more hiding or pretending I didn't know. I had to be straightforward.

I sucked in a deep breath before plunging in. "That's funny that you said that, because—"

Shouting sounded on the other end of the phone. I couldn't tell if it was the crowd at the horse track, cheering their bet on toward victory, or a fistfight that had broken out. Whatever it was, I didn't like it.

"I have to run, Holly," Chase rushed. "If I can, I'll check in again, okay?"

Before I could say anything, the line went dead.

***

I'd been quiet for most of the ride back home. I had too

many thoughts, and none of them were worth voicing.

When we reached Northern Kentucky, Jamie pulled off the interstate to get some gas. As she climbed back in and put the van into drive, she surprised me by stopping at the back of a parking lot in a large shopping center anchored by Walmart. A couple of fast-food restaurants as well as the gas station were located closer to the street. Jamie put the van in park.

"Haven't we had enough of parking lots?" My feeble attempt at a joke fell flat.

Jamie ignored me, looking at me instead with determination in her gaze. "Talk to me."

My smile faltered, and I glanced down at my hands, trying to find the words. "Things weren't supposed to work out like this for Chase and me."

"Where's all that optimism you're known for?"

"I don't know if I've ever really had my heart broken before, Jamie. I've always been so careful with guys. I saved my first kiss for the man I was going to marry."

"Chase." Jamie sighed. "You're in love with him. Of course you're upset. If you weren't upset, then something would be wrong with you."

"It's just hard to let go and accept change sometimes. I originally wanted to help him, but now I'm starting to think that's a bad idea. He wants space, so I should give it to him."

"Keep praying about it. And remember—we still don't have all the facts."

"There's also the dead body. That has made all of this even more complicated."

"The police are handling that. We did our part, albeit a bit unconventionally."

I leaned back in the seat, grateful to turn my thoughts away from my broken heart for a moment. "Let me just think out loud for a minute, because none of this makes sense. Chase is seen with Peyton at the track. Chase leaves the track. Men follow him and leave a gun by his Jeep. The men also leave a body, most likely shot with the gun left near Chase's Jeep. The said men then call the police. Fast-forward to the next day. Chase is heatedly arguing with a man."

"And the Creeper Van finds us at the track. Don't forget that."

"How can I? Add all that, and what do you have? I'm clueless. These secrets are killing me."

"Only time will give us the answers."

I rubbed my forehead, knowing her advice was spot on. "These are going to be two of the longest weeks of my life."

Jamie cocked her head and raised her eyebrows. "Girl, it wasn't that long ago that doctors gave you less than a year to live. Are you sure these two weeks will be the hardest and longest?"

I leaned back and sighed. "When I thought I had only a year to live, every moment seemed to go by too quickly." I frowned. "Now that I'm waiting to hear about Chase, time is dragging. Life is complicated like that."

"Ain't that the truth?"

"I'm just going to return to normal life, Jamie." I shook my head with determination. "I'm going to forget about everything I've seen. I'm going to let Chase come back to me with answers. I'm going to let the police figure out what happened to the man left in the woods. It's the only solution I can live with. I can't continue to spy on my boyfriend. And, since I can't speculate on murder, I'm going to have to face the fact that I can't solve the world's problems."

"Admitting that is half the battle."

I elbowed my friend. "When the time comes, when Chase

returns home, I'll own up to my mistakes. Maybe he'll own up to his also."

As soon as the words left my mouth, my throat constricted.

"What is it?" Jamie asked.

I pointed to the traffic light. "It's the panel van from every horror movie ever made."

"What?"

"The van that dumped the dead body. It's right there."

CHAPTER 7

"We've got to get out of here," I mumbled, panic trying to seize me.

Jamie's bottom lip dropped as she shook her head and stared at the van. "It doesn't make sense how they located us. It's like we have bright, flashing lights saying, 'Over here!'"

She had a point. There was something more going on here. We'd lost that van in Louisville, and somehow the driver had found us again. I didn't have time to ponder it now.

"I think we should ditch the van," I mumbled. "At least for the moment. It's too recognizable to them."

"Listen to you—sounding all professional and everything." Jamie looked me up and down like I'd morphed into a different person. "I agree. Maybe we should distance ourselves from the van and see what happens."

I glanced around, trying to assess my options. It was times like this I wished I did have some Navy SEAL training. Finally, my eyes stopped on a building. "Think we can make it to Burgerville over there?"

"I say it's worth a try." She patted the dashboard. "Be safe, Love Bug."

"Since when do you call your van Love Bug?"

"I didn't until now. Okay, let's go."

Carefully, we climbed out of the van. We remained low, ducking behind other vehicles as we hurried across the parking lot. Hopefully, those men would assume that we'd gone into

Walmart. That was, if they even saw our van at all. It was dark, and there were a lot of cars here. Really, the odds of them finding us were small.

I popped my head up to check their status. As if in response to my thought, the van turned into the shopping-center lot.

My stomach sank. How were they tracking us?

There was so much here that didn't make sense. I didn't have time to squat and analyze at the moment. *Hide first. Analyze later.*

"Jamie, they're onto us," I whispered, still moving toward the restaurant. "Somehow they know exactly where the van is."

She peered up before jerking down behind a car again. Her eyes were wide, and I could tell she wanted to do the Diva, but it was too hard to execute while in a hunched position.

"To say I'm floored would be an understatement," I muttered. "You just need to color me stupid right now."

"Stupid isn't your color. It looks awful with your complexion."

Her reply surprised me so much that I snorted. "We need help—on more than one level."

As we came to the edge of the line of cars that concealed us, I glanced back. The van was nowhere to be seen, but that didn't mean much. It could be anywhere.

I wasn't going to stick my neck out enough to see. They had the potential to be close, and I didn't want to give away our presence.

Quickly, we darted across the open space between the rows of cars. We only had about five more rows to go until we reached the burger joint in the distance.

We followed the same routine for row after row. Stop, check, go. Stop, check, go.

Finally, we reached the safe haven of Burgerville. We

straightened as we walked inside, trying to appear normal—even though we felt anything but. There were probably seven people inside, most of them eating grease-laden sandwiches and sipping bubbly, sugar-infused sodas at various tables and booths scattered throughout the space.

The smell of grease turned my stomach. That, on top of the blaring AC, made me feel sick, almost feverish, even though I knew I wasn't. We bypassed the counter where employees waited to take our order and grabbed a table by the window instead.

"Do you think they saw us?" Jamie's jaw hardly moved, almost as if she feared someone overhearing us.

She was spooked. I hardly ever saw my brazen friend spooked.

But we were dealing with killers here, and they weren't exactly being secretive about their obsession with us. Back at the horse track, they hadn't even tried to hide the fact they were following us.

I straightened as something in the distance caught my eye. The van was creeping by Jamie's, scoping it out to see if we were inside. "There they are. They're looking for us."

"We're in public. They wouldn't do anything to us here, would they?" Jamie asked.

"I hope not." I glanced around at all the people in the restaurant. Thank goodness there were no children. But there *were* four college-aged adults, two middle-aged women, and a fiftysomething man who looked like he might be a trucker. Had we put all these people in danger?

"Should we call the police?" I asked.

"What if they ask questions about what happened at the Belmont Apartments?"

My stomach sank. She was right. The more information we

revealed, the better the chance that we'd look guilty. We had to play it safe.

How were these men continuing to find us? That's what bothered me the most. It just didn't make sense.

I supposed they could have seen us fleeing the van. Or they could assume we'd come into the restaurant, since it was the closest building. Or . . . "Jamie, what if these guys are somehow tracing our cell phones, just like I'm tracing Chase?"

She narrowed her eyes in thought. "How would they have gotten our cell information?"

"I'm not sure."

"There's only one way to find out," Jamie mumbled. "Do you still have that bag of cashews in your purse?"

I nodded. "Of course."

"I need it."

I set my purse on the sticky table in front of me, trying to make a mental note to sanitize it later.

I didn't ask any questions. I handed it to my friend, and she emptied the nuts onto a napkin and then stuck her phone in the Ziploc bag.

"I need yours too."

I fished it from my purse, gave it to her, and watched as she added my cell to the collection.

"I'm going to put this in the bottom of the trash can in the restroom. If those men aren't tracing us, I'll come back and pick it up before the restaurant closes. If they are, then these men will end up in a women's restroom."

"Have I ever told you that you're brilliant?"

"A girl can't hear those words enough." She did a cutesy shoulder bump but quickly sobered.

As she disappeared into the bathroom, I kept my eyes on the parking lot. Sure enough, the van started to head this way.

My heart raced at the realization. What would those men do if they got their hands on us?

I didn't want to find out.

I rushed to the bathroom, almost knocked over by the obnoxious odor of bleach. "Jamie, we've got to go."

She had her nose turned up and her hand halfway down the trash can. On a normal day, she'd never reach into a public waste disposal. In a fight for her life, absolutely. "Coming."

We rushed out the door on the opposite side of the building. The only thing I saw was a Dumpster at the edge of the dark lot. I grabbed Jamie's hand, and we ran in front of the drive-through window until we reached our hiding spot. In the distance, I saw the van pull up to the restaurant.

If those men were tracking us, how exact was their location device? They'd obviously have to have money in order to afford the kind of technology that would pinpoint us down to the precise place. Based on their van, they weren't that rich.

The bad feeling in my gut continued to twist harder and harder, deeper and deeper.

"They're going inside," I whispered. "Jamie, we're in trouble."

Just then, a *bleep bleep* sounded directly behind us.

I turned around and spotted a police car there.

And based on the look in the officer's eyes, he thought Jamie and I were up to no good.

CHAPTER 8

"I'm sorry, did you say you think someone is following you?" The police officer was on the younger side, or maybe his baby face made him look that way. But his attitude was the polar opposite of his appearance: it made him seem callous and old, like he'd heard one too many stories to easily accept what we told him.

I knew our story sounded a little off the wall, but the officer could give us the benefit of the doubt, at least.

Apparently, someone at the restaurant had called the police on us after surmising we'd left a suspicious package in the restroom. I couldn't blame the caller. We had looked sketchy.

Police lights flashed behind us, illuminating our faces. Meanwhile, the zip of traffic from the interstate created a type of static noise in the background. Every detail seemed ingrained in my head.

"It's true," I told the officer. "There was a black van that followed us here from Louisville."

I glanced behind me. A crowd had gathered inside the restaurant at the floor-to-ceiling windows, staring at us. Who needed to go to the movies when you could watch your fellow citizens be humiliated in public?

An employee emerged holding our cell phones. His shoulders were puffed up, like he'd just cracked a major case, as he handed the cashew bag to Officer Bunch.

"What was in this?" The office turned his nose up at the

dirty bag.

"Cashews."

He quickly shoved the bag toward me. "Nut allergy. Take this. Please."

What I really didn't want was for Officer Bunch to ask for my name. All I had to say was "Paladin," and he'd most likely know I was related to the state senator from Ohio. Stories like this had a tendency to make the front-page news. Reputation was very important to my family, so that turn of events wouldn't be well received.

The officer stared at the notes he'd jotted on his pad of paper. "And this so-called van appeared out of the blue at Wyndmyer Park in Kentucky?"

"So-called van? I think I know what a van is. It was definitely a van." Sarcasm, as unbecoming as it was, tinged my voice. I turned my back to the audience at the windows. "But, yes. When we pulled over for gas and saw the van pulling into the shopping center, naturally, we were frightened. The van is recognizable. We knew it was the same one."

"So you hid your phone in a trash can in the bathroom?" He both squinted and scrunched his nose as if disgusted.

I sighed. This officer hadn't even given us a chance, and that was unfortunate. Meanwhile, the real bad guys had gotten away. "I know it sounds crazy, but we thought maybe these guys were tracking our cell phones somehow."

"How would they have gotten ahold of your cell phone?"

Jamie seemed to sense my rising frustration and stepped forward. "We have no idea. Remotely, maybe."

He shook his head, looking unconvinced. "I'm pretty sure that's not possible."

I tapped my foot, ready for this crazy ride to end—all of it. I just needed to resume my boring life of working and

CHRISTY BARRITT

volunteering. Part of me wondered if that was even a possibility. I knew it wasn't, not until I'd done everything I could to help Chase.

"Well, technology is amazing, and when you're scared, anything seems like a possibility," I murmured.

His expression remained unchanged. "Where are these men now?"

"They must have seen you here and driven away," I said.

He finally lowered his pad of paper. "Would you like to file a report?"

I glanced at Jamie. Did we want to? It might be nice to have something on file. On the other hand, this might eventually link us back to the whole fiasco at the apartment complex. I couldn't take that chance.

"It wouldn't do any good," I finally said. "We don't have a so-called license plate or even a make and model."

"You sure?" Officer Bunch looked like he couldn't care less, and if he heard my so-called jab, he didn't give any indication.

I nodded. "Yeah, I'm sure. It looks like they're long gone now."

"I'll let this go, then. This time. You two ladies stay safe and stay out of trouble." He gave us a stern glance, something similar to what a father might give a child who denied eating out of the cookie jar.

I didn't bother to say thank you. Instead, we climbed back into Jamie's van, feeling spent. What a night. What a week.

What a life.

Jamie cranked the van and started down the road. We'd have time to talk as we traveled. Parking lots appeared to be full of bad luck and bad memories, so I had no desire to stay here any longer than we had to.

"I'm getting scared, Jamie," I said. "This has all blown up."

57

"You can say that again. These guys are after us. *They* have to know that *we* know what *they* did."

"Are they trying to kill us?"

"That's my best guess."

I shivered. "What are we going to do?"

"We just need to sleep on it right now. I'm not thinking clearly. I only want to react."

We crossed the Brent Spence Bridge into Cincinnati. Just a couple of hours ago, I couldn't wait to be home. Now I wasn't so sure.

My house was located only a few minutes over the bridge in an area called Price Hill. The neighborhood itself had gone downhill in the last several decades, but some buildings offered glimpses into the treasure it had been at one time. I liked to think my family home was one of those places. It was Tudor style with an immaculate lawn and a spotless interior.

Jamie slowed as we approached my house. "Is your mom still out of town?"

"Yeah, she's visiting some family down in West Virginia. Why?"

"You shouldn't stay by yourself tonight."

I sucked in a breath at her implications. "You think those men know where I live?"

"At this point I don't know what to think. How about if we both camp out here tonight? In case they are tracking us, I don't want to lead these guys back to my house. Especially not with my brothers being there."

She had three kid brothers, adopted from Haiti. She liked to act like she didn't like them, but she was actually a mix between mama bear and mother hen when she was around them.

"I'd actually feel a lot better if you stayed here. Thank you."

She found a space on the street and put the van in park. I

took a glance down the road as I climbed out. I didn't see the black van anywhere. That was good. Maybe we'd somehow lost them.

I wished I could be confident they wouldn't find us again.

I doubted my theory about the cell phones now. At first I'd thought someone could have tracked them remotely, but Officer Bunch made it sound like a near impossibility. It would be a long shot. Besides that, I hadn't been away from my phone, other than when it was in the trash can. The likelihood that someone had grabbed it and begun tracing me seemed slim.

That still didn't make me feel better, though.

I walked into my silent house, remembering that night when Chase was over. When we'd stood somewhat awkwardly in the living room while Chase told me he had to go somewhere and do something.

He had to go to Kentucky and meet with his ex. I was sure there was more to it, but those two facts remained. As much as I might want to drop this, my actions had tied me to a crime, and now killers were tracking me.

This wasn't only Chase's life in jeopardy now. Jamie and I were also in the line of fire.

***

At 3:00 a.m., I got out of bed. I couldn't sleep. My thoughts were too tumultuous. Every time I closed my eyes, scenes from my life haunted me.

Jamie slept in the guest room across the hall. And she was sleeping. I could hear her snoring even with the door closed, though she'd be horrified if I ever told anyone. Apparently, divas shouldn't snore.

Quietly, I crept downstairs. Maybe a cup of chamomile tea

would help me get some shut-eye. Or baking some cakes, cookies, brownies, and maybe a pie or two. Baking always made me feel better.

After I put the kettle on, I plodded into the formal living room, pulling my robe closer around me. I ran my hand across the coffee table. A thin layer of dust was there, but only because my mom had been away visiting relatives in West Virginia for almost a week.

Mom prided herself in keeping a clean house with everything in place. That was my family for you. When they did something, they did it well. That was about all I had in common with them—that's how it felt most of the time, at least.

I really just wanted a simple life. I wanted to be able to go to sleep at night knowing I'd done my best. That I'd tried to help people. That I'd lived for a purpose higher than my own desires.

I tried to put others before myself, to love my neighbor as myself, to store up my treasure in heaven instead of earthly rewards. My family, although Christians, didn't quite understand that.

I lowered myself onto the couch and replayed my last face-to-face conversation with Chase. My heart panged at the memory. My gut, at the time, had been correct. Something big had been wrong.

Not that long ago, I'd pictured my future with Chase. I'd determined that we'd have one boy and one girl by birth, and at least two that we adopted, probably from the foster-care system. While we all ate peanut-butter-and-jelly sandwiches around the lunch table, I'd tell them stories about Chase and me—about how we met in high school, how I'd had a crush on him but was certain I was invisible, how he'd reappeared in my life a decade later. I'd tell them how Chase was the only man I'd ever kissed, and how he'd saved my life.

All those potential conversations were on the line.

I stood and paced to the window. Out of curiosity, I nudged the curtain aside. My eyes widened.

It couldn't be . . .

It was.

The panel van.

It was parked outside my house.

I released the curtain before anyone spotted me and slowly stepped back. My heart stammered into my rib cage. They'd found us. Again. The thought was disturbing on so many levels.

Where were those men now? Were they inside the van still? Or were they plotting ways to get into the house and murder Jamie and me?

My thoughts might seem dramatic, but my fear was real.

The kettle began screeching in the background, tightening my nerves even more.

I quickly ran into the kitchen and pulled the boiling water from the burner. So much for my tea. I had bigger issues right now than getting to sleep.

I rushed up the steps and barged into Jamie's room. I didn't bother to try and be polite. I grabbed her shoulders and shook her until sleep was a distant dream.

"Jamie, you've got to get up. Now!" I kept my voice low but urgent.

She startled awake, sitting up with wide, crazy eyes that clearly stated she wanted to slap me. "Are you trying to give me a heart attack?"

"Jamie, they're here." My words sounded haunting and still, like a catchphrase from a horror movie.

Jamie became eerily quiet, her crazy eyes looking even crazier when combined with her flaring nostrils. "The men are here? The *killer* men?"

I nodded, the blood draining from my face at her reminder. "The van is outside the house. I don't know where the men are, though. I just know we've got to get dressed and get out of here. Now." My words collided with each other, each sentence coming faster than the previous one.

She didn't argue. She threw her legs out of bed and grabbed her clothes.

I hurried across the hall. My hands trembled uncontrollably as I pulled my own clothes on. I grabbed some extra outfits and tossed them into a bag, along with some toiletries. I slung the bag over my shoulder and met Jamie in the hallway.

"What now?" Jamie said.

"We've got to figure out where those men are. I haven't heard them downstairs, but maybe they're just really good at being sneaky and evil."

"Sneaky, evil people are bad. Very bad."

I had to do a double take to see if she was being funny. She looked dead serious.

We tiptoed downstairs. Every creak made my muscles feel wound up tighter than a jack-in-the-box. My heart beat so fast by the time we reached the living room that I thought I might pass out. Jamie went for the window, and I didn't try to stop her.

"They're still there," she whispered. "I think they're still in the van."

"How do you know?"

She peered through a slit between the curtain and the window frame, squinting against the darkness. "I think I see a silhouette in the driver's seat."

"Let's check the backyard. We have to make sure we're not ambushed."

We stayed close as we ventured to the other side of the

62

house. We might have even held hands like two schoolgirls confronting the boogeyman.

We kept the lights off, which only squeezed my nerves. The shadows seemed like such obvious places for people to hide. Darkness and criminals were natural conspirators.

I cautiously approached the back window. I could hardly breathe as I moved closer. I imagined that jack-in-the-box again, the one that had been winding up inside me. At any minute, I expected to startle when something popped out.

I leaned closer to the glass. Nothing jumping out. Not yet.

My dark backyard came into view. Nothing looked out of place. All the patio furniture was there. No figures lurked behind the maple tree or near the deck. Thank goodness.

But that still left Jamie and me stuck inside. That wasn't going to work. We couldn't just stay here and wait for these guys to attack.

"Any brilliant ideas?" Jamie whispered, stepping back and taking refuge against the wall.

I thought a moment, hoping for a flash of "eureka." Praying for wisdom and brilliance. Settling on anything other than staying here and waiting to be a victim. Finally, I had an idea.

"We can take my mom's car," I said. "It's parked in the garage, which leads out—"

"To the side street." Jamie slowly bobbed her head up and down, as if my plan impressed her. "If we idle out of the driveway, there's a chance they wouldn't see us, based on where their van is situated."

"Exactly!"

"I say it's worth a try. We've got to ditch my van anyway. It's obviously way too recognizable."

"Let me grab my mom's extra set of keys." Mom always liked to rent cars when she went away on trips. That worked to my advantage right now. I couldn't take my own car. The '64½ Mustang drew attention wherever I went.

Thankfully, the extra set of keys was close—in a table by the back door. With a plan in place, I turned to Jamie. "Let's do this."

"Traveling mercies," she muttered.

I hesitated a minute as my hand connected with the back door handle. This could either be clever or blow up in our faces. Best we could tell, those men weren't in my backyard. They most likely assumed we were sleeping inside the house and totally unaware of their presence.

Their plan perplexed me. Were they going to tail us again in the morning? Break inside while we slept and kill us? I had no idea, and I didn't want to find out.

Slowly, I twisted the handle and pulled the door open. The sound of crickets wafted to my ears, and I took the first step onto the patio.

My skin crawled as I glanced around. Everything appeared normal. My senses were heightened with anticipation and adrenaline.

Jamie stepped out behind me and carefully shut the door, making sure it locked. Like secret agents, we moved along the wall, behind the tree, along the edges of the pergola. Finally, we darted toward the detached garage.

Jamie was right—some Navy SEAL training could come in handy.

My hands trembled as I tried to insert the key into the garage lock. I finally managed to get it in and twist it to get the side door open. We wasted no time slipping inside and shut the door. Obstacle one: completed.

Darkness surrounded us. I sucked in another breath, praying that we were in here alone. That the men hadn't spotted us.

That they'd perhaps fallen asleep.

"We can't risk turning on the light," I whispered. "We're going to have to feel our way to the car."

I took my first step forward and banged my knee on something hard and sharp. Pain shot through me. "Owie!"

"Shhh," Jamie said.

"It hurt," I mumbled as my hand hit cool metal. "Here's the car."

I skirted around the trunk, past the back door, and found the driver's side door. I manually unlocked the door, fearing the *beep beep* of the key fob would alert those men to our presence. The dome light inside offered just enough light for me to slip inside and unlock Jamie's door.

I had to raise the garage door by hand. The electric opener would be too loud. My anxiety ratcheted to a whole new level at the thought of how many things could go wrong.

This was the point where I would figure out whether or not our plan would work.

Our lives depended on it working.

I gripped the handle, turned it, and slowly raised the floodgate.

CHAPTER 9

The garage door slowly rolled open. The scene on the other side revealed itself inch by inch, like the opening act of a play. I held my breath, waiting to see if this particular production would be a serene drama or an intense action thriller.

Please, not a thriller. Please.

An empty street stared back. An apartment building backed up to the right side of my house, and an abundance of cars were always parked along the street. There were also a couple of trash cans—tomorrow was trash pickup day, I remembered. Too late to do anything about that now.

Everything was silent.

I let out the breath I held and started to run back to the car. I didn't want to press my luck.

Just then something darted in front of me. My hand went over my heart as fear pulsed through me.

I nearly screamed, but by God's grace I didn't.

It was a cat. A cat.

I nearly laughed, except I didn't want to draw attention to myself.

The critter scampered off, looking just as frightened as I'd felt.

With labored breaths, I ran back to the car and carefully closed the door. I put the car in neutral, and Jamie and I slowly pushed it out of the garage.

"I'll close the door," Jamie whispered once we cleared the

building.

I nodded, my apprehension still getting the best of me. I craned my neck toward the front of my house. From where I was, I couldn't see the van. But if they had men on the ground, then we'd be toast.

The garage door closed, and Jamie ran back to the car. We pushed it into the street and all the way to the corner—in the opposite direction of the van.

I didn't dare crank the engine until we were a block away. I kept my eyes on the rearview mirror, waiting to see the van reappear. The street remained vacant.

I relaxed my shoulders and glanced at Jamie. "That was close."

"More than close."

I scanned the street as we crept farther and farther from my neighborhood, headed toward downtown. There were plenty of hotels in the area, but hotels required money, and money wasn't something either Jamie or I had much of.

"I can call a friend from work or even Ralph or Alex." Alex was my older sister who'd just gotten married. I really had no desire to spend time with the honeymooners, but I would if desperate. "Either of them would let us stay there."

"We should keep other people out of this, as much as possible. Besides, Ralph and Alex would ask way too many questions. I have another idea."

"What's that?"

"We're going to do what every person on the run has done at one time or another in their life in order to flee from danger. We're going to take refuge at a church."

***

The next morning, with a major kink in my neck, I managed to get myself cleaned up in the ladies' restroom of Jamie's church. Her dad was the interim music minister for the congregation, which met in an old strip mall in lower Price Hill, only minutes from the downtown area.

The church was small and poor, but it was full of life. I loved it there. However, the pews weren't ideal when used as beds. That worked in favor of the preacher, but not in favor of a girl on the run.

After I dressed, I sat down on the end of the pew and waited for Jamie to wake up. I stared at the cross at the front of the building. It was a great reminder of what my perspective should be. Not myself. Not my own happiness. But loving Jesus. Loving others.

A year ago I would never have done any of this. I liked my peaceful little life. I'd been given an inaccurate diagnosis of a year to live, and my perspective had changed. I had no idea how much time I had left on this earth, and I wanted to make the most of each opportunity I was given. Since then, I'd started jumping in with both feet. I'd taken more risks. I loved harder. Made more mistakes. Danced in the rain.

In essence, I'd tried to seize each moment and live out all the pithy sayings that decorated people's walls.

Jamie groaned on the other end of the bench, stirring from her sleep. As she sat up, she did a double take at me. "What an awful night," she muttered, rubbing her eyes.

I sighed. "I know. Now it's a new day and a new set of problems."

"Hey, you're the optimistic one here. None of that negative talk."

I shook my head and smoothed the edges of my black shirt. "I thought about it all night, Jamie. I couldn't sleep. I don't think resuming normal life is an option right now. I think these guys are going to keep tracking us until they get what they want."

She rubbed her eyes and paused midway through her yawn. "What do they want?"

"To silence us? I'm not sure. But I don't really want to find out."

"So we don't resume normal life. What do we do?"

I sighed again. "I wish I could tell you. I suppose we need to find answers. We need to figure out who these guys are before they find us again."

"Somehow Chase is connected with all of this. You do realize that. Right?"

"If only I could deny it."

"But before you write him off completely, remember what happened to you not so long ago when that crazy man threatened you."

I frowned at the memory. A man bent on revenge had threatened me, saying that I had to break up with Chase or he'd kill him. Also per his instructions, I couldn't tell Chase what was going on. In the end, when the truth finally came out, Chase was upset, but thankfully we'd resolved things.

Jamie was right. I did need to give him the benefit of the doubt. Crazy things happened in life.

"I'm going to keep searching for answers," I told my friend. "You don't have to do this with me, Jamie. But I'm going to take the rest of the week off from work. I'm going back to Louisville, and I'm going to figure this out."

"Of course I'm with you, Holly. Friends through thick and thin, right?"

I smiled, thankful for Jamie. "Through thick and thin."

"Through fat and skinny."

"Through fat and skinny," I agreed.

"Through black and white."

"Through black and—how long are we going to do this?" I asked.

"I was going to see how long you'd last." She sighed and stood. "First, I've got to stop by my house and get some clothes. And you're making me want a sausage biscuit. Do you know how long it's been since I've had a sausage biscuit?"

"How am I making you want a sausage biscuit?"

"Because my family used to always go through the drive-through and get a sausage biscuit when we left early in the morning for a trip. That's why."

"If I had more time, I'd try to whip up one made from almond flour and oat fiber just for you. But I don't have any time."

"You'd do that for me?"

"You know I would."

"You see, that's why we're such a good team. I risk my life for you, and you would make me gluten-free goodies."

I couldn't help but laugh. "Sounds like an even trade."

***

Three hours later, Jamie and I were back at the racetrack. I'd checked on the entire drive here for the Creeper Van, but I hadn't seen it. Maybe we'd finally lost them. Thank goodness.

Jamie and I had already arranged to stay with one of Jamie's friends who lived in the area—not far from the apartment complex where we'd seen Chase, for that matter. Jamie's friend Magnolia apparently worked for the local paper, and since she was single, she had a lot of flexibility and two extra bedrooms. We might not have had any other plan, but at least we had a place to sleep.

I sighed and stared at the huge arena in front of me.

Truth was, my Friend Finder app didn't show that Chase was here now. It showed he was in the middle of nowhere. Seriously. There was absolutely nothing around the area marked on the map where Chase was located, not even a street. It looked like he was wandering through the woods.

I found that odd.

But at least he wasn't at the racetrack.

I'd checked the race schedule on my phone, and there were no events going on now. However, Peyton's truck was in the parking lot.

I bristled at the thought of running into her.

Did Peyton know about me? Did she know I'd dated Chase? Or was I still dating Chase? I didn't know. Until I knew what the status of his relationship with Peyton was, I wouldn't have an answer to that question.

"What now?" Jamie asked, staring at the huge Wyndmyer Park sign in front of us.

I glanced around the entrance, at a loss myself. Was there a connection between the racetrack and the panel van/dead body? I couldn't be sure.

All I knew was that Chase had a connection to this track and Chase also had a connection to the dead body. That meant the racetrack was as good a place as any to start.

I pointed to a newsstand located near the entryway. "Do you mind grabbing a copy?"

"Sure thing."

I pulled up to it and Jamie climbed out, paid for a newspaper, and then hopped back into my mom's Lexus.

"Got a hankering for an update on the stock market?" Jamie asked, plopping the paper in my lap.

I rolled my eyes. Miss Manners would not approve of the

reaction, but I did it anyway. "I want to see if there are any updates on the body we found."

The scent of ink wafted up to me. There was nothing quite like the smell of newsprint. I found most of my news online nowadays, but I needed to change that. What was more old-fashioned than actually holding a newspaper in your hands?

As soon as I unfolded the paper, a face on the front stared at me.

"There he is," I whispered.

I'd never forget him. The man from the woods. He looked much better in this picture. He looked . . . alive. And vibrant. Like he had his whole life ahead of him.

"Aidan Jennings. Twenty-four years old. He worked as a stable boy for Golden Equestrian," I read aloud.

"Golden Equestrian? Equestrian means horses, and we're at a racetrack. Maybe that's our link. Maybe *he's* our link." Jamie peered at the paper. "Chase isn't mentioned in that article, is he?"

My stomach tightened. "No."

"Any persons of interest mentioned in the article?"

"A black van with at least two men, probably in their thirties, Caucasian."

"That's exactly what you told the police," Jamie said. "At least they didn't ignore you."

"I wish I'd had more to go on."

I flipped through the paper, seeing if anything else caught my eye. The front page of the business section contained a picture that seemed vaguely familiar.

"Jamie, isn't that the man who was arguing with Chase?" I showed her the picture.

She studied the photo a moment. "It looks like it. Who is it?"

CHRISTY BARRITT

My eyes scanned the article. "His name is Alexander Cartwright. He owns three of the top two hundred fifty racehorses in the world."

"Explains why he was by the stables."

I shook my head. "But it doesn't explain why Chase would be arguing with him. How does this fit in with everything else that's happened?"

"You got me." Jamie's eyes lit. "But I have an idea."

CHAPTER 10

I put the car into park, waiting to hear her brilliant plan.

"I'm going to write an article on horse racing."

"But you write community news for Cincinnati."

"I know people in Cincinnati come here. I'm sure there's some kind of community tie-in that we can find."

"What do I do?"

She handed me something from her purse. "You're my photographer."

"Fine." I held up the DSLR. "But what if we see Chase?"

"His car isn't here. Your app says he's not here. This is the only way I can think of to get information. Our lives are on the line here. Desperate times call for desperate measures, right?"

"That's what they say."

"Then let's do this." When Jamie was determined to do something, there was no stopping her. I just hoped this all didn't blow up in our faces.

We slipped past the gates at the track. The doors were unlocked, and no one was there to stop us. We paused once we were inside.

A few employees walked here and there. One carried a broom and dustpan. Another had a cloth and a spray bottle. Out on the field, someone mowed the grass.

"Where do we start?" I mumbled.

"I say let's head to the office. It's our best chance."

Before we could step that way, a voice sounded behind us.

"Can I help you?"

I turned around and saw . . . Peyton. My stomach clenched. Up close, she was just as beautiful as I'd imagined. I mean, really, people should not be that pretty. I could see why Chase had fallen in love with her.

She wore those skintight jeans that showed off her shapely legs, cowboy boots, and a tight black T-shirt. Her hair was glossy and neat, and her teeth were bright white, contrasting nicely with her tanned skin.

When she'd been married to Chase, she'd been a hairdresser. So what was she doing here now? Did she work here?

"I'm with the *Cincinnati Times*." Jamie extended her hand. "I'm doing an article on things people can do in the Louisville area for weekend fun. I'm hoping to include the Wyndmyer Park."

Peyton stared at Jamie's outstretched hand a moment, cynicism in her gaze, before finally returning the handshake. "We usually like a phone call before agreeing to anything. Just to keep things on the up-and-up."

Jamie shrugged. "I don't really need any interviews. Just information. This is also my photographer."

I smiled and held up the camera I'd strapped around my neck. I figured I looked more like a professional this way.

"We're hoping to take some pictures, at least," Jamie continued. "I can get the rest of the information via a phone interview later, if necessary."

Peyton crossed her arms, still carefully observing the two of us. "We need approval from management."

I noticed her gaze was on me, so I pushed my sunglasses up higher on my nose. Certainly she didn't recognize me. I mean, why would she? We'd never met.

"You look familiar." Peyton narrowed her eyes in thought.

I shook my head, trying to remain casual. "I have one of those faces."

She continued to stare until I shifted uncomfortably. Finally, she looked back at Jamie. Either the woman was shrewd or she was paranoid. I wasn't sure which.

Peyton's phone buzzed. She glanced down at her screen, and her face went pale. Just as quickly, she slipped the phone into her back pocket again.

"Everything okay?" I ventured to ask. I didn't want to cross any lines, but something had spooked her.

Her gaze flickered toward me, amber eyes blazing with some kind of unspoken emotions. "Yes, of course."

But the way she glanced around only confirmed that something was wrong.

This was about more than Chase potentially getting back together with Peyton. Something else was going on in addition to that possibility.

Just then, a man walked up to Peyton and whispered something in her ear.

I looked away, trying to appear uninterested and like I was giving her privacy. But, of course, I was trying to hear whatever I could.

"Cartwright is out of town. Now's the time," he whispered.

Something raced through her gaze. Fear? Excitement? I wasn't sure.

That had to be the same Cartwright I'd read about this morning. Alexander Cartwright. The man I'd seen arguing with Chase. The millionaire.

The tall, lanky man stepped back and, without a glance at us, started on his way.

"Thanks, Larry," Peyton said.

Larry? That was the name Chase had used that night in the parking lot. Maybe we were getting closer to the truth.

Peyton turned back to us, a new tension to her shoulders, to the set of her jaw. "I really do need to run. Call before you come next time."

***

Jamie and I wandered back to the car, realizing we hadn't gotten very far in our quest for more information. We had seen Larry, the same man Chase had mentioned in the parking lot. And we knew that Peyton had some kind of connection with the racetrack; we just didn't know what.

Despite the fact that there were hardly any cars here, I'd still parked in the same general area near the stables. Perhaps I was a creature of habit.

We leaned against the car trunk a moment, still processing what had just happened and enjoying the unusually warm and sunny early autumn day.

"She's not very nice," Jamie muttered. "I'd say I could see why Chase fell for her, but I can't."

"Believe me, while he takes responsibility for their failed marriage, he never made her out to be a saint."

"Did he try to get back together with her after he stopped drinking?"

"Yes, he did, but it was too late. She was either married or already dating someone. I can't remember. Anyway, she didn't want anything to do with him."

"The words 'gold digger' came to mind when I was talking to her," Jamie said.

"She definitely liked to live big."

Jamie and I turned toward a noise in the background. A man

was walking from the stables. He was probably in his thirties and looked a bit like a cowboy. His eyes lit when he saw us, and he tipped his hat.

"Morning, ladies."

Jamie's eyes lit. "This is our chance," she whispered before stepping forward. "Hello there. You work here?"

"As a matter of fact, I do." He stopped beside us, his chest puffing out. The man's teeth were a jumbled mess and yellow to boot. He also had a spare tire around his midsection, and all the plaid shirts in the world wouldn't cover it.

But the man's demeanor made it obvious that he liked having attention from ladies. His hands went to his belt. His eyes sparkled with excitement. He leaned back, almost like he was attempting some swagger. His eyes clearly showed he thought he was doing us a favor.

And, little did he know, he was.

"What can I help you lovely ladies with?" He practically preened as he waited for our response.

"We're just looking for more information on the track." Jamie appeared more innocent than I'd ever seen her look before as she clasped her hands in front of her and tilted her head sweetly. "We've never been to the races before."

He continued grinning. "What would you like to know? I've worked here for fifteen years. I can pretty much tell you anything."

"Fifteen years? You sound like just the person we're looking for." Jamie actually batted her eyelashes.

I nearly rolled my eyes, but I stopped myself just in time.

"I started when I was fresh out of high school. I've seen this place go through a lot of changes—good and bad."

"How are things here lately? On the right . . . track? Maybe I could look for a job here."

I had to look away in fear I'd burst out laughing.

The man shrugged. "I wouldn't recommend anyone work here at this point."

"Things must be bad, then."

"I don't know. I just have a few suspicions." He wagged his eyebrows. "None that I can talk about, of course."

"Are you sure?"

He nodded. "Oh, I'm sure."

Jamie shifted, obviously changing tactics. "I'm such a history buff, but I love current events too. I just adore stories about places and the people who work there. You know what really fascinates me? All the stories about horse racing. Hearing about the winners. The champions. The winning by a nose."

"Oh, there are some good stories out there." He seemed interested again. "I could talk about the races all day. I've seen some nail-biters."

"Then there are also the scandals. The horse juicing, and tension between jockeys and horse owners, and risky gambling."

"Those tales have been around for near a century," the man said. "The industry truly is fascinating."

"Any of that happen here?" Jamie asked, lowering her voice.

"Now, what kind of question is that? You trying to get me to lose my job?" He laughed nervously.

"Is that a possibility?"

"Oh, there have been threats of layoffs. No one wants to really talk about it, but I've heard the track is in trouble. I'd sure hate to see it go through a hard time again. It seemed like this place was just returning to its former glory, and now . . . it's anybody's guess what will happen."

"Why is it in trouble?" I asked.

The man cringed. "I'd better not say. If my boss man finds out I was talking, I could get fired. I'm sure there'd be someone here waiting to spill the beans as soon as he returned from his trip."

"He's on a trip right now?" Jamie said. "In the middle of racing season?"

"I heard he's visiting family. Let me tell you, it's been a regular soap opera around here. He's gone. His wife is hanging out with a new man while he's gone. We're all walking on eggshells."

"That doesn't sound good," I muttered.

"Yeah, his wife is a piece of work." He shook his head, as if he wasn't impressed.

"She stayed here while he went on a trip, huh?"

"That's Peyton for you."

My face went pale. "Peyton?"

He nodded. "Peyton Andrews. Yes, she kept her maiden name. Some type of last-ditch effort to maintain her independence or something. That's not surprising. Everyone knows she married Winston for his money."

CHAPTER 11

"Peyton is married to Winston?" I shook my head as I sat in the car. "I shouldn't be surprised."

"It's like I said: gold digger." Jamie did the Z-snap hand-on-the-hip Diva.

"And she's been hanging out with someone else while Winston's been gone. That would be Chase." I sighed, not wanting to believe it.

"On the bright side, at least we're getting somewhere. Wyndmyer is in trouble, right? Then we heard Larry whisper something about Alexander. Maybe he is connected with all of this."

"Let's find out." I pulled out my phone and typed "Cartwright" and "Wyndmyer" into the search engine. Sure enough, I hit pay dirt.

"Well?" Jamie asked.

"There are numerous articles on the man. He has a stunning horseshoe collection. He's going to be at an art show this weekend that features paintings showcasing equine life." I scrolled down farther. "Oh, now we're getting good. There have been allegations of horse doping against him. He's had several award-winning horses. But other horse owners are accusing him of using steroids and paying off vets to remain quiet about it."

"Interesting, but I'm not sure how it helps us."

"Let me keep looking." My eyes widened. "Get this: he owns Golden Equestrian."

"The place where Aidan Jennings worked?"

"Bingo!"

"I say we pay a visit to Aidan Jennings's family."

"Really?" I'd done my fair share of difficult house calls as a social worker, but I would never purposefully put myself in a position to make someone's grief worse.

"I know. Let's look up the articles about his death," Jamie said. "If there's an article on him, maybe the reporter quoted someone—a friend, maybe. We could start there."

I scanned the first article I came across and then nodded. "Sure enough, his best friend Calvin Williams was quoted. He might be a better starting point. But we're going to have to choose our words carefully."

"You know I don't like doing this either, right? But considering there are homicidal maniacs chasing us, we don't have much choice. It's like you said earlier: either we find these men or they find us again. If they find us again . . . I'm not sure what will happen next time."

I wanted to argue, but I couldn't. We had no choice but to push ahead.

***

Thanks to social media, we discovered that Calvin Williams was a mechanic at a local repair shop. We decided to introduce ourselves to him there. When Jamie and I walked into the bay area, the three men who were working stopped and gave us a look of approval. The youngest stepped our way first.

"How can I help you two ladies?" The man had blond hair that was a little too long. It was slicked back from his face and had a touch of wave to it. I wasn't sure if it was gelled or greasy, but either way, I didn't care for the look.

Not that anyone had asked me for my opinion.

"We were hoping to speak with Calvin," Jamie said.

He tossed a stained rag over his shoulder. "That's me. What can I do for you?"

"We wanted to talk to you about your friend, Aidan Jennings," she continued. "We're so sorry for your loss."

"So am I." A cloud seemed to darken his face. "What about him?"

I stepped forward. "We read what you said in the paper about your friend deserving justice, and we're trying to figure out what happened to him."

"Did you know Aidan?" Calvin asked, his eyes narrowed skeptically.

I decided to take a . . . gamble. Gulp. Bad thought choice. "We know of him from down at the tracks. Jamie's a reporter, and she's actually doing a story on the fall of Wyndmyer Park. We understand he has connections there."

Calvin nodded slowly but surely. "Something's going on. I've been saying that for weeks. Ever since Gold Standard won the Belmont Crown, everyone has hoped things will turn around."

"But you don't agree?"

He shook his head. "Bad leadership. Winston Kensington just bought the place for the prestige of it."

"You know him?" I asked.

"No, but everyone around here knows that. Besides, my dad used to work at the racetracks. It's a small world, and word travels fast."

"Listen," Jamie started. "We know you're working, but we have more questions about Aidan."

That seemed to calm him. His shoulders softened a moment before he looked behind him at a man in the distance. "Harry, can I take five?"

After the man raised his chin in a nod, Calvin led Jamie and me outside, away from anyone who might hear. We stood on a sidewalk brightly lit with sunlight. Colorful air dancers swayed by the street, presenting an overly cheerful atmosphere considering our conversation.

"What do you want to know?" Calvin started. The scar across his cheek looked old and gave him an air of toughness, like he'd lived a rough life, as did the choppy cadence of his words.

"Any idea who might have wanted to kill your friend?" I asked.

He raised his chin in a half nod, half jerk. "I have a few theories. Aidan was a good guy. But he got mixed up in a few things he should have stayed away from."

"Like what?" I prodded.

"Gambling. Nothing big time. But big enough that he owed some people some money."

Was this all about a gambling ring? Had Chase—in just the few days he'd been back here in Louisville—gotten himself mixed up in some kind of dangerous underworld based out of Wyndmyer? Was that the reason these men were chasing us down now?

Maybe Chase owed them money and everything was somehow connected with that.

I shifted on the sidewalk, trying to process what Calvin was saying. "So you think these men found Aidan and gunned him down because he hadn't paid his debts?"

He didn't hesitate this time. "That's exactly what I think."

"Do you know who these men are?" Jamie asked.

"I think they might have worked at the stables where Aidan worked. But that's all I know."

"Golden Equestrian, right?" I said.

"That's right. There's another arrogant jerk. Alexander Cartwright. He thinks he owns the thoroughbred business in the area. Still denies he juiced his horses. Just like he denies he was involved in that other murder a few years ago."

My blood went cold. "Murder?"

He nodded. "Another stable boy. Forget his name. Anyway, Cartwright was never implicated in public, but there was plenty of talk around the stables. People lived in fear of the man."

Interesting. We were finally getting somewhere.

We had a horse track, a horse owner, and a stable boy with a gambling problem.

How did all those pieces fit together?

I needed to figure it out. My life depended on it.

CHAPTER 12

Jamie and I grabbed lunch at a sit-down chain restaurant. Jamie had ordered steak and a double order of steamed broccoli. I splurged on chicken scampl. Pasta with rich, creamy sauce and plenty of cheese? Yes, I was stress eating.

That was never a good sign.

"What now?" Jamie asked, taking a bite of her broccoli before adding more salt to her pile of veggies.

Heaviness settled across my shoulders—across my heart—as I twirled some angel hair pasta around my fork. The more I learned, the more disturbing all of this became. "We have to go back to the racetrack tonight."

Jamie's eyebrows shot up. "Really?"

I nodded. "I know each time I go I increase the likelihood I'll run into Chase. But the answer somehow goes back to that place. I'm here in Louisville. I can't just sit around and not do everything within my power to find the truth. I'm going to have to go back to work soon. You too. We can't stay here forever. Our lives are in Cincinnati. However, the pressure of having time constraints is making me feel like I'm going to crack."

"How did Ralph take the news that you were taking a few days off?"

I shrugged, still swirling my pasta. The creamy sauce was beginning to look cold and lumpy. "He couldn't say anything because I had the time coming. But he suspects something."

"What did you tell him?"

"That you and I were going to help out a friend in Louisville. I said the details were private, and that stopped him from asking too many questions. For now, at least. He did ask me to text him the address of where I'm staying."

"Really?"

I shrugged. "He's the protective older brother. What can I say? Besides, it wasn't a bad idea, just in case I don't come home and the police need to know where to start looking."

"True that."

"What did you tell your parents?"

"I said I was following a story lead in Louisville. But I actually turned in a couple of articles early, so I'm good. How was I to know just how fortunate that would be when I worked ahead?"

"Fortunate."

Jamie ate the last bite of her meal. "Okay, let's see what time the race starts tonight."

I pulled it up on my phone. "At five."

"I have my scarf to pull my hair back. You?"

I glanced down at my gray A-line dress. I wore a jean jacket and red Converse shoes with it. "I'll pull my hair into a bun and wear my sunglasses. It will have to be fine."

After we finished eating, we headed toward the track. I didn't see any vans following us as we traveled. That was a good thing. But I was still nervous as we pulled into the parking lot, locked up the car, and walked to the entrance. I tugged my hat lower, feeling uncomfortable.

A crowd had already gathered. Racing was obviously a big business, a fact that I found incredibly sad. If people would put their money toward feeding the poor instead of gambling, it could really make an impact on society. But, of course, I had frivolous expenses I could sacrifice also. Not gambling, but getting manicures or lattes.

I sighed. The answers sometimes seemed simple, when they were in fact quite complex.

"One time we were in a gas station," Jamie said beside me as we walked.

I had no idea where she was going with this. "Okay . . ."

"You told me that if the man of your dreams was there but he was buying a lottery ticket, you couldn't date him."

"That sounds a little harsh, doesn't it?" I shrugged. "But I still stand behind that sentiment just because I feel like there are better ways to spend money. I don't want to link my bank account with someone who gambles—even if it's just the lottery or a horse race."

"And if you see Chase gambling? How are you going to feel then?"

My heart thudded in my chest. "I'll cross that bridge when I get there."

My eyes searched the crowd as soon as we entered the building. There were too many people here. It would be almost impossible for me to spot Chase.

Except I did.

It seemed like a near miracle. But there he was. At one of the machines where he could make a wager.

I must have let out a gasp, because Jamie followed my gaze. Her hand went to my arm, as if she knew I was going into shock.

In the back of my mind, I'd tried to believe the best. I'd held out a ray of hope that all of this was a misunderstanding. But looking at Chase now, I couldn't deny what was happening.

As Chase turned to leave, Jamie and I quickly stepped behind a fat cement column and out of sight. After he walked past, I peered around the edge in time to see Peyton meet him near the seats. He said something quietly to her.

I couldn't take my eyes away. It was like a car crash: you

didn't want to look, but you couldn't stop yourself.

Chase, almost as if in slow motion, leaned toward Peyton.

I held my breath.

He pulled her into his arms. Her arms went around his neck.

They stepped closer, lingering in each other's embrace as if relishing it. Enjoying it.

Tears rushed to my eyes.

My worst fears were confirmed. They were back together. Friends didn't linger in embraces like that. My respect for Chase plummeted.

"Holly . . ." Jamie squeezed my arm.

I shook my head, trying to communicate to her that there were no words. I didn't want her to offer me platitudes. I knew what I was seeing, and I had to deal with it.

My heart ached, panged inside my chest. The Jaws of Life wouldn't even be able to save it from the turmoil permanently trapped there. My rose-colored glasses were off, though in reality they'd been sliding farther down my nose for a long time.

Finally, they stepped back, but Chase kept a hand around Peyton's shoulders as the two of them went to find their seats.

"Holly . . ." Jamie repeated.

I raised my hand again, trying to stop her. There was nothing she could say to make me feel better. Nothing.

"No, Holly. Really." She tugged my arm, her voice changing from compassionate to spooked. "Look."

I followed her gaze and saw two men walking toward us. They wore black T-shirts and jeans, as well as black stocking caps that were pulled down low. Their steps were brisk, urgent.

My gut told me these guys weren't part of security. No, these were the men from the van, who'd been trying to track Jamie and me down. They were here now.

Jamie and I hurried away from them, resisting the urge to

run because it would only draw attention to us. We had to somehow figure out how to get away from these guys.

I stole a glance over my shoulder. The men were still behind us. They were gaining speed with each step.

Urgency pressed on me. I reached for Jamie's arm as my gaze scanned my surroundings, looking for an escape route.

Who were these guys? Why were they fixated on Jamie and me?

It had been one thing when their actions seemed covert. But they were becoming bold. They were pursuing us in public now.

We dodged in and out of the crowd, between vendors and families and groups of businessmen.

A bathroom was ahead. But I didn't want to be cornered.

Finally, my gaze stopped at a group of concession workers. They were standing by a door that led to an "Employees Only" area. Someone, a manager, based on his bossy tone, was speaking to them.

They were trainees, I realized. They all appeared green and a touch nervous. They had too many questions to be seasoned employees.

This could be our chance. Our only chance.

Just as I spotted the workers, I sucked in a quick breath.

Chase.

He walked our way, purpose in his steely gaze as he stared ahead. His head didn't turn our way.

Not yet.

But there was a good chance he could.

I glanced behind me. The men behind us were only steps away.

My nerves ratcheted up to near-record levels.

I grabbed Jamie and pulled her into the mix of employees

flooding through the "Employees Only" doorway. No one seemed to notice us—not right away, at least. As soon as I was inside, I slammed the door and leaned against it, twisting the lock in place.

I closed my eyes, held my breath, waited.

The handle turned. It jiggled.

Someone was trying to get in.

Those men were trying to get in.

But the door didn't budge.

I released my breath. We'd done it. We'd gotten away from them. At least for a moment.

As my eyes wandered from Jamie, I saw the group of workers. Staring at us with curiosity in their gazes.

I offered a feeble smile. "It looks like we've got some 'splaining to do."

***

A security guard had led Jamie and me to the administrative offices while all the new trainees watched with wide eyes and maybe even a few snickers. The good news was that we hadn't seen the men who were chasing us, *and* this had distracted me from the emotional fiasco of seeing Chase and Peyton together.

We were in an administrative office located on the perimeter of the building. The room was decorated in burgundy and mahogany and featured gold-framed pictures of racehorses all around the room. The strange mixture of leather and Lysol filled my nostrils.

The man who sat across from us at an oversized desk was none other than Larry Mullins. We were informed he was the assistant manager here at the track.

Being in his office seemed like both a great turn of luck and a great act of misfortune. I didn't want to get in trouble with the law, but maybe I could make lemonade out of lemons and get some answers.

I swallowed, not used to getting in trouble. The only time I'd ever gotten sent to the principal's office was when I interjected myself between the school bully, Hank Starns, and his prey—a quiet, nerdy boy named Melvin. Melvin was about to get a wedgie, and a group of Hank's friends had gathered around to watch the show. I'd put myself between Melvin and Hank and, in a grim turn of events, had ended up with a day's suspension after I'd shoved Hank away.

"Why did the two of you sneak into an 'Employees Only' area?" Larry asked.

"We got lost," I tried to explain.

"Lost? Haven't heard that one before."

"We were trying to find an exit, and we saw a mass exodus," Jamie explained.

"A mass exodus?"

"The Red Sea practically parted and showed us the way," Jamie said.

Larry nodded slowly, but my underlying sense indicated the man thought we were loony. "I see. You should understand that we have tight security here at the tracks."

"Of course," I said.

"We take potential threats seriously, and we just don't want trouble."

"Neither do we," Jamie said. "In fact, if you let us go, we'll be on our way."

Except I wasn't ready to leave yet. This might be my only chance to speak with Larry, and I could feel the conversation starting to wrap up.

"Aren't you friends with Chase Dexter?" I blurted. "I feel like

I've seen you with him before."

Larry's eyes narrowed, and his muscles visibly tightened. "Why would you ask that?"

"I thought I saw you with him the other day. I had a big crush on him back in the day." I flashed a big, dopey smile. "You know, when he played football."

"Men in tights," Jamie added. "We love them."

Larry released a seething breath and shook his head. "No, I don't know him."

I wasn't ready to drop this. "That wasn't you and that brunette with him? What's her name again?"

"Peyton Andrews?" His words sounded dull, annoyed.

"Yes!" I threw my hands in the air. "That's her. I thought I saw you all together."

He narrowed his eyes even more, until they were almost slits. "Yes, she's my boss."

I leaned closer. "He was married to her at one time, right? Did they get back together?"

His jaw flexed. "I don't see where this is any of your business."

"Is it true that Wyndmyer is having trouble?" Jamie asked. "That it might shut down?"

"Where did you hear that?" His voice rose in pitch. Our welcome was outlived. But we'd also struck a nerve.

"What about Alexander Cartwright? Do you know him?" Jamie continued. If she had a microphone in her hand, she could be a one-woman media section at a press conference.

His fists hit the desk, and he pushed himself to a standing position. "I don't know who you think you are—"

"Okay, I'm going to be honest," Jamie interjected. "I'm a reporter, and there are several things I've found very interesting about Wyndmyer."

"A reporter who accidentally wandered behind the scenes?" His cheeks reddened. "You need to leave."

"Can you just answer this—are the police investigating Alexander?" I threw in, desperate for answers.

"The police? What? You're out of line." His voice trembled now, and veins protruded at his temples.

"What are you hiding?" Jamie continued.

"That's it! I'm calling security." He picked up the phone.

Acting on impulse, I pressed down the receiver in front of me. "You don't have to do anything if you answer our questions. We can keep all this between us. I know you don't want any dirt to be released on this place. On you and how you're doing your job. We've heard about the scandals, and this place doesn't need any more bad PR."

His face reddened even more as he stared at me. I swallowed hard. I hadn't meant to talk tough. I wasn't even sure where my nerve had come from. But what I'd said was already out there, and now we were all having a stare down, waiting to see who would relent. Who would win.

Finally, Larry put the phone back on its cradle. "Look, I don't owe you an explanation. Let me make that clear. But I don't want you making up stories either. The only involvement we currently have with Cartwright, other than racing, is hosting an event for a charity he's started for retired racehorses. It will be good PR for the track. It's not a secret that we've been hurting financially for a while now."

"Why is that a secret?" I asked. "I heard you tell someone that Alexander was out of town and now was the time."

His frown deepened. "You two are good. Yes, I did say that. Alexander was out of town for the day, and we're trying to arrange for Baldwin Irving to be here for the charity event. We're arranging with Alexander's staff for Baldwin's appearance to be a surprise."

"Baldwin Irving?" I questioned.

"He's a horse-racing legend. Won the Triple Crown."

Realization washed over me. That was why they'd mentioned Alexander was out of town.

"You're not trying to help Peyton get away with having an affair?" Jamie asked.

"What? No. I help her with day-to-day operations here. Now we're done. If I were you two, I wouldn't show your faces around here again. Next time I won't be nearly as polite."

With that said, we left. The air remained emotionally charged as we walked toward the car. We stopped by my mom's car in the parking lot—again, probably a terrible idea, given our track record in parking lots as of late.

"Larry may not have anything to do with this," I muttered. "I think he's simply Peyton's employee."

"I agree. But why did Chase say his name in the parking lot at the apartment complex the night we found Aidan Jennings's body?"

"Maybe Larry was discouraging Chase and Peyton from hanging out." I shrugged. "After all, that could be bad PR for the track. He seemed pretty intent on keeping Wyndmyer's reputation clean."

My thoughts went back to Chase and Peyton's earlier interaction. The lingering hug. Stolen glances. The arm around her shoulders.

My gut twisted at the memory. If Jamie's theory was right, then Larry was onto something. Chase and Peyton weren't doing each other any favors.

"Maybe it didn't mean what it looked like," Jamie said, seeming to read my thoughts.

"Why else would they hug like that unless they were back

together?" I shook my head, wishing I could erase my thoughts. "Besides, Peyton is married. That makes all of this worse."

"We just need to take a few steps back. Maybe there's something we're not seeing."

"I don't know, Jamie. I've put a lot on the line to try and help Chase. And, at each turn, I just feel like Chase hurts me even more. I don't know how much longer I can do this."

Jamie turned squarely toward me, a no-nonsense look in her gaze. "Remember: this isn't about you. This is about helping Chase. Isn't that what you said?"

I didn't want to admit it, but I finally nodded. "Yeah, I did say that."

"Then let's sleep on it. In the morning, maybe your perspective will become clearer."

She was right. My emotions felt too big right now for me to make any decisions. Maybe things would be brighter in the morning.

CHAPTER 12

Thirty minutes later, we pulled to a stop in front of an older-style bungalow located about fifteen minutes from downtown. The streets here were narrow and filled with cars parked on the edges. The main highway that ran by the neighborhood was busy and bustling with lots of old shopping centers and power lines that were strung from poles instead of buried beneath the ground. Jamie's friend Magnolia lived here.

Apparently, her name was Magnolia, and she had big blonde hair, wore heavy makeup, and had perceptive eyes. Also according to Jamie, Magnolia was the epitome of a Southern belle. But, similar to sugar alternatives, she was initially sweet with a bitter aftertaste.

We walked to the front door, but before we could even knock, it opened. Magnolia stood there, just as Jamie had described her. She offered a wide grin, showing bright white teeth.

"Well, if it isn't Jamie and her friend Holly!" Magnolia's voice sounded unusually high and Southern.

She pulled Jamie into a hug. As soon as she pulled away, Magnolia grabbed me and pulled me into a hug also. She smelled like roses, and her hairspray made her poof of hair crackle next to my ear.

"I'm so glad to meet you."

"Sorry we're late, and thanks for letting us crash here," Jamie said, stealing a quick look at me. "As you've surmised, this is Holly."

Magnolia grinned wider. "Of course. She rivals me when it comes to manners. I've heard all about you."

She ushered us inside. I quickly observed her decorating style: lots of flowers and pastels. It also smelled like potpourri and cookies, and there were a lot of knickknacks inside. Like, *a lot* of knickknacks. Precious Moments figurines. A spoon collection. Glass birds.

Magnolia turned toward us. "I have tea in the dining room. Let's sit and talk. My knickers have been in a knot since you called."

Knickers in a knot? Interesting. We sat down at the table. Tea was already waiting there for us.

Jamie had assured me that Magnolia was smart and in the know about all things Louisville. So I told her almost everything. An unbiased, objective opinion seemed so tempting and right.

I paused when I finished and waited, trying not to play with my hands as they rested in my lap.

Magnolia stared at me before letting out a long sigh and frowning, a deep V furrowing into her brow.

"What?" I asked.

"You really want to know?"

I paused a moment before nodding. "Yes, I do."

"You ask me, sugar, and it sounds like he's cheating on you, drinking, gambling, or all three."

My heart sank as my stomach dropped.

Maybe I'd hoped for a new perspective. Maybe I'd hoped for hope—for a reason to hope. I hadn't gotten it. I couldn't deny my hurt after seeing Chase and Peyton.

"There could be another explanation," Jamie said, laying her hand on my arm.

Magnolia shrugged. "Maybe, but probably not."

Jamie gave her a dirty look, but she shrugged. "You know that saying: 'You've got blinders on'? That comes from horse racing. Horses wear blinders so they can keep their focus and not get distracted by anything around them. People put on blinders, and all they see is what they want to see."

Now I not only felt bad, but I felt irritated.

"You don't know Chase like I do," I finally said. "Besides, why would someone be hunting Jamie and me down if this was all about Chase's personal problems?"

"Maybe someone's after Chase," Magnolia said. "Maybe he owes them money. Maybe if they get to you, they figure they'll get to him."

My frown deepened. I hadn't thought of that.

"Our own preconceived notions, mixed with our own desires, cloud our judgment, honey," Magnolia continued. "When you put all the pieces together, that's the logical conclusion."

She said it so matter-of-factly, like she had to be right. And she had to add that "honey" to the end, like that would make everything sound a little bit nicer.

A new somberness came over me.

"Remember: assumptions are bad manners," Magnolia finished with the innocent bat of her eyelashes.

My mouth dropped open. Now she was accusing me of not being courteous? I suddenly wasn't liking Jamie's friend very much.

Magnolia shifted and sighed. "I can see I've caused a bit of trepidation here. So I want to make you feel better. I asked some questions about Alexander Cartwright."

"I told her about the argument when I called earlier," Jamie added.

My spirit perked for a moment. "And?"

"People think he's corrupt, but no one can prove anything. People think he dopes his horses and pays people so he can get away with it."

"What?"

She nodded. "It's true. Your boyfriend wasn't gone anytime last week, was he?"

I searched my thoughts when one memory in particular made my stomach drop. "He did have to do a special training in Lexington. It was all day. Something with Homeland Security or something."

"What day?" Magnolia asked.

I swallowed hard. "Wednesday."

Magnolia frowned just as widely as she smiled. "Because Wednesday is the day Aidan Jennings disappeared."

***

I woke up the next morning feeling angry. Really angry. Mostly at Chase. A little bit at myself.

I couldn't believe he would do this to me. I couldn't believe I'd be naïve enough to fall for it. I couldn't believe he'd cast aside the massive strides he'd made in his life and go back to everything he'd left behind.

But I also awoke with a new conviction. I had to help Chase. No matter how much he'd hurt me and how I felt, I had to stop this downward spiral he was on. That's what you did when you loved someone. You didn't abandon him or walk away. You tried to be part of the solution.

"How do you propose to do that?" was the first thing Jamie asked.

"I'm going to talk to Chase's friend Josh."

"Who's Josh?"

"When Chase's life fell apart—the first time—there was only one person who called him out on it. Josh was a chaplain at the police station, and he's been Chase's accountability partner since then."

"You're going to visit him?"

I nodded. "That's right. And, unfortunately, I need to go alone."

"I'll stay here and see if I can find out anything about Aidan Jennings or Alexander Cartwright or Larry or Peyton. So many possibilities. I shouldn't get bored."

"Thanks, Jamie."

I looked up Josh Caraway on Magnolia's computer and discovered he worked full-time as a pastor at a local community church. I knew a lot of police precincts had volunteer chaplains who held other jobs too. That was apparently the case for Josh.

An hour later, I pulled up to a small, traditional-looking church building in the suburbs. It was made of red bricks and had an A-frame roof, with a cross at the front of the building.

I hadn't told Josh I was coming, and I hoped all this didn't backfire in my face. I felt jittery when I stepped onto the brownish-orange carpet. Across the foyer was a corner office with glass walls on two sides. That's where I headed.

My voice sounded squeaky when I asked the salt-and-pepper-haired lady there to speak with Josh. A moment later, a man appeared at the door behind me.

I blinked when I saw him. Maybe I'd expected meek and bookish. I wasn't sure why. I'd seen enough pastors to know they came in all shapes and sizes.

Josh Caraway was probably just under six feet. He had spiky black hair, an oval face that was a touch too long to be considered handsome, and a glimmer of mischief in his eyes.

"Can I help you?" he asked.

I licked my lips, suddenly nervous. "Yes. I was wondering if I could have a moment of your time?"

"And you are . . . ?"

I flushed, entirely too self-conscious. "I'm so sorry. Where are my manners? I'm—"

"Holly Anna Paladin," he finished.

I blinked. "How'd you know?"

"As soon as you said *manners*, it all clicked in my mind." He grinned affably. "Of course we can talk. Come on into my office."

My nerves only intensified as Josh ushered me into his office. It was packed full of books on three walls, and a gigantic desk sat in the middle of the room. Atop the desk was a well-worn Bible, open to the book of Matthew.

A Bible that's falling apart usually belongs to a person who isn't.

I'd seen that saying many times, and it had often proven true.

Would my life prove it? I was beginning to doubt it. Lately, I'd put an awful lot of faith in people. In my future. In my plans.

Maybe God was trying to teach me another lesson: a person falling apart usually meant their Bible wasn't.

CHAPTER 13

"What brings you here, Holly?" Josh didn't sit behind the desk but instead took one of two padded chairs against the wall. At Josh's direction, I sat across from him. Everything inside me screamed that I shouldn't be here, though. This was all a mistake. A huge mistake.

But losing Chase as my boyfriend was worth saving his life.

"So you're Holly." Josh shook his head, leaning back in his chair and observing me a moment. "Chase has told me all about you."

"Has he?" To say I was surprised would be an understatement. I felt like he'd easily thrown away our relationship.

"He seems like a new man since he met you, Holly. I've been anxious for the chance to meet you myself, but I've never had the opportunity. I keep meaning to make it up to Cincinnati, but my little congregation here keeps me busy. I'm not complaining, though."

I forced a polite smile. Josh was good. He knew how to put people at ease, to start with gentle conversation, to mirror people's body language in order to make them feel at ease.

"I'm not sure I should be here," I started, smoothing the skirt of my navy-blue dress.

"Don't be silly. Any friend of Chase's is a friend of mine." His expression sobered. "Whatever is happening, it must be important if you took the trip all the way from Cincinnati to

Louisville."

"I beg you to use your discretion with what I'm about to tell you," I said. "I'm here because I'm concerned about Chase. I know that he looks up to you. He's always spoken very highly about what you did for him back when his life fell apart."

"I was only doing what the Holy Spirit put on my heart to do. Chase is my friend; I couldn't watch him throw his life away. I couldn't watch him drowning and do nothing to save him."

"Exactly!" Maybe Josh *would* understand why I was here. I'd used that analogy many times before. "I'm worried about Chase."

A knot formed between his eyes. "What's going on?"

I told him everything. Well, almost everything. I tried to dampen the parts about me following Chase and the other parts where I sounded like a stalker. Instead, I emphasized the horse-racing facilities, Chase's ex-wife, the van that had followed us back to Cincinnati, even the dead body.

"Dead body?"

"It's a long story."

"Did you say in the parking lot behind the Belmont Apartments?"

I blinked in surprise. "How did you know?"

"Because I live there."

My bottom lip dropped. "Chase is staying with you?"

Josh nodded. "I haven't seen him a lot, but yes. He's staying with me."

"This is going to be an odd question, but humor me if you will. What happened on the night that dead body was found?"

He thought about it a moment and shrugged. "I can tell you what I know. Chase had stopped by the apartment to pick up something. He went back outside and apparently ran into someone he knew—someone who'd been on the force with him

104

at one time. They discovered the gun that had been left under his Jeep. The detective took it into evidence and left. Chase left. Then the police came again after an anonymous call about the dead body."

I nodded. Something bothered me, but I didn't know what. "Does that help?"

"I'm not sure. But thank you for sharing. Chase told you that?"

Josh nodded. "That's right."

"That's actually not why I'm here, though. I'm here about Chase."

"It sounds like you care about him a lot, Holly."

I told him all of that, and this was the conclusion he walked away with? I was surprised and maybe even a little irritated. I wanted him to be as shocked and concerned as I was. "I do care about him."

"I can see where everything that's happened would make you worried."

"I'm afraid he's slipping back into his old patterns. I don't want to see him go down that dark hole again."

"Addictions are a dark hole. You realize that there's a part of Chase that will always struggle with alcohol, right? A person is never really cured."

"I'm a counselor. I do realize that."

"Of course," Josh said, smoothing the leg of his jeans. "But sometimes even counselors need reminding." He leaned toward me. "What do you want me to do?"

What did I want him to do? I didn't know. "He's shut me out, Josh. He doesn't know that I know any of this. He doesn't even know that I'm aware of where he is. It's a long story how I found out. Let's just say I'm resourceful."

"I've heard that also." He smiled, but the action quickly

morphed into concern. "You want me to talk to him?"

I rubbed my lips together. "I suppose that is what I want. I just feel like he could use a voice of wisdom right now."

"Are you afraid of losing him?"

"I'm more afraid that he's going to mess up his life. I don't know how to help."

"Sometimes we can't help. We have to let a person learn for themselves."

Did he know something I didn't? "Are you saying that's true for Chase? Because that might work in some scenarios, but not with addictions."

He raised his hands. My voice must have risen as my emotions got the best of me.

"I understand that. I agree that we need accountability. But the choice is ultimately up to the person whose life is wrapped up in their choices. You know that as a social worker, I'm sure. I pushed Chase in the right direction five years ago, but he was the one who made the choice to change."

I nodded reluctantly. His words were true. I knew that. I wanted a formula or the option to wave a magic wand and make everything right. If only life worked like that.

If only God worked like that.

Josh must not have interpreted my agreement, because he continued. "There were other guys at the station I tried to help. It didn't always work. Even after I confronted some people with the truth about their lives, they continued to do what they wanted. It didn't matter what I told them. They kept going on the path they were on."

"That's pretty common."

He leaned toward me, lowering his head and his voice. I had a feeling there was a sermon coming on. I wasn't disappointed.

"I'll call this 'The Tale of Two Officers.' There was another officer at the station who had problems around the same time Chase got off track," Josh started. "The guy ended up stealing some drugs from the evidence lockers and got himself into a heap of trouble. I tried to speak life into this man also, but he only got defensive and acted out more. Instead of turning from his ways, he dove in deeper. He ended up losing his job, going to jail, and basically turning to a life of crime."

"So you're saying that could have been Chase?"

He nodded. "That's exactly what I'm saying. Chase could have gone off the deep end. He didn't. He came to a point in his life where he had to choose which path he was going to take. He chose wisely. Unfortunately, we come to a lot of those paths in our lives. We have a lot of moments where our decisions will define the foreseeable future."

"I understand. And I agree. I've been there before myself." When I'd been given a year to live, I'd chosen to embrace the future I had left instead of mourning the time I was losing. I waited, unsure of how to read between the lines. I supposed in some ways, I was at that fork in the road now also. I could walk away from my interference in Chase's life, or I could dive in deeper.

I was diving in deeper. Almost to the point of no return.

I frowned. "So, all that said, you'll help?"

Finally, he nodded. "I'll talk to Chase. See if I can find out what's going on. I'll make sure he's okay. I'll also see what I can find out about that security footage."

"You'd do that?"

"Of course."

Relief flushed through me. If anyone could connect with him, I had a feeling it was Josh. "Thank you. I just don't want to see him ruin his life."

"He's blessed to have someone like you, Holly."

"When he finds out how I've been snooping around, he may not feel that way. I'm usually not this nosy. I promise I'm not. But one thing has just led to another . . ."

"You don't have to explain." He offered an affable smile. "Your secret is safe with me. But I do want to urge you to be careful. I don't know what's going on with the van that's been following you or the dead body, but it doesn't sound good."

"Thank you for your time, Josh. I really do appreciate it."

He flashed a sincere smile. "Anytime, Holly. I meant what I said earlier: any friend of Chase's is a friend of mine. If you need anything, let me know."

***

When I got back to Magnolia's, Jamie ushered me to the kitchen table, where she'd prepared a garden salad with grilled chicken and homemade ranch dressing. While we ate, I recounted everything I'd learned.

"So Josh was hot?" Jamie wiped her mouth and looked at me with wide eyes from across the table.

I scowled and stabbed a piece of lettuce. "I just told you all that, and you're walking away with the fact that Josh is hot?"

She shrugged and resumed eating, unaffected by my conversational expectations. "I'm a single lady. I just like to know what options are out here."

"Let's focus, Jamie."

"Right. Focus. Well, I discovered something today. I actually called Golden Equestrian, and now I have a job interview there tomorrow."

My eyes widened this time. "Really? I'm not sure it's safe. At least not if our suspicions are right."

"It's a huge place, and it's a job interview. If two people

108

associated with the place are killed within a week of each other, the police will be all over it."

I hesitantly nodded, still unsettled. "I know I can't talk you out of it."

"There's one other thing. I went ahead and put the stables into my GPS so I could figure out how long it would take to get there. Get this? It's in the middle of nowhere."

I shook my head. "I'm not following."

"Just like Chase was in the middle of nowhere the other day."

My jaw went slack. "Really? That's where Chase was the other day?"

Jamie smiled and ate the last bite of her salad. "Bingo."

"This just keeps getting stranger and stranger." I stabbed another piece of lettuce, taking my frustrations out on my poor salad. "Where does this leave us?"

"That's a good question. I'm still not sure how all this is connected—or if it even is. Maybe we're making it more complicated than it actually is. Maybe Chase really has reverted to his old ways. Maybe he did get in too deep, and now someone's trying to get money back Chase owes him. That would explain the van that followed us. They could use you as bait and put more pressure on him to pay up."

I frowned. "I don't want to think that's true. Besides, shouldn't they snatch *Peyton* to put pressure on him?"

"It's better to face reality, though. I feel like we're skirting around the real issues here because we don't want to be hurt or disappointed in someone we've put a lot of faith in."

I put my fork down, most of my salad eaten, and slowly wiped my mouth. "I don't think a guy is the answer to all my problems, Jamie."

"I know that."

I crossed my arms and leaned back, feeling gloomy. "I don't expect Chase to ride into my life and make everything right. I don't think falling in love is the pinnacle of my life. But I do think that finding someone you want to spend your life with—someone who you respect and who respects you—can be a beautiful thing."

"I know you're grounded, Holly. You don't have to tell me that." Jamie squeezed my hand. "I just hate to see you hurt."

"I guess I'm telling you because I did let myself dream. Maybe this is a reality check. Maybe my emotions and all the fairy tales I ever listened to in my life did begin to play with my psyche."

"Let's keep looking for answers, okay? I don't have another article due until Monday, so we've got some time. We'll keep checking out Alexander and maybe even Peyton."

"I think I can help."

I jerked my head up. Magnolia stood in the doorway. I hadn't realized she was home, but she appeared to have just woken up from a nap, based on her lopsided hair and droopy eyes.

"What are you thinking?" Jamie asked.

"My old college roommate works for the racing commission."

"What?" The question shot from my mouth like . . . well, like a horse hearing the firing pistol at the start of a race.

Magnolia nodded. "It's true. I talked to her, and she's willing to meet with you tomorrow."

"Yes! I'd love to."

"Here's the thing: she could get into a lot of trouble, so the meeting has to be hush-hush. She wants to meet you at a park, and you can't ever mention her name to anyone."

"I can agree to that. Thank you."

"I'm glad to help. Besides, I'm always up for a good story."

I mentally took a step back, realizing Magnolia could have some ulterior motives. "I don't exactly want this to be front-page news."

She waved her hand as if to dismiss me. "I didn't say it would be. That would be rude. But I want first dibs if this turns out to be something."

Unease churned in my gut as I imagined the possible outcomes of this. It was one thing to have my personal life as a disaster for friends and family to see. It was another thing to broadcast my mistakes and Chase's mistakes to the world. "I don't want you to make Chase look bad."

"Even if he is bad?" Magnolia said.

My unease churned even harder. "He's not bad. You don't know him like I do."

"All this positive thinking on your part might not mean anything when your boyfriend realizes you've been spying on him." Magnolia's words seemed to make even the air go silent. There were no barking dogs or honking cars or loud neighbors. Everything was quiet.

I opened my mouth, wanting to argue. But I couldn't. I knew I'd gotten myself in a pickle.

"My dad always said that a person of character does what's right, even if it means taking a personal loss," I finally said. "Regardless of the consequences."

"There aren't many people of character around." Magnolia shrugged. "You know what I say? Bless their hearts. All of them. Every blessed one, because they need all the blessing they can get."

I wasn't sure if she was insulting me or not, but my defenses were going up. The fruit of the Spirit began repeating in my mind. Love, joy, peace, goodness, kindness, gentleness, and self-control.

Not anger. Not self-righteousness. Not snappy comebacks.

"I'll meet with your friend," I finally said. "But I'm not promising any paybacks. Call me rude. Call me ungrateful. Call me un-Christian. But I'm putting my foot down."

***

After Magnolia left to do an interview, Jamie and I stared at each other for a moment. I'd cleaned up our mess, even scrubbing her toaster—it had crumbs in it. Take that, Martha Stewart! I wanted to leave the kitchen better than I'd found it, lest she say I had bad manners again.

She'd even had the nerve to remind us to lock up when we left. Sure, she'd also said something about a string of burglaries in the area. But she didn't have to treat us like adolescents.

"What now?" I asked.

"See where Chase is," Jamie suggested.

With a touch of hesitation, I pulled the app up on my phone. I hit Chase's name, and several seconds later, a little dot appeared on a map. I blinked in confusion.

"What?" Jamie asked, peering over my shoulder.

"He appears to be in the suburbs."

"Do you have a street name?"

"St. Helens."

Jamie pointed to a button on the app. "Go to satellite view."

"You really know your way around a digital map." I glanced over my shoulder long enough to show her I was impressed.

"One of my many talents."

I hit the button, and the map changed to digital satellite. I zoomed in on the area. It was slightly blurry yet amazingly clear at the same time.

"It's a neighborhood," Jamie said. "A nice neighborhood."

"I wonder why he's there." Researching horses to bet on? Spending time with Peyton? Avoiding questions the police might have about Aidan Jennings?

"We could find out . . ."

I glanced at Jamie, surprised by her idea. "Really?"

"We'll be subtle. Smooth. Invisible." She spread her hands out, as if gliding across the ice, and got a far-off, dramatic look in her eyes.

"That sounds good in theory, but in reality . . ." I could see so many things going wrong.

Jamie snapped from her thespian moment and frowned. "Yeah, I know. We have a bad track record. I say we give it a shot anyway. If Chase is with Peyton again, then it won't matter if he thinks you're psycho."

"Unless he issues a restraining order against me." Wouldn't the media love to get ahold of information like that?

Jamie snorted. When she saw my face, she covered her mouth and tried to look apologetic. "I'm sorry. I didn't mean to laugh. It's just that . . . the idea of you having a violent bone in your body is just funny. Absurd, really. I mean, you're my peace-loving friend."

"Who always seems to get in the middle of conflict and messes," I reminded her.

"It's almost like that's where God wants you. In fact, it's almost like these messes find you instead of the opposite. Maybe that's your purpose in life, Holly. You are supposed to clean up messes in people's lives."

"I need to figure out how to clean up the messes in my own life."

"Don't we all? Don't we all?" Jamie stood and stuck her plate in the dishwasher. "Ready to go?"

I nodded. "Like you said, what do I have to lose?"

CHAPTER 14

We sat in my mom's Lexus in a very, very affluent neighborhood. Sure enough, Chase's Jeep was in a driveway of a very, very nice house. And this whole scenario felt very, very creepy.

Jamie cut the engine and we slouched in the seats. We'd parked a street over from Chase's location, at a place where we could still see the massive house. It was white, wide, and tall, and had black shutters and neat landscaping.

"Who do you think owns it?" Jamie asked. She took a sip of some tea we'd gotten at a drive-through on our way here. I'd opted for some coffee to keep myself alert. I usually added lots of cream and sugar, but I'd kept it black and now I regretted it.

Black coffee was disgusting.

"A jockey?" I offered.

"Maybe." She took another sip of her tea and sighed, almost sounding content. "Our first stakeout. I feel like a real private eye."

"Yeah, PIs. Not stalker chicks," I added.

"Exactly."

The next five minutes felt like an hour. Just sitting with my thoughts was a challenge because they kept going places I didn't want them to go. Mainly replaying Chase and Peyton last night.

"One thing they never mention on those stakeouts on TV is

just how boring stakeouts are," I mumbled.

"Your brother suspicious of your time off?" Jamie asked.

I looked at my chipped pink nails and shook my head. "I don't think so. I told him that you and I were having some girl time in Louisville. I haven't taken any vacation time since I started working for him, so he seemed okay with it."

"I didn't have any stories lined up. I told my mom the twins were driving me crazy and I needed some NASCAR and horse racing."

"I'm sure she believed that." Mama Val was no fool.

"Nah, but she trusts me."

I straightened as a Mercedes started down the road. I held my breath, waiting to see if it would go to the house where Chase was.

The driver continued past, without so much as a look our way.

I released the air from my lungs. I wanted a lead, yet I almost feared knowing the truth.

"What if he stays here all day?" I asked, drumming my fingers on the top of my coffee.

"It would be torture. We've only been here fifteen minutes."

I nearly slapped her arm with surprise. "Take it back! It has to have been at least an hour."

She shook her head and glanced at her watch again. "You're wrong. Fifteen minutes. My tea is still hot."

"I'd make a terrible PI. I don't have the patience." I grabbed her arm the moment I spotted a new clue driving our way. "Jamie, look! It's the van."

"Oh, girlfriend. We're in trouble if they see us. They shouldn't recognize the car, though."

Thankfully the Creeper Van was approaching from the other

side of the neighborhood. If it didn't turn down this street, they probably wouldn't see us. Had they followed us?

My gaze swerved to the very, very nice house where Chase was parked. My eyes widened when I saw Chase step outside . . . with Peyton.

What . . . ?

Almost as if in slow motion, the van pulled into the driveway—apparently Peyton's driveway.

A man stepped out of the driver's seat. I couldn't tell much about him. He wore black, all the way up to his stocking hat. He met Chase and Peyton . . . even shook Chase's hand.

My mouth gaped open. What was going on?

Nothing was making sense.

"Please tell me I'm seeing things," I whispered.

"You're not seeing things," Jamie said. "But this is like living out a Lifetime movie." She shook her head, as if realizing what she said. "Except much more horrible. I wouldn't wish it on anyone, especially not my best friend."

The three of them talked for just a minute. Then the man went back to the van, pulled out of the driveway, and left.

Chase put his arm around Peyton, and they walked inside the very, very nice house.

And my heart broke in two.

***

Jamie and I got caught in rush-hour traffic. Halfway through the battle, at 5:30, we decided to stop and eat dinner at Chick-fil-A. Neither Jamie nor I said very much during the meal. Jamie tried to theorize several times, but I wasn't really in the mood.

I wanted answers, but I needed time to process everything.

We should have followed the van, I realized in retrospect.

I'd been in too much shock to think of it at the moment, though. Now it was too late.

We got back to Magnolia's at seven, and I was wiped out and ready to be by myself for the rest of the evening. I said good night and escaped to my bedroom. After changing into my pajamas, I sat in bed and pulled the covers up around me in the dark.

It might sound pitiful, but I had so much on my mind. All the conclusions I was drawing only added to the burden I felt like I was carrying. I'd put my faith in a person, and now I was suffering the consequences.

A knock sounded at the door. It was Magnolia.

"Come in," I muttered. What else was I supposed to say? It *was* her house.

She stepped inside. "I just wanted to confirm that my friend can meet with you in the morning. Are you still good?"

"I am. Thank you." My gaze went to the ten-gallon aquarium in the corner with five tropical, colorful fish inside. I was no expert at fish, so I didn't know what kind they were, other than relatively flat and about an inch long not including their tails.

But a bright yellow fish swam at the top of the aquarium. I thought he was dead when I'd first glanced into the tank yesterday. But when I tapped on the glass, the fish would begin wiggling again. He'd swim around, lopsided at that, but eventually he'd end up floating on the surface again.

"He's been like that for two weeks," Magnolia said, following my gaze.

I raised my eyebrows. "Two weeks? Wow. That little guy is determined to hang on, isn't he?"

She frowned and nodded. "Yep. I kind of want to put him out of his misery, but I can't bring myself to do it. To keep him alive seems cruel, yet so does killing him."

"I see."

"I'll let you rest. Talk to you more in the morning."

As she closed the door, my eyes were riveted on the little yellow fish.

Suffering.

That was the word that came to mind. That little fish was suffering. In a way, I could relate. I felt like I'd been going through a season of suffering as well. I'd lost my father after a long battle with cancer.

Just over a year later, the doctor had told me I only had a year to live. Thankfully, he'd been wrong and my condition was treatable.

Then a maniac had pulled me into a deadly game that had messed with my relationships and caused me to hurt the people I loved. I'd thought maybe my trials were over for a while, but apparently they weren't.

That's where that word came back into play. *Suffering.* Alive, yet feeling like living was so painful.

Initially, I'd dealt with everything okay. But, as time went on, the realities sank in even more. While I was incredibly thankful to be alive and to be in good health, I was living life a little shell-shocked for everything I'd been through.

Like rushing water over a rock, I was beginning to feel worn down. I closed my eyes.

Dear Lord, help me. Please.

Because I was tired of just barely surviving. Of trials. Of suffering.

CHAPTER 15

The next morning, I pulled into a scenic park not far from downtown Louisville. It boasted lovely stone bridges, cheerful flower beds, and the start of changing fall foliage.

This was where I was supposed to meet Crystal Hanson from the Horse Racing Commission.

I felt a bit like a CIA agent who was meeting with an informant as I pulled the car to a stop at the far end of the parking lot and waited. I'd dropped off Jamie on my way for her job interview at Golden Equestrian. I was antsy about her being there, but I hadn't been able to talk her out of it.

Since I'd arrived a few minutes early, I glanced around the car, trying to pass time until Crystal arrived. I picked up a packet of scented beads my mom kept in the car that made the entire vehicle smell like lavender. That was my mom for you. I smiled.

I really needed to call and check on Mom, but I was afraid she'd ask too many questions, questions I didn't want to answer. She'd easily see through me, and I didn't want to lie any more than I already had. She deserved to enjoy some time away from home.

A piece of paper sticking between the seats caught my eye. I picked it out and saw that it was some kind of letter. Maybe a bill.

To kill time, I opened it. I gawked at what I saw written there.

It was a bill for my mother. From an oncologist. From an appointment that had taken place three weeks ago.

Oncologist. My mom.

What was going on? Was my mom sick?

I searched the bill, looking for a sign of what the bill was in reference to, but all the terms seemed generic.

As a surge of panic welled in me, tears heated my eyes. What if something was wrong with my mom? I couldn't lose both of my parents before I reached thirty. I didn't want to ever lose either of them, but I knew that wasn't reality. Eventually, more people I loved would die. But my heart needed more time to heal.

My soul quivered at the thought of what-ifs.

Please, Lord. Not my mom. Can't we just have a season of peace? And wisdom. I could really use wisdom.

I needed some insight, especially since I was losing hope and faith. After seeing Chase gambling last night. Seeing him meet with those rough-looking guys. Seeing him hug Peyton.

I was unable to deny the truth anymore.

I was going to have to confront Chase soon. I'd tried to hide in the shadows until I had proof, but time was running out. He was getting in deep.

My phone rang. I didn't recognize the number, but I answered anyway. I had my Bluetooth speaker in my ear, and I shoved my phone into my pocket. A static-sounding voice said something on the other line. I couldn't make out anything that was being said.

"Jamie?" I questioned. I couldn't be sure it was her.

The person said something else. Something about her voice sounded urgent. I plugged my other ear, trying to make out what she was saying. It was no use. I couldn't understand anything.

Finally, I climbed from the car and paced toward the woods, trying to find a better connection. "Jamie? Is that you?"

A scrambling noise sounded over the line.

I pulled the phone from my pocket and looked at the number. It wasn't Jamie's. But what if she was calling from her job interview? What if something had gone wrong during her interview and she needed help?

Just then, something screeched behind me. I jerked my head toward the sound. A van pulled up beside me. The one from the parking lot. The one that had followed me to Cincinnati.

I tried to scream, but I didn't have the chance. A masked man opened the back door and reached out. Rough, strong hands grabbed my arms. I tried to dig in my heels, but it did no good. The man jerked me into the van. My shoulders jammed against the floor, and pain shot through me.

I had to keep fighting.

I kicked. But it was too late.

They had me.

The door slammed shut, and the van squealed away.

Before I could gather my surroundings, a black bag was pressed over my head.

CHAPTER 16

Fear rippled through me as the man pressed his knee into my back. My face felt ground into the floor. He jerked my arms behind me hard enough that my joints ached. Plastic zip ties—maybe—went around my wrists.

Not being able to see anything only ignited my fears more. These men could have a gun or knife to my head, and I wouldn't know it. I was at the mercy of killers. Panic seized me at the thought, causing my lungs to constrict.

Pay attention.

I tried to keep my sanity by storing away each new piece of information. Dirty carpet underneath me pricked my arms. The scent of old French fries and stinky shoes wafted through the fabric at my nose. The road bumped, but there were few stops and starts. Maybe we were in the country?

What would happen next? The question made nausea rise in me. I couldn't puke. Not now. Not with a bag over my head.

Lord, help me. Please.

I'd prayed that prayer numerous times in my life. Too many times? I wasn't sure it was possible to pray too much. I desperately needed Jesus, and the sooner we all admitted that, the better off we'd be.

Before I could dwell on that any longer, voices drifted through the dark fabric over my ears. I tried to hear what they were saying.

All I heard was "make her talk," "do what it takes," and "put an end to this."

I swallowed hard. I was going to end up like Aidan Jennings, wasn't I? The nausea in my gut grew even stronger.

Finally, the van screeched to a halt. I tried to figure out where we were. But I could hear nothing. No sounds of traffic. Not the noise of tires on gravel. No church bells or sirens or boats blowing their horns.

It was quiet.

Had they taken me out of town? Somewhere secluded? I felt sure I was at a location where no one could hear me scream.

Another bolt of fear shot through me.

One of the men jerked me upright. His fingers were harsh and like steel on my arm.

In one motion, he pulled the hood from my head. As light hit my eyes, another surge of nausea hit me. Before I could stop it, the contents of my stomach expelled all over the man's legs.

The masked man let out a few choice words. The driver chuckled and threw him a towel that was stained with motor oil.

The man continued to mumble as he wiped the barf from the legs of his jeans. "You think this is funny?"

The driver sobered. "No. Not at all."

I didn't bother to say, "Sorry."

I quickly took in my captors. There were three of them. All wore black ski masks. I could only see the flash of white around their eyes. One sat in the driver's seat, peering back. The other two were back with me, the more dominant one leering in my face.

I tried to remember everything I'd ever learned in my self-defense classes. Did I act compliant? Try to run for my life? Give them a piece of my mind?

I didn't know what the best method was. But I was probably going to have a lot of trouble making myself act any certain way. My fear wanted to control me. That was evident in the way my entire body trembled, the way my stomach churned with upset, the way I could hardly get a breath.

I waited for them to speak first. I'd already puked on one guy. I didn't want anything else to upset him.

"Who are you?" my barf recipient asked.

"You don't know?" I was honestly surprised.

The man's hand connected with my cheek with enough force that my head felt like it might wobble off me for a moment. My face stung. My eyes watered.

"Come on, LJ. Was that necessary?" the driver asked.

"You're asking me that? After what you did last week?"

"You're really going to bring that up now?"

LJ visibly bristled, and I feared the driver might come to the back of the van and rough up the man in front of me.

It was the third man who acted as a voice of reason. "Come on, guys. You have time for that later. Let's get on with business."

I wasn't sure I wanted them to get on with business, not until I knew what that business was, at least. My fear bit down deeper.

"Who are you?" LJ repeated.

The pain spreading across my face made my answer easy. "I'm Holly."

"Why are you following us?"

I swallowed hard. "I'm not. You're—"

Before I could finish, the man slapped me again. This time, I let out a gasp. Tears poured down my cheeks. My jaw ached at the impact of what he'd done.

His voice turned to a growl. "Why are you following us?"

"Please don't hit me again. I promise you—I'm not following you. I'm trying to lose you."

The man raised his hand again, and I cowered. Up until this point, I'd thought I'd hold my head up high no matter the danger I faced. But my face hurt. I was sure bruises would pop up soon enough.

All I wanted to do was protect myself. Maybe that made me a wimp. I didn't know. At the moment, I didn't care.

"What did you see?"

"What did I see?" Tears pooled in my eyes. Somehow I sensed that there wasn't going to be a good outcome to this situation. I was in the back of a van in the middle of nowhere. Would this end with a bullet through my head?

How many times could my life flash before my eyes before I crumbled beneath the burden of life's fragility? I tried to live life to the fullest, but the reminders only made me live with guilt. Living with guilt wasn't living to the fullest, either. The balance between making the most of your days and living as God intended could be a difficult balance to obtain.

The man wrapped his fingers around my throat. My airway closed as his hand clamped around it.

"Stop playing games." LJ's voice had moved from growling to downright evil.

I tried to speak but only a squeak emerged. My legs flailed as panic encapsulated me. He was going to kill me.

"LJ!" the driver shouted. "Let her go."

Finally, he dropped me back to the ground. My backside hit the floor, and pain shot up my spine.

But I was alive. I sucked in air, attempting a long, deep breath. It didn't work. I could only pull in short, shallow gulps. My throat ached.

"I'm not playing games," I said, my voice raspy. "I was

following my boyfriend, and I happened to see you."

The men exchanged glances. My story had obviously surprised them. But at least I had a moment to catch my breath.

"Following your boyfriend?" my interrogator asked. "Chase Dexter is your boyfriend?"

I nodded, scooting back as far away from him as possible. "I was worried about Chase. Thought he might be getting himself in trouble. I wanted to make sure he was okay."

The man let out a long, low chuckle. "Are you kidding me?"

I shook my head. "No."

"He looked awfully cozy with his ex," LJ continued.

I licked my lips. This man was hitting me everywhere it hurt, not just physically. "Call me naïve. I thought we had something special. I was obviously wrong."

"You telling us the truth?" He ran a gloved hand over my throat. "Because I have other ways of getting the truth out of people."

I shivered. "I've told you everything. I never wanted trouble. I just wanted answers."

"Are you any happier now that you're getting them?"

I shook my head after a moment of thought. "I can't say I am."

"You need to stay out of our way."

"Gladly," I croaked. I hoped he believed me. And, at the moment, I couldn't think of anything I wanted to do but run far away from these men. Forever. Always. Fast.

LJ glanced at his friends, and I knew this was a turning point. The moment they decided what to do with me.

Kill me. Let me go. Or keep me.

Jesus.

That was all I could do—mentally mutter the name of my Savior. To cry out for him.

He knew the rest of my prayer, the rest of my thoughts.

"She might be fun to keep around." The driver looked me up and down. "She's pretty."

I shuddered at his implications. Bile rose in me again. My entire body ached. The worst of this could very well be yet to come.

My interrogator ran his hand across my throat again, this time letting his fingers linger too long, too suggestively. I tried to pull away, but I had nowhere else to go. My throbbing head hit the back wall behind me, and my ache intensified.

"She could be fun. You're right." His index finger went under my chin, and he tilted it up. "It's been awfully lonely just hanging out with these two guys."

"Guys, she's a liability!" the third man said. "We've got to get rid of her. Soon."

LJ dropped his hand. "You going to talk?"

I shook my head, knowing good and well that I could very well talk. I'd be stupid if I didn't. But I was desperate. I wanted to hang on for dear life for my life.

"You want to know what will happen if you do?" he continued.

As a matter of fact, no, I didn't want to know.

But before I could say anything, he rammed his fist into my stomach. Circles danced in my eyes, my head. I wasn't sure which. Both?

His elbow came down over my head, and everything went black again.

CHRISTY BARRITT

CHAPTER 17

Something scratchy pricked my face. My legs brushed against something unfamiliar and rough—some kind of coated fabric with little splinters embedded in it. And pain radiated throughout my entire body.

I opened my eyes with a start.

Blackness surrounded me.

Blackness?

I sucked in a breath. No, the hood was still over my face, I realized. I wanted desperately to pull the obstruction off. But I had to be careful, to plan my moves.

Where was I? In the van? Was that dirty carpet still scraping my legs or something else?

I remembered the man who'd snatched me. He was close now. I could sense it. But what I couldn't sense was what he was doing.

Maybe I should pretend to still be unconscious.

I listened. There were no sounds, except for a bird squawking. And I was cold. So cold. Especially when air moved over me.

There was no bumping. No movement. I didn't think I was in the van. I didn't think I was inside, period. My gut told me I was outside. Maybe in the woods?

I waited several minutes, but I didn't hear any sign of human life. Maybe the men were gone. Slowly, I moved my hands. The ties were gone around my wrists. But my wrists

129

were sore and tender. I knew there would be red marks there where the restraints had cut into my skin.

My body ached as I moved my hands up. My stomach muscles. My back. Everything hurt.

More slowly than I would have liked, I jerked the hood from my head. I blinked as bright light hit my eyes.

I wasn't in the woods. I was . . . where was I?

All I could see around me was a field. There were some trees in the distance. A telephone wire. But otherwise I saw nothing but dry grass and a few rocks.

I sucked in a deep breath. Maybe I would be okay.

With trembling limbs, I managed to stand. My knees shook terribly, to the point I wanted to sit back down. I forced myself to stand.

I glanced around. My phone. They'd actually left my phone? It had been in my pocket and must have fallen out when they'd dumped me here.

I grabbed it and dialed Jamie's number. It went straight to voice mail.

She must still be at the stables. Of course she wasn't answering. She'd told me she had to keep her disguise, and that meant not always being on the phone.

Who else? Magnolia was doing an interview an hour south of here. She'd told me she had no cell phone reception in the area where she was.

Tears wanted to spill over again. No, I had to hold it together. This wasn't hopeless. If worst came to worst, I could call my brother or sister. But it would take them at least an hour and a half to get here, and I wasn't even sure where here was.

I could call Chase. But I wasn't sure I could trust Chase. I would rather walk ten miles in my battered state than run to him right now.

My hands trembled as I stared down at my phone. I pulled up my recent calls list.

Josh Caraway's number stared back at me. Funny, I hadn't even spoken to him on the phone. I'd dialed the number but then chickened out before calling him. I'd decided to speak with him face-to-face instead.

This was either a smart move or a really dumb one. Either way, I called him. My face stung as I placed my cell against my ear.

I remembered the blows I'd received. The memory of each made me flinch. I'd always been a nice girl. I'd never been hit before, nor had I ever hit anyone. I was ill prepared for how painful the whole experience might be.

He answered on the first ring with a perky "This is the day the Lord has made. How can I help you?"

I swallowed hard, my throat achy. "Is this Josh?"

"Speaking."

"Josh, this is Holly Paladin."

"Holly." His voice changed from perky to concerned, almost as if he could sense my distress. "How are you?"

"Not good. Can you pick me up? I hate to inconvenience you, but I have no one else."

"Pick you up? Sure. Of course. Where?"

"That's the problem. I have no idea. But I do have this app on my phone . . ."

***

Josh's eyes widened when he pulled up beside me on the road. That's when I knew I must look terrible. Really terrible.

I didn't need a mirror to know half my face was swollen. My lip was busted. I probably had a black eye. I was also limping

131

and shaking, and my eyes wouldn't stop watering.

I climbed in the passenger's side door and sat down, thankful to have a place to rest and feel safe. No, I didn't know Josh that well, but my gut told me he was trustworthy. That was good enough for me for now.

"Holly, what happened?" He didn't start driving. He just sat there on the side of the road, studying me with his gaze as worry and concern entrenched his eyes. His car, slightly messy with forgotten coffee cups, water bottles, and church bulletins, brought a certain measure of comfort.

So I told him. Everything. This time I didn't hold back. I didn't skirt around details, fearing what he might think of me. I laid it all on the table. Even the letter from my mom's oncologist.

"Suffering happens so the works of God might be displayed," Josh said. "I know that probably doesn't make you feel better now. But one day it will. You're the type of person who uses your experiences to help others. To build your compassion. To offer comfort."

I nodded. He was right. I didn't feel better. I just wanted my heartache to end.

"I'd say someone was watching out for you if you got away from that alive," he said quietly.

I nodded. "I agree."

"Praise God."

"I haven't stopped thanking Him."

He continued to stare. "I should get you to a hospital, Holly."

I shook my head. "I'll be fine. I just need to get cleaned up. Maybe rest. This is nothing that some frozen peas and Band-Aids can't fix."

"I don't know. You should file a report at least."

"Please, just get me back to my car. I'll get this figured out."

With noticeable reluctance, he put his car in drive and started down the road. Silence stretched between us for several minutes. Maybe we were both formulating our thoughts. I knew I was. I hadn't stopped running everything through my head since I regained consciousness.

"Did anything else happen since you talked to me last?" Josh finally asked. "Anything that might have . . . provoked this? Not that I think any of this is your fault. But I can't wrap my mind around what might have precipitated them doing this to you."

I pressed my lips together a moment. "We started looking into Alexander Cartwright. Does that count?"

"He's . . . powerful. I suppose it might, especially if there were accusations involved."

"I don't know about accusations. We're still in the process of digging."

Josh frowned. "I asked one of my friends on the force about the death of Aidan Jennings."

I sat up straighter. "And?"

"It's strange. He said all the security footage at the apartment complex disappeared."

"What?" Surprise shot through me.

"Apparently the manager stepped outside to talk to the police. When he came back inside, the door to his office was open. The footage was gone."

Chase . . . would Chase have done that? Why?

I didn't know what that meant or where it left us. But it was strange.

"Holly, correct me if I'm wrong, but it doesn't sound like these guys are really after you. It sounds like you made them nervous because they thought you were a threat. Maybe now that they know you're not tracking them, they'll leave you alone."

"Maybe."

"But you would have to truly start leaving them alone. Maybe go back to Cincinnati."

I shrugged and stared out the window a moment. Apparently, I'd been right on the outskirts of town, because we were already seeing strip malls and traffic lights. "I think my work here is done. I'm not even sure what I was fighting for anymore."

"What do you mean?"

"I saw Chase yesterday, Josh. He was placing a wager on one of the horses down at the track. Then he gave Peyton one of these long-drawn-out hugs. Not the kind of hugs that happen between friends. This was one of those intimate ones."

"I see."

I glanced at him sharply. "What does that mean?"

Something about his words had struck me. He hadn't denied or urged me to look at the situation in a different way. He'd just accepted my words.

"I actually talked to Chase last night, Holly." His voice held regret.

The tension in my back pulled tighter. "And?"

He sighed. "Do you really want to know?"

I wasn't sure if I did or not. People always said the truth was the best thing. But sometimes the truth was hard to handle, and ignorance really could be bliss. But I'd come this far. My heart already felt broken. So why put off the inevitable?

CHAPTER 18

"I do want to know," I told Josh.

Josh sighed again, keeping his gaze focused out the front window. "I asked him why he was really in town. I said I hoped he wasn't falling back on his old habits."

"And?" I was nearly on the edge of my seat—figuratively speaking, of course.

"He got defensive." His voice almost sounded apologetic.

"Defensive?" People usually got defensive when a nerve was struck. That usually happened when the truth was within touching distance.

"I don't know. I expected him to deny it. He told me he was coming here as part of his work. That a lead in an old case had popped up. I had questions about that, since he has no jurisdiction in this area. But I wanted to trust him."

"You don't anymore?"

"He wouldn't give me a straight answer. And when I asked him if he'd been drinking again, he wouldn't even answer me."

"You think something is going on too?" I said as he pulled to a stop by my car.

He frowned. "I do. I don't know what, but I'm worried, Holly. I'm really worried."

***

When I got back to my car, I felt even more determined. Maybe it made me stupid. Maybe it made me brave. I didn't know.

I pulled down the visor in the car and flinched at what I saw. My lip was split. A bruise had already formed around my eyes. My hair looked like a Stylist-of-Doom had practiced her skills on it.

But even more than that was the look in my eyes. My fear was all too evident.

But I couldn't let fear stop me. Life was too short for that.

I found my purse and tried to cover the imperfections on my face. But every time I touched my sensitive skin, I wanted to cry.

Maybe makeup wasn't a good option right now. Instead, I pulled my hair back into a ponytail. I grabbed a hat and slid it on, along with sunglasses. I also had a jean jacket in the back that I pulled over my bloodstained shirt. I still wasn't a pretty sight, but this was going to have to do.

My ribs ached with every motion. My head throbbed. My throat felt swollen. I should have driven to the hospital, but I didn't have time.

I found the address for Golden Equestrian and headed that way. I didn't know if I'd get in or not, but I had to at least try.

It took me forty minutes to get there. On the ride, my entire body throbbed. I needed some painkillers, yet I didn't want to take anything. I needed to remain lucid.

I could do this.

Rolling hills passed as I traveled toward the outskirts of town, deeper into an area that screamed "affluent." Ancient-looking stone fences surrounded some of the land, and black fences surrounded the rest.

I pulled up to the gate. I knew it was there. I'd seen it when

I dropped Jamie off this morning. But, after everything that had happened, I'd forgotten. I needed to get my game face on.

"Can I help you?" a man about my age asked. He had freckles, reddish-brown hair, and a stain on his shirt that could have easily come from the chips and dip behind him.

I licked my lips and tried to smile, but it hurt too much. "I'm here for an interview."

"Name?"

"Anna Pala . . . wicky." Palawicky? That was the best I could come up with?

He conferred with his clipboard. "There's no one named Anna Palawicky on the list."

"It was a last-minute interview. I assure you, I'm a world-class stall mucker."

He stared at me a moment before a smile spread across his face. "World class, huh?"

"Only the best for Alexander Cartwright." I shrugged. "Besides, I really need a job before I get kicked out of my apartment. You know how that goes."

"Yeah. I do." He frowned. "Look, James—he's the stable manager—should be finishing up an interview right now. You can probably squeeze in. He's in the last building you'll come to. Just say there was a scheduling mix-up. Okay?"

I attempted another smile. I was certain it wasn't pretty. "Thank you. I appreciate this more than you know."

The gate rose, and I drove inside. That had been easier than I'd anticipated.

Now my hands trembled again. My body couldn't seem to give me the chance to hide my anxiety. It was always out there for anyone observing me to see.

I drove past several buildings before coming to the end of the parking lot. There was a building here, but also another in the distance. Which one had the man at the gate been talking about?

I pulled into the last parking space and stepped out. Everything around me was immaculate and breathtaking. Several horses grazed in the fields.

Was I at the right place? I wanted to think so. This was where Jamie had told me she'd had an interview. Now I just needed to find her.

I stepped toward the closest building and frowned. The man at the gate had said the last building. With that thought in mind, I started up the hill to the barn at the top of the hill. My ribs and lungs and every other part of me cried out in pain with every step.

But I was determined to get my friend and go home.

I reached the stable and stepped inside. I paused by the entryway. The building was actually much older than I'd anticipated. Whereas the other stables had looked clean and new, this one even smelled old and stuffy, like the wood inside had seen more years than most of the horses who had at one time occupied it. Small streams of sunlight slithered in through the cracked boards of the roof and walls. Traces of hay sprinkled the floor, and frayed ropes hung on tacks against the wall.

Not surprisingly, I found no one inside. No horses. No people. No Jamie doing an interview.

My walk up the hill and the ensuing pain had all been for nothing.

Despite that, I started walking down the long row of stalls, imagining for a moment what it would be like to own this kind of place, to work here, even. Far beyond what luxuries I'd ever been permitted or blessed with. But I liked my little life, as simple as it was. I'd take contentment any day over wanderlust.

Except when it came to love. Wasn't that truly the case? I

wanted what I'd seen my mom and dad have.

I thought I'd found it in Chase. I'd been wrong. Deeply wrong.

The thought almost made me feel like I'd been stabbed in the heart.

I reached the end and turned around. Just as I'd suspected, no one was here.

It looked like I needed to walk back to the other building. My body felt tired, exhausted. Even the thought of trying to drag myself that far made me want to give up and curl into a little ball instead.

But I was Holly Anna Paladin. I wasn't a quitter. I was a fighter. I fought for the people who were voiceless, who were powerless to help themselves.

But who was I really fighting for now?

A man who'd gotten back together with his ex-wife without even bothering to tell me first. Without the courtesy of breaking up with me. Without being respectful enough to speak the truth to me.

Anger burned inside me at the thought.

I wasn't fighting for Chase. I had been. Maybe against my better instincts.

Right now, I had to fight for myself. I had to find Jamie before I ended up getting her too deeply into this mess as well.

As a creak sounded in the distance, my steps faltered. What was that? No one was in here. I'd checked myself.

Despite that, fear grabbed at me again, desperate to pull me back into its clutches. Maybe I'd never escaped its grasp in the first place.

I took a tentative step. I had to get out of here one way or another.

Besides, this place was empty, I reminded myself. The noise

had probably been a bird or maybe a mouse.

Voices sounded outside. I looked out one of the open windows and saw two men walking this way. My breath caught. I didn't want to be caught in here.

Just then, arms reached out of nowhere. Grabbed me. Pulled me into the dim isolation of a stall.

CHAPTER 19

My heart hammered in my ears. Using the last of my energy, I kicked against the man. I threw my elbows back and into a rock-solid abdomen. It didn't matter; I was no match for his strength.

Was it one of the men from the van? Had he followed me here to see what my next move would be? To make good on his promise?

The swift staccato of my heartbeat drowned all other sounds. My captor kept one hand over my mouth, and the other pinned my arms in place. He was waiting for the men outside to pass, I realized. I froze, waiting also. Maybe those men could help. When the voices faded, my heart plummeted.

Despair threatened to bite deep. I had to fight it. But my fight was dying. Waning. It was as if I was playing Russian roulette with my life by taking too many chances.

"Calm down," a gruff voice whispered.

I heard the growl in his tone and complied. I was clearly outmuscled and would need to rely on another way of getting out—brains, wit, luck—whatever worked.

The seconds ticked past as I waited, anticipating his next move. Finally, he released his hold and turned me toward him. I resisted the desire to cower and kept my chin up instead. If I was going to die, it was going to be with dignity.

I sucked in a deep breath when I saw his face.

"Chase?" My voice sounded breathless with surprise.

"What do you think you're doing?" His voice sounded hard, which matched well with his gaze. His eyes were narrowed, and he hunkered over me, all brawn and testosterone.

My anger surged to life. At one time I'd feared how Chase might feel when he learned the truth about what I'd done. But his truth blew mine out of the water. "I could ask you the same thing."

"Did you follow me?"

I wanted to deny it. I wanted to pretend all my actions had been honorable and above reproach. But I couldn't do that. "I was worried about you."

His jaw flexed and he stepped back. "I asked you for space."

"I wonder why." My voice held sarcasm and scorn, and I hated myself for it. But I couldn't deny how hurt I was. I might be Mary Manners in regular life; in matters of the heart, maybe I was just as immature as the next person. I'd have to work on that. On a different day.

He lowered his voice, his eyes still narrowed. "Do you have any idea what you've gotten yourself into?"

"Apparently I don't. Apparently the man I thought loved me has been lying to me. When were you going to tell me the truth, Chase? Didn't I deserve that? I at least deserved for you to break things off before you returned to your old life."

"Returned to my old life?" Chase raised his chin, his eyes still containing that hard edge, one I'd never seen directed at me until this conversation. "I asked you to trust me."

"I saw you were on a downward spiral, and I didn't want you to go there."

"I didn't see you trying to stop me." He still glared down at me, the look in his eyes disapproving and distant, with a touch of anger.

"If you only knew what I'd been through. I was gathering

142

the facts first and trying to believe the best in you."

He stepped closer, his shoulders slumping as if he was going through the stages of grief: denial, anger, bargaining, depression, and acceptance. "You're lucky you weren't killed, Holly."

"I almost was." I slid off my sunglasses and watched as his face muscles went slack. Before I could lose the full effect, I unbuttoned my jacket and showed him my bloodstained clothes. I took off my hat, so no shadows would conceal my bruises. "Is this what you want to see? Is this the point you want to drive home?"

"Oh, Holly." He closed his eyes, his features pinched with regret. He turned away, as if he couldn't stand to see me this way. "I never want to see you hurt. Never."

"Well, this is what happens when someone you love lies to you."

His eyes opened and he reached for me, that soft look in his eyes that I always fell for. The one that made my insides turn to jelly and made me think with my heart instead of my head.

"Holly . . ."

I shook my head and stiffened my back. This was no time to get soft. "Don't 'Holly' me. Don't act like you care, because we both know the truth."

I almost jabbed him in the chest with each word, but I held myself together.

His eyes widened. "What are you talking about? Of course I care about you."

I only stared at him, refusing to respond. It seemed so inconsequential to share what we both already knew. He was in love with his ex. Into gambling. Associating with unsavory characters. Who knew what else? Voicing it out loud would only humiliate me.

His fingers skimmed the tender area around my eye. "Who did this to you, Holly?"

I froze, his touch sending shivers across my skin. "I don't know."

He dropped his hand, his anger dissipating and replaced with somberness and regret. "Holly, there's a lot you don't understand—"

Before he could finish, voices drifted toward us from outside the stable. Chase grabbed my arm and nudged me against the wall. He stepped in close, blocking me, sheltering me.

Even as angry as I was toward him, my body again reacted differently than my self-control dictated. My skin burst to life at his closeness. When I smelled the familiar scent of his woodsy cologne, my heart quickened.

Chase still had that effect on me, whether I liked it or not.

I had so many questions that I wanted to toss on him like grenades onto a battlefield. How had he even found me here? There was no time to ask him that. Not now.

Chase put his finger over his lips, motioning for me to remain quiet. For a moment, I forgot how upset I was with him. His heart pounded against me. His chest rose and fell. His muscles felt tense, taut.

I froze, conscious of every moment, every breath. The voices drifted again.

What was going on? Chase acted like this was life or death. That realization didn't make me feel better.

He pressed harder against me as the men's voices grew louder. They were in the stables now. Close. Maybe on the other side of the gritty wooden wall.

"I can't do it anymore," one man said. His voice sounded soft, almost whiny.

"We'll make that choice." The second man's voice was gruff and all business. I imagined a burly, scary-looking man with a shaved head and a gold tooth.

"I don't think you understand. I'm done."

"We've paid too much money to you for you to walk away," Gruff Man said.

"What's that mean?" Whiny Man's voice rose higher in pitch. He was becoming frightened, and rightfully so.

"It means I need for you to see things our way," a third voice said. This one had a touch of country twang.

"Is that a threat?"

Tension crackled in the silence that followed.

"*Threat* would be a strong word." Gruff Man half chuckled, half growled.

Footsteps shuffled across the dirt. "I'm done."

"You might want to rethink that," Country Twang said. "We can't let word of this leak."

"I have just as much at stake here as you. This is my reputation. My career." Each of Whiny Man's words sounded punctuated with powerless assertions.

He was a goner, I realized.

"We have to ensure you remain quiet," Gruff Man said.

"Is . . . is that a . . . a gun?"

Someone chuckled. "Just as backup. In case this doesn't work."

A groan sounded. Then another. And another.

Scuffling. Shuffling. Scraping.

Gruff and Twang were beating up Whiny, I realized. I sucked in a breath, but Chase's hand went over my mouth, silencing me. His eyes locked on mine, calling me down from the ledge. I stared into their blue depths, all my bitterness disappearing in a moment as his strength captured and reassured me.

"Consider this a warning," Country Twang said. "Get him out of here."

Footsteps sounded, ever so slightly. A steady, consistent sound followed their steps. They were dragging Whiny Man, I realized. Was he dead?

My heart pounded into my rib cage. What if they spotted us? We were relatively out of sight. But if the men walked any farther, if they leaned against the stall door, then Chase and I would be goners.

Chase pressed his hand over my mouth now, and I knew that if I made any sound, our lives would be on the line. We weren't just hiding so we wouldn't be caught. We were hiding to protect our very being.

I waited, listening for a sign of what was going on. I prayed Whiny Man was okay, that my mind had exaggerated all this. But my thoughts went to dark, non-rose-colored places, which messed up my equilibrium. Was Chase somehow caught up in all this?

Just then, I heard another footfall. One of the brutes had come back, I realized. Would he see us?

Please, Lord . . .

My gaze traveled beyond Chase. There was no way out of here. If the man spotted us, we'd be trapped with no escape.

What had I gotten myself into?

Finally, the footsteps faded.

Chase's grip on me didn't, though. We remained frozen for what seemed like hours. When the silence had gone on for an uncountable amount of time, Chase finally moved.

"We've got to get out of here," he whispered. "Fast."

I didn't argue.

He gripped my hand, motioned for me to stay behind him, and then edged forward. Slowly, he peered beyond the wall before tugging me forward. Moving at a fast clip, we slipped from the stall.

Chase pulled me toward the back of the stables. Just as the sunlight warmed our faces, a sound screeched from my pocket. My cell phone blared "Unforgettable."

Before we could even turn around, someone shouted.

I glanced at the other end of the stable and saw a man. With a gun. Aimed at us.

CHAPTER 20

Chase must have seen the man a split second before I did. He no longer tugged at my arm. He jerked it.

We darted in the opposite direction, toward the woods beyond the building.

A bullet whizzed past.

I knew death could come quickly. In the blink of an eye. Before I could mutter the sweet name of Jesus.

But Chase wouldn't let up. Despite the way my legs burned, he pulled me. Even though I couldn't catch my breath, we continued running for our lives.

An open field waited in front of us. There'd be no cover, no protection, in the field. Just Chase and me out in the open.

This would be a hard run on a good day. But my lungs and ribs still ached. My stomach revolted. My face hurt.

Chase pulled me to the right. Thick trees waited beyond a black fence.

But could we make it?

Chase didn't slow down. Moving at lightning pace, we reached the fence.

Another bullet rang out.

I wanted to look behind me, but I couldn't waste the time. I had to focus on my goal: anywhere but here. Anywhere but the men behind us.

I pictured myself hurdling the fence. But before I could even try, Chase swooped me up in one easy motion and carried me with him across the divide.

He slowed, though barely, as we reached the woods.

It was only once the darkness of the forest swallowed us that Chase allowed us to stop.

I sucked in air, in a very unfortunate manner, as I leaned against a huge rock behind me. Somewhere in the process of escaping, water had started streaming from my eyes. I wasn't crying. At least, I didn't think I was. But that didn't stop the liquid from flowing down my cheeks as if I was.

"Are you okay?" Chase leaned toward me. He didn't look nearly as winded as I did. Sure, sweat stained his shirt and he drew in deep breaths. But he otherwise appeared fine.

Everything about my body hurt at the moment. But I couldn't admit that. I didn't even know why, but the words wouldn't leave my lips.

Instead, I nodded, continuing to double over and gulp in air.

"You're not okay, Holly."

I shook my head now, a little too hard. My whole world tilted, and my hand jutted out. I pressed it into the rock, trying to steady myself. "I'll be fine."

"We can't stay long. We've got to keep moving."

I closed my eyes, my body aching at the thought of more exertion. "Where are we going, even?"

"My Jeep is parked in the distance. If we can make it there, we'll be okay." His voice turned soothing as he leaned down until our gazes were level. "You can do this, Holly. I know you can. You're resilient and tough."

I hated the boost of confidence his words gave me. He didn't deserve to have that effect on me anymore. But this wasn't the time to analyze that. There'd be plenty of opportunity for that later.

Chase grabbed my hand again, looked over his shoulder, and tentatively started forward. Our pace was slower this time—just below a jog—but urgency still lingered in the air.

Run. Move. Get outta here.

A quiet voice in my head kept urging me on.

Was the man still chasing us? Had he brought out his recruits? Exactly what was going on?

Survive, Holly. Just survive.

It didn't take that long until the woods cleared. Chase's Jeep appeared there, just out of sight from the road.

I'd never seen such a blessed sight.

Chase ushered me inside before climbing in. Moving quickly, he jammed the keys in the ignition, cranked the Jeep into reverse, and sped from the hiding space.

He didn't let down his guard. His shoulders remained tight. His gaze looked serious.

If anything, I could read Chase. I knew even though we were literally out of the woods, we weren't out of the woods yet.

Thank goodness he'd been there to help, though. I sometimes had what I called "sitting duck syndrome," also known as "deer in the headlights malady," where I simply stared at trouble as it came toward me.

Maybe we could at least finish our conversation now. I still had burning questions and uncountable hurts that I wanted to address before I went back to Cincinnati. I didn't want to be a brat, but . . .

"So, are you going to explain—?"

"I can't talk now, Holly." Chase glanced into the rearview mirror again.

"But—"

"Holly, you're the sweetest girl in the whole world. You really are. But right now you've got to stand down. Our lives depend on it."

I clamped my mouth shut, knowing I couldn't argue with him. He'd never told me to stand down before, and I wasn't sure how I felt about it.

As if his words were a prophecy, I craned my neck in time to see a car appear behind us. A fast car. With men hanging out the windows. Men with guns.

"Get down!" Chase yelled.

He put the pedal to the floor. Just as we swerved around a bend in the road, his back glass shattered. I screamed.

I didn't mean to, but I did.

I'd been scared before, but I felt downright terrified right now.

I knew from driving to the stables that we still had a good ten minutes before we emerged from the countryside and into anything that vaguely resembled the suburbs. Could we make it that far on this hilly, windy road?

My only comfort was in the fact that Chase, if anyone, knew what he was doing. He'd been trained for this type of thing. I grasped the door handle and closed my eyes a moment.

Dear Lord, please help us. Please.

Chase remained in control. His hands gripped the wheel, and his upright posture screamed *focused* and *capable.*

If it had been Jamie and me, we'd be crashed in the woods by now.

Jamie . . .

How could I have forgotten about my friend? Was she okay? Was she still at the equestrian center?

My stomach clenched at the thought. How could I have forgotten about her? I was a terrible friend.

Another bullet took out my side-view mirror.

I supposed the best-case scenario was that these men were

after us and probably not paying any attention to her at the stables. I found a moment of solace in that.

A curve, so sharp it was practically a U-turn, appeared ahead. I remembered it from the drive here.

"You've got to stay down, Holly!" Chase said.

I ducked lower again, squeezing my eyes together. My stomach went one way and my body seemed to go another as the Jeep swerved.

My mind turned in circles. What was happening?

I held my breath.

Finally, the Jeep righted itself and we moved forward again.

He'd done it. Chase had conquered the turn.

Thank You, Jesus.

Just as the words fluttered through my brain, the sound of metal crunching filled the air.

CHAPTER 21

The other car hadn't been as lucky, I realized. They'd crashed. Smoke rose behind us.

Chase eased off the accelerator, glancing in the rearview mirror again. His shoulders relaxed, so I took that as a sign I could return to my regular seated position.

I didn't even know what to say. There was so much on my mind, yet nothing seemed adequate, or maybe I didn't know where to start.

"I need to get you to the hospital," Chase said.

I shook my head. "I'll be fine."

"You don't look fine, Holly. You weren't supposed to get involved in any of this."

"Any of what?"

He pressed his lips together. "I can explain things, Holly, but I need time."

Time to formulate his story? To figure out if he wanted to be with Peyton or me?

Or was I overreacting here? Could there be an honest explanation that made sense?

"Turn here," I muttered, crossing my arms.

Awkward silence fell between us. Why had Chase been at the stables? None of this was making sense. No matter what angle I looked at it, I still came up confused.

Finally, he pulled to a stop in front of Magnolia's house and put the car in park. The sun was beginning to sink toward the horizon in the distance, and several maple trees on the street had a touch of reddish orange to them.

The moment, by all appearances, was serene. But nothing felt serene about my heart.

"We need to get some ointment on those wounds," Chase finally said.

"I'll handle that in a minute. I'm sure Jamie's friend has a first-aid kit inside."

"Holly . . ." He reached for me, but I pulled away until his hand dropped. I had too many questions and uncertainties to easily give my trust back. Even if he was the love of my life.

Maybe it made me smart. Maybe it made me stupid. I wasn't sure. But I only hoped I was making the right choices.

Heaviness settled between us. I hated it. I hated the change. Hated that the something beautiful we'd had was reduced to this.

"You deserve an explanation, Holly," Chase said. "I'm sorry I haven't been forthcoming. I've been helping an old friend."

"Is that what they're calling it these days?" I wanted to slap a hand over my mouth at how rude I sounded. But it was too late to take my words back.

"I guess I deserved that one."

I shook my head, squeezing the skin between my eyes. Part of me wanted to take his words at face value. I wanted to believe him. The other part of me knew that being a Pollyanna wasn't always wise or helpful to my emotional well-being. "I saw you with my own eyes, Chase. You and Peyton exchanging a more-than-friendly hug."

He sucked in a slight, sudden breath, so subtle that I almost didn't notice it. "You saw Peyton and me together?"

"Yes. More than once, but most recently at the racetrack

yesterday. Wyndmyer. You two were cozy."

"You were there?"

I nodded. "Unfortunately. I also saw some strange men in a van deposit a gun by your Jeep."

"You're the one who called the police in the parking lot of the apartments." His voice sounded raspy with disbelief that morphed into what almost sounded like admiration.

"That van has been following me," I said, remembering the exchange between Chase and the driver. "They're your friends. They did this to me."

He shook his head, leaving no room for doubt as to how he felt. "They're not my friends. You can't take things at face value. Especially not anything that's happened with those men. They're trouble."

"Then tell me the truth," I pleaded with him. Certainly my eyes showed it. I didn't want to be desperate. But deep down inside, I knew I was.

He closed his eyes and lowered his head ever so slightly before meeting my gaze again. "I can't."

I let out a long sigh, not bothering to hide my frustration. Keeping up appearances at this point was futile. If there was ever a time to be direct, it was now. "What is going on, Chase? Why won't you talk to me?"

"The truth will come out soon. But I've made promises, Holly."

"Promises to whom?"

He didn't say anything.

I wiped a hair from my face, the action reminding me of the tender skin at my scalp. I flinched, realizing that my entire body would ache even worse tomorrow. "Should I even bother to ask you why you were at the stables?"

He stretched his hand across the back of our seats, his

fingers dangerously close to my back. If he touched me, I might flip out. These mixed signals were making me go crazy.

"I was looking for something, but then I saw you. Or I thought I saw you. You can imagine my surprise when it actually *was* you. I thought you were in Cincinnati."

I held up my phone. "That Friend Finder app we both installed? It showed you were at the Wyndmyer Park. I was afraid you were getting into trouble, and I became worried. Apparently, I was right to be concerned. Everything spiraled out of control fast from that point."

His hand brushed the bare skin at my neck, sending shivers up and down my spine. "I should have known. You've never been one to let things go. I've always loved that about you."

I suddenly lurched forward. Was that what he told Peyton also? I wasn't in the right emotional state to think about it.

"I only want to keep you safe, Holly." Chase's words sounded raw as his voice cracked with emotion. His gaze looked haunted, pleading, real. I wanted nothing more than to pull him into my arms.

Instead, I licked my lips, about to say something. I didn't know what. That I believed him? That I trusted him? Or would I call him out on his deceit? I wasn't sure.

Before the words left my lips, Chase's phone beeped. He pulled his gaze away from me and glanced at the screen. His face tightened, and when he looked back up, there was an apology in his eyes.

"Holly, I want to keep talking. I want to explain everything. But I've got to go. There's a window of opportunity that I've been waiting for. Please tell me we can talk more later. Please try and trust me."

I didn't say anything.

With one last glance at Chase, I pulled the door open and

slid out. I felt broken and battered, both physically and emotionally. Even Josh had sounded doubtful about Chase's true reasons for being here, so I knew it wasn't just me. Other people who knew Chase were also worried.

"Good night, Chase." The words hurt my throat. Would this be the last time I told him this? Would the next time we spoke be the end of Chase and Holly forever?

***

I closed the door to the house and leaned against it for a moment. My heart had been through so many wretched emotions over the past few days. From fear and anxiety, to betrayal and suspicion, to confusion and uncertainty.

I'd been abducted and feared for my life. I'd heard someone possibly lose his life, separated only by an old wood wall. The man I loved still refused to explain anything to me.

I pinched the skin between my eyes, trying to control my breathing and calm myself. If I let myself, I could easily break right now.

"Holly?"

I jerked my head toward the kitchen, nearly jumping out of my skin. I didn't think anyone was here.

Jamie's face came into view. Jamie. She was okay. She was more than okay—she was alive!

"What are you doing here? How'd you get home?" Before Jamie could answer, I quickly closed the space between us and pulled her into a hug.

Thank goodness, my friend was okay.

She patted my back slowly, as if I'd lost my mind. Maybe I had.

"I'm fine, but you look like the walking dead." She stepped

back to observe me, her lips pulling back in a mix of concern and disgust. "You look . . . you look like you got trampled by a horse or something. Are you okay? What in the world happened to you?"

I pushed a hair behind my ear and frowned. My body wouldn't let me forget the ordeal I'd been through. If I stopped long enough to think about it—to really think about it—I might completely fall apart. I couldn't do that now. I had too many other things to accomplish before I could allow myself to have any kind of breakdown.

"I know I look terrible." I shook my head, trying to process everything. Like Jamie being here when she was clearly supposed to be at the stables. "How'd you get here? You didn't have a car."

She shrugged as if it wasn't a big deal. But her eyes still looked worried as she studied me—most likely my busted lip, black eye, and who knew what else was out of place or abnormal.

"I got a ride from one of the other workers," she said. "He said he had to come by this way and could give me a lift. I tried to call, but you didn't answer your phone."

"I was a little busy."

She led me to the couch and lowered me there before sitting across from me, her eyes narrowed with questions and concern. "What in the world happened to you? I feel like I should go beat someone up because they messed with my best friend. But maybe beating up someone wouldn't even be justice."

Where did I start? The events of today had seemed devastating enough to cover an entire week. Had everything really happened in less than twenty-four hours? Was that possible?

I sighed and leaned back into the couch. As I tried to formulate the words, my head pounded with enough intensity that I had to shut my eyes. "I'd be happy to tell you. But can you get me an ice pack, some Tylenol, and some water first?"

"Of course." Jamie stood up and hurried toward the kitchen, casting one more glance at me before disappearing through the doorway.

I pressed my eyelids tighter together. Everything felt surreal. Had I dreamed all of this? Could I wake up and discover this was all a nightmare?

No, I wouldn't be that lucky.

My head pounded harder as I replayed everything Chase had said and tried to make sense of it.

Please tell me we can talk more later. Please try and trust me.

How could he possibly have an explanation for all this? Before I could even dwell on that, I remembered the man who'd been beaten up mere inches from where I'd been hiding. Who was he? What was his connection to Alexander Cartwright?

Jamie returned to the room with everything I'd requested.

I downed the Tylenol. Hopefully that would help ease some of the ache in my head. Just in case it didn't, I put the ice to my temple.

I closed my eyes, trying to figure out where to start.

"I talked to Chase," I started.

Her eyebrows shot up. "Chase? What? Really? Where? How?"

"You're not going to believe this—" Before I could finish, a knock sounded at the door.

Jamie bustled through the room and answered.

A familiar figure stood on the front stoop. The man wore a rumpled suit and had hair so short it almost made him appear bald, and huge bags hung beneath his eyes.

I squinted. Where had I seen him before?

Almost as if it was happening in an alternate universe, I heard him speaking. "I'm Detective Victor Rollins. Can I come in?"

CHAPTER 22

Detective Rollins? That's when I remembered.

He was the detective we'd seen in the parking lot that night we'd found Aidan. Chase had known him.

What was he doing here?

"I'm looking for Ms. Holly Paladin and Ms. Jamie Duke," he continued.

Jamie glanced over at me, looking a bit speechless.

"I'm Holly Paladin," I volunteered. "Is everything okay?"

"And I'm Jamie."

"May I?" He extended his arm toward a chair across from me.

I pushed myself upright, but my head throbbed with such intensity that I sank low again. "Yes, please excuse my manners. Have a seat."

He lowered himself into the chair, but his posture was so stiff that it was almost like he was here to deliver bad news. The tension between my shoulders pulled tighter as he studied me.

"I have a few questions for you." He looked at me, his eyes intense and perceptive. "But before I start, I should ask you: Are you okay, Ms. Paladin? You look . . ."

"Horrible?"

"I was going to say like someone tossed you around like a rag doll."

Should I tell him what happened? Not yet, I decided. I

needed to know why he was here. There were too many
possibilities.

"I'll be fine," I said. "How'd you know we were here?"

He tugged at his pant legs as his eyebrows flickered up.
"Interesting story. I surveyed the security footage at the
Belmont Apartments after the body of Aidan Jennings was
found. We saw a van pull away. I ran the plates and made a trip
to Cincinnati trying to track you both down. Ms. Duke, your
mom told me that you'd gone to Louisville with your friend
Holly Paladin. I tracked down Holly's brother, and he shared this
address."

Drats! That must have been Ralph calling earlier at the
stables.

"That's some detective work," I muttered.

"That's why I get paid the big bucks." He offered a wry
smile.

"What did you want to see us about?" Jamie asked.

His gaze flickered between the two of us. "As you probably
know, the body of Aidan Jennings was found in the woods that
evening. I understand you were both at the scene. Did you see
anything suspicious?"

"We saw a van pull up, and someone deposited a gun by a
Jeep," I said, surprised by how even my voice sounded. "Then
that van backed into an open spot and dumped Aidan Jennings's
body into the woods. We called the police and explained
everything that happened."

His gaze flickered again as he processed what we told him.
"Why didn't you stick around?"

"We got scared, I suppose."

"Running does convey guilt. You both realize that, right?"

Jamie and I looked at each other before nodding.

"Yes, we do," Jamie said. "But the only thing we were guilty of is being in the wrong place at the wrong time."

He shifted, tugging at those pant legs again. "That's not actually the main reason why I'm here."

I bristled and waited.

Detective Rollins leaned toward me, his elbows on his knees. "Ms. Paladin, what's your relationship with Chase Dexter?"

"Chase?" I mumbled. "Why? Is he okay? Did something happen?"

I tried to tell myself I didn't care about him anymore, but I knew I did.

"Physically, he's fine."

My shoulders sagged with relief. For just a moment I'd wondered if those men had found him after he dropped me off. I'd pictured them killing Chase, just like that other man had died. My heart wouldn't be able to handle that.

"Your name has come up in conjunction with his."

"Is . . . is Chase helping you with this?"

Detective Rollins leveled his gaze. "No, ma'am. I'm afraid you misunderstood. I'm investigating Chase Dexter. We suspect him in a murder."

My mouth dropped open. Had I heard him correctly? "What?"

He gave a curt, serious nod. "We believe he was involved in the murder of Aidan Jennings. We believe he's trying to frame Alexander Cartwright for the crime."

All I could hear was my heart, pounding in my ears. Murder? No. I didn't believe it.

"You're his friend," I muttered. "I heard you talking that night."

"We worked together in the past," he corrected.

"How did you know Chase and I were connected?"

"All one has to do is check your social media profiles."

He had a point, I supposed. I had to stop being suspicious at every turn. "What could you possibly think Chase's motive would be for killing Aidan Jennings?"

Detective Rollins squinted at me a moment, almost as if he was confused. "His motive? That's simple. Alexander Cartwright was the prime suspect in the murder of Chase's brother, Hayden Dexter. He's had vengeance on his mind ever since."

CHAPTER 23

I nearly fell over. Thankfully, I was sitting on the couch. My arm darted out, and I caught myself before I tumbled into a horizontal position.

Why hadn't I pieced that together?

"Are you okay, Ms. Paladin?" Detective Rollins continued to watch me. Did he think I was lying? Did he think I was in on this?

I managed to nod. "Yeah, I'm fine."

"Have you heard from Chase lately?"

I nodded, anxiety churning in my gut. "Today."

"Today? Where?"

"At Golden Equestrian."

His eyes widened with surprise. "What were you both doing there?"

"I was picking up a friend from a job interview. I ran into him."

"Why was Chase there?" the detective continued.

I swallowed hard. "That wasn't clear."

"What was his demeanor?"

I remembered it clearly. "He seemed agitated."

"Did he hurt you? Did he do this to you?"

I touched the tender skin around my eye. "Chase? No, he would never."

He twisted his head and narrowed his eyes as if doubtful. "I'm not certain about that. I urge you to be cautious."

"I will be."

He put his notepad back into his pocket and nodded. "If Chase tries to contact you again, call me. It's of utmost importance that we bring him in for questioning. Do you understand?"

My throat went dry. He wanted me to turn Chase in? Turn on the man I thought I would marry? I didn't know what to say. I wasn't sure if I could actually do it. "I . . ."

"You don't want to impede an investigation," the detective warned. "You do understand how serious those implications are?"

I nodded. "I understand."

He stood and took a step toward the door but paused before leaving. "I urge you to be careful. Don't try to confront him yourself. He's dangerous."

I didn't even have to contemplate that. I simply shook my head. "Not Chase. He would never hurt me."

"Maybe not in everyday life, Holly. But he's panicked right now. He's drinking. And he's desperate. That's a deadly combination."

I remembered how he'd acted when I was with him earlier. Had it been panicked? Maybe, but that was only because there were two men willing to kill in the building with us.

But I didn't want to be stupid, either. People could change. People on substances could change.

"Do you understand, Ms. Paladin?" Detective Rollins repeated.

Finally I nodded. The detective handed me his card as he stood. "You may want to consider staying somewhere else. It's only a suggestion."

***

I escaped to my bedroom, desperately needing to process everything. Magnolia had returned home shortly after the detective left. Jamie had filled her in, but I didn't want to hear her opinions. Not right now, at least. I just wanted to be alone.

I leaned against the headboard in my room, my thoughts churning. As my gaze drifted to the aquarium, I spotted that little fish, still hanging in, skimming the top of the water and barely hanging on to life.

Every time I closed my eyes, I remembered Chase pulling me into the stall. The man being beaten up. My haunting conversation with Chase when he'd dropped me off.

Despite my qualms with Chase, I didn't believe he was a killer, as Detective Rollins had implied. Besides, the men in the van had all but admitted that they'd killed the man. But what *was* Chase's connection with the death of Aidan Jennings?

But that detective had swept in and dropped a bombshell, and now I didn't know how to begin picking up the pieces.

A knock sounded at the door. Before I could answer, Jamie stuck her head inside.

"Can I come in?"

I nodded. "Please do."

She gingerly sat on the edge of the bed, looking more nurturing than I'd ever seen her. "You've had a rough day."

"I can't believe I didn't know about Chase's brother and his connection with Alexander Cartwright." I shook my head, feeling another headache coming on. When Calvin had mentioned two deaths connected with Alexander, I had no idea Hayden was one of them. "Not only that, but I can't put the pieces together. Now I'm really confused."

"Let's talk it out," Jamie said.

"Here's what we know. Chase met with his ex-wife. A dead body was dumped outside the apartment where he's staying, and the man who died is connected with the same man who possibly murdered Chase's brother."

My head pounded. "This string of events is in a great big knot, and I have no idea how to untangle it."

"The good news is that Chase may not have been cheating on you," Jamie said.

I jerked my eyes toward her. "What do you mean?"

She shrugged. "I mean, maybe he just needed Peyton's help with something. She works at the track. Maybe she has connections to Alexander Cartwright."

She had a point. But other things still didn't add up.

"Then why wager?"

Jamie shrugged. "I have no idea, only guesses. He could have been posing for some reason."

"Let's say all that is correct. It doesn't make sense why he couldn't tell me." The questions just poured out of me. I didn't expect Jamie to have the answers. Not really.

"Maybe the less you knew, the better. Maybe he was trying to protect you," Jamie offered. "It could be one of those 'the less you know is better' type of things."

Maybe assumptions were bad manners, just as Magnolia had said.

"The detective said if Chase contacted me again, I had to call him. I don't know if I can do that."

"You could be arrested if you don't." Jamie shifted. "Tell me about Hayden, Holly."

I sucked in a long breath. "I don't know how much I really know. Hayden was two and a half years younger than Chase. They'd only met a year before that. I know he was shot in the back while he was at the park. No one saw anything. No one knew anything. It tore Chase apart."

Silence fell between us as we both processed everything. I

pulled my knees to my chest and turned to face her better, trying to formulate my words. "Jamie, do you remember when you were in two car accidents within a three-month period?"

"None of them were my fault!"

I raised a hand to halt her thoughts. "That's not where I'm going with this. I promise. But do you remember how for the next year, every time you got into a car with me and noticed anything remotely dangerous—a car driving too close behind us or one that was all over the road or someone speeding— whatever it was, you got nervous."

She nodded. "I tensed all over. My body was preparing for another accident, I guess. Why are you bringing that up?"

I sighed and stared at the fish again. "I guess that's how I'm feeling about my life lately. You go through death and grief and health scares, and suddenly you get paranoid. Your experiences have conditioned you to look for the worst, to prepare for it."

She squeezed my hand. "I get that."

"I found an oncology bill for my mom stuck in the seat of her car," I continued.

"Oncology?"

I nodded. "She didn't mention anything to me about it."

"Well, now I know where you get it. You're pretty secretive about things sometimes too."

I frowned. "I guess I just don't understand life sometimes. I see some people who glide through their days, their weeks, their years, and everything seems easy. I mean, I'm sure it's not. I'm sure they have struggles. But they're all alive, and they're all whole and healthy. Their family units are intact."

Jamie murmured something to let me know she was listening.

"Then I look at my family and everything we've been through. It's seemed like trial after trial, and I have to ask myself, why? Why does God allow so much suffering for some people of faith and hardly any for others? And please don't tell me it's because He's trying to grow my faith or He only gives people that He has big plans for that kind of hardships. Maybe it's true, but it doesn't make me feel any better."

"I wish I had some answers for you. I only know that life's hard. We all experience that in one way or another eventually. Some people learn that lesson earlier in life, and others not until later. It's not fair. It's not easy. It doesn't make a lot of sense. I guess we really have no choice but to deal with it, though. You know?"

"Unfortunately."

"I know that's not deep. It may not even be helpful. But we can let those experiences overwhelm us and make us sad. Or we can take the time we've got left here and make the best of it, despite the hard times."

I bobbed my head up and down slowly. No, her words weren't that deep or philosophical. But they made sense. She was right.

We couldn't control what happened to us in life. We could only control how we reacted to it, what we did with our pain, how we handled the bad times. We could only pick up the pieces and try to learn and grow throughout the experiences.

"Don't give up hope, Holly," Jamie finished.

"I haven't. I just wish God would cut me slack sometimes."

"You've taken everything that's happened, and you've used that ugliness and turned it into something beautiful. You're an inspiring person, Holly. You pour your life into others. You've been a great example of what it looks like to really live out your faith. Never forget that. You may not be able to see the truth through your pain, but other people can see God shining through you."

"That means a lot. Thank you." I was going to buck up. I had to give Chase the benefit of the doubt. I'd want him to do that for me. "I'm not giving up, Jamie."

CHAPTER 24

Jamie and I went to church at a local congregation less than a block away. Time with God in His presence could be more powerful than weeks and weeks of trying to do things on my own. Both Jamie and I knew that well from experience, so despite the urgency of the situation, we made sure to find a church.

We'd walked there and then back to Magnolia's afterward, since my car was still at Golden Equestrian. I was right—I was sorer today than I'd been yesterday, and my bruises had only deepened and darkened. It made exerting myself difficult, but I wasn't going to let anything hold me down.

We arrived back at the house just in time to meet Jamie's friend who'd given her a ride home yesterday. He took us to the stables. My mom's Lexus was still there—thank goodness—so we drove back with no trouble.

Magnolia was waiting at the house with an assortment of food from a local deli. We set up everything on the dining room table and prepared ourselves for a powwow.

I knew we had to get down to business. Our time here was coming to a close. I couldn't stay indefinitely, so I had to make the most of my time.

I finished my chicken-salad sandwich, most of it anyway, and leaned back. I straightened my shoulders and waited until Jamie and Magnolia looked my way.

"I need a plan," I announced. "We have responsibilities to get back to at home. Chase may be in trouble. And I need answers. My life depends on it."

"Everything seems to be pointing to Alexander Cartwright, if you ask me," Jamie said. "I think he's the one who has those answers."

"But how do I get close to Alexander Cartwright? He's rich enough to hire an army to protect him."

"That's a good question," Magnolia said, wiping her pink lips. "Besides, even if you did, it's not like he would just fess up. Am I right?"

"But maybe I could see his eyes. You can tell so much about a person from their eyes."

"So you think you're going to look at him and be able to know whether or not he's telling the truth?" Jamie repeated.

"I'm not saying anything. I'm just throwing out ideas."

Magnolia excused herself for a moment. She grabbed a tissue and walked out of the room.

"Chase asked you to trust him," Jamie reminded me, lowering her voice. "How does that tie in with talking to Alexander?"

"I have no obligation to listen to Chase." I paused, realizing how much emotion my voice held. Each word sounded like a verbal punch.

Jamie stared at me, worry in her gaze. "I see."

My shoulders slumped. "Sorry I'm being snappy. I'm just desperate for answers."

Jamie didn't say anything for a moment. "Well, if you're going somewhere, I'm going with you. Safety in numbers and all. Besides, you need someone to watch your back."

"Thanks for always being that person, Jamie."

The sound of a throat clearing behind us interrupted our

Hallmark moment.

"Someone is here to see you," Magnolia said, a satisfied look in her eyes. "I didn't think you would mind."

Someone here to see us? Who could that be? Another detective? I prayed it wasn't someone bringing more bad news.

Jamie and I exchanged a glance before walking into the living room.

A woman I'd never seen before waited in the entryway. She was in her late twenties, if I had to guess, and sported heavy makeup, wide, loopy blonde curls that had probably taken considerable time to get in place, and a lot of gold jewelry.

She offered a tight smile when Jamie and I came into view.

"I'm Crystal Hanson," she said, clutching an expensive-looking purse.

The woman I was supposed to meet yesterday from the Horse Racing Commission, I realized.

I extended my hand. "Crystal! So nice to meet you. I didn't mean to stand you up yesterday. Please forgive me."

"Something came up at the last minute, and I tried to call, but our connection was terrible. Anyway, I heard you have quite the explanation for it."

I touched the bruise on my cheek and attempted to smile. "You could say that."

"Magnolia said it was urgent that you talk to me?" Her knuckles whitened around her purse in her hands. She was nervous, I realized.

"Yes. I'm afraid a friend of mine is wrapped up in something that somehow ties in with horse racing. I wanted to learn more, and I heard you were just the person."

She sighed before motioning toward the couch. "Do you mind?"

"Where are my manners? No, of course not. Have a seat." I

sat across from her, clenching and unclenching my hands as I waited to hear what she had to say. Instead, I fell back on my standard banter. "Would you like some tea?"

"No, thank you." She rubbed her lips together, her gaze squirrelly. "Is there anything specific you want to ask me? Because there's so much I could say about horse racing."

I shrugged. "I guess anything about Alexander Cartwright, Peyton Andrews, and Chase Dexter, if you've heard of him."

"Chase Dexter?" She let out a small chuckle and flung a curl behind her ear. "I used to have a huge crush on him."

"You know him?" Surprise rippled through me.

She shook her head and waved her hand in the air, almost looking giddy. "No, but everyone around here did for a while, back when he played football for Louisville."

I released my breath. "I see."

"Okay, I'll get back to Alexander Cartwright. Everyone knows he's a major player in this industry. He's invested millions in horse racing. But you need to know about Peyton as well?"

I nodded. "If you wouldn't mind."

She rubbed her hands on her slacks. "I don't know much about Peyton. Most people don't like her. Well, I take that back. Most men like her. I wonder why?"

I shouldn't have smiled, but I did because I knew exactly what she was getting at.

"She married Winston Kensington, and she acts like she owns the track. I don't really know much more about her."

"How about her husband, Winston?"

Crystal shrugged. "He's a nervous guy. Not very attractive but loaded with money. His mom seems to have a lot of expectations for him, even though he's in his forties. But she's ill now, and he's been down in Georgia visiting her."

"I'm sorry to hear that."

"It's bad timing, since fall racing season is under way at Wyndmyer."

"I heard the track was having some trouble."

"I heard those rumors also. I believe there are several reasons, including poor management, high turnover of employees. Then there's Starting Gate Gate. And, no, I didn't stutter."

I drew my eyebrows together in curiosity. "What's Starting Gate Gate?"

"A couple of the starting gates didn't open like they were supposed to. A few of the jockeys and horse owners were upset. The race got thrown out. It was a mess."

"Wow. Who was guilty?"

Crystal shrugged. "No one knows. No one owns up to it, and everybody is pointing fingers."

"Sounds like a mess."

Crystal sucked in a quick breath. "Okay, on to Alexander Cartwright. He's built an empire. He's a cutthroat, and you don't want to come between him and his money. What else do you need to know?"

That seemed succinct enough. "All that said, do you think he's capable of murder?"

Crystal's eyes widened, and she let out that nervous laugh. "Murder? Now that's a new one. I thought I'd heard them all. He's been accused of juicing his horses, paying off veterinarians to stay quiet, firing jockeys when they had one bad performance, threatening anyone who pushes too hard. But I've never heard anything about murder. It's possible, I suppose."

"It sounds like you're not a fan."

She shook her head. "I've never been a fan. Alexander sees animals as a means to profit. I see them as beautiful creatures to be held in awe. Plus, I've met him probably ten times and he never remembers me. Never. My impression is that he thinks of women the same way he thinks of his horses: only the best make the cut to be showcased. The rest aren't important."

Ouch. So Alexander liked his horses fast and his women beautiful. I kept that in mind, even though I doubted it had anything to do with this whole fiasco with Chase. "Crystal, I fear that somehow Chase is connected with Alexander and not in a good way."

"You don't want to get on his bad side."

"I need to talk to Alexander. Any idea how I can do that?" I waited hopefully.

A light ignited in her gaze. "I know the perfect way. He's going to be at a museum tonight—Harbor House, just outside of Louisville. He's a donor. Anyway, I was given two tickets to the event because of my job. I have no intentions of going, though. Would you like the tickets?"

I glanced at Jamie and nodded. "Yes. Would we ever."

"He'll have a team of men around him, so he'll be hard to get to. But if you're up for a challenge, I'd say go for it."

I nodded. I was up for a challenge. I had no other choice.

CHAPTER 25

"We have no idea what we're doing here," Jamie mumbled in my ear.

I nodded. "I know."

I surveyed the art museum one more time. It was located in an old church with a beautiful stone exterior. The main exhibition room had beautiful, glossy wooden floors and stained glass that captured my attention more than the pictures of thoroughbreds around the room. The place smelled like perfume and polished wood, and occasional wafts of savory foods wafted toward me.

I wasn't out of place. I loved stuff like this. I'd accompanied Ralph to fancy events on more than one occasion.

But my anxiety rested solely in the fact that I didn't know how my confrontation with Alexander Cartwright would go. That's what made me nervous. Was I showing my hand? Would I tip him off and only make things worse? I had no idea. I wasn't a gambler. I had no poker face. And I was most likely in over my head here.

At least I felt beautiful. I'd borrowed a ruby-red gown from Magnolia. Jamie wore a bronze cocktail dress, and together we looked like two Southern belles out for a classy evening of art and rubbing elbows with the town's wealthiest. With enough makeup I'd even managed to cover the bruises on my face, and my busted lip made me look like I'd just had the "Angelina Jolie" done by a plastic surgeon.

I raised my goblet of sparkling apple juice to my lips, mostly to conceal my mouth and my words. I'd never been a huge fan of alcohol, but when Chase and I started dating, I'd vowed to stay far away from the stuff.

"Do you see Alexander anywhere?" I whispered.

Jamie scanned the room. "Not yet."

"Do you see Chase? Peyton?"

"This has nothing to do with horse racing. They shouldn't be here."

"There are a lot of things that shouldn't happen," I mumbled, keeping my head up and my shoulders back as I surveyed the crowd.

Servers wearing black and white carried trays with drinks and finger foods. A long table covered with a white linen cloth at the back of the room had a steady assortment of foods arranged artistically on various tiers. My stomach rumbled smelling them. I wasn't sure what the food was, but the scent of basil and roasted tomatoes and bubbly cheese made me want to taste test everything.

If only we were here for fun.

Even if all of this somehow turned out to be a gigantic misunderstanding, where would that leave Chase and me? I obviously had a big gap in my life when it came to trusting him. Could I ever get past that? Would Chase ever forgive me for the oversight?

My gut was starting to believe that Chase was innocent. I still had a few doubts—such as that hug I'd seen him exchange with Peyton. But I wanted to give him the benefit of the doubt.

"What we're seeing is just the tip of the iceberg," Jamie continued. "There could be a huge mountain just beneath the surface that will help us to understand all of this eventually."

"I hope you're right." I took another sip of my drink in order to conceal my frown.

"If Chase contacts you, are you going to call the police?"

No amount of drinking could conceal my frown this time. I'd struggled with that question since Detective Rollins talked to me. I didn't know what I'd do.

"I have no idea," I said. "I don't want to think about it. I have to do the right thing. The problem comes in when I don't know what the right thing is."

As if she didn't hear me, Jamie elbowed me. "There he is!"

I followed Jamie's gaze. Sure enough, Alexander Cartwright had stepped into the room. The air seemed to change in his presence.

White hair at his temples made him look distinguished. He was thin, and he held himself well. But his eyes were shifty. I noticed it right away. How could other people not see that?

Three men in black suits had followed him inside. Did he have his own security detail? That's how it appeared. The man had somewhat of a celebrity complex, and maybe he deserved it. As soon as he arrived, several people started toward him.

He kissed cheeks and hands and glowed under the attention.

He wasn't one of the men who'd come after Chase and me, I realized. But, as I glanced at the three men with him, I realized that he had people who would do stuff like that for him, so that didn't mean anything.

"How are you going to make your move, Retro Girl?" Jamie whispered.

"In an overwhelmingly clever, smooth-as-ice way." I watched him as he talked to several people in the room. Charming. That's what he was. Did these people truly like him? Or when you were that rich, did everyone want to be your friend because of what you could do for them?

I would probably never have a chance to face that dilemma, and I was okay with that. My moments of want and need only served to draw me closer to God.

"How exactly do you plan on being smooth and clever?" Jamie asked, her eyes still on Alexander.

"I have no idea. But I know that I have to time it right."

"As long as you have a plan . . ."

I watched as Alexander walked toward the food table in the back. When he went to grab some more shrimp, I saw my chance.

"This is it," I whispered. "Wish me luck."

"Luck has nothing to do with it. I'm going to pray to God Almighty that He'll watch over your soul and protect you just like a shepherd protects all those stupid sheep."

"Thanks . . . I think."

I paced toward the refreshment table, casually picked up a shrimp, and dabbed some cocktail sauce on an elegant white plate.

Natural, I reminded myself. *Be natural.*

"Nice gallery," I started.

Alexander glanced up, at first skeptical, but then he looked again and straightened. A flicker of interest filled his gaze as he looked me over. "It is."

He didn't recognize me, I realized. He might be a grubby jerk who thought of women as being disposable pieces of meat, but he had never seen me before. There was no flash of recognition.

That was interesting.

Now for the hard part—planning what to say next. I wasn't great at doing the flirty thing or being fake, for that matter. But I had to remember the bigger issues that were at stake here.

"I know about the man beaten to a pulp in the stables at the

Golden Equestrian Riding Center yesterday," I blurted.

He dropped his shrimp, and it hit the floor. The cocktail sauce that had covered it splattered like blood from a fresh kill. My heart pounded erratically at the thought.

Bad analogy.

Alexander looked around to see if anyone had noticed. When no one did, he placed his plate on the table. "I don't know what you're talking about."

"I think you do."

He raised an eyebrow. "Do I know you?"

I gripped my plate so hard that I feared it might crack in my hands. "I think you're trying to hurt a friend of mine. Chase Dexter."

The man's body went completely rigid. "Chase Dexter? He's always wanted to point the finger at me, mostly because he can't find anyone better. It's like I told him a few days ago: I'll have him—and you—arrested if you don't leave me alone. I'm tired of these threats. Find someone else to blame."

He wasn't getting out of this that easily. This might be my only opportunity to talk to the man. "Who was the man beaten on your property this week?"

"Do you know whom you're talking to?" Steam practically came from his ears as he leaned toward me, narrowing his eyes.

The men around him stared me down, remaining on the edges of the room and ready to pounce if necessary.

"Of course I do. That's why I sought you out." I batted my eyelashes innocently, even though I knew exactly what he was implying.

He swallowed hard, his gaze locked with mine. "What do you want from me?"

"Just some answers."

He looked around again, smiling at someone in the distance

and waving his hand in the air as if he had no worries. "Meet me out back in five minutes. Come alone."

Those were the words a girl never wanted to hear.

And now I had a choice to make.

Take a risk or play it safe.

***

"You shouldn't do this," Jamie whispered.

I hoped my voice sounded strong as I said, "I have Girl Genius as lookout. What could go wrong?"

Her eyes widened dramatically. "So many things. Pain. Torture. Death. Need I go on?"

Yeah, I'd thought of those things also. I'd hoped I was just being paranoid. "He just wants to talk," I insisted. I was trying not to show it, but I was nervous and doubting myself. But I needed answers.

"I strongly discourage this." She put her hands on her hips and tapped her foot.

She looked just like her mom when she did that, but I didn't dare say those words aloud.

"I don't have time to think of another plan, Jamie." I glanced behind me, noticing that Alexander was making his way toward the door, but people kept stopping him to talk. "This is my one chance. Call the police—maybe even Detective Rollins—if anything goes wrong. Okay?"

"I should go with you."

"He insisted I go alone. I don't want anything to mess this up. It's important, Jamie. Important enough that I'm willing to take a huge risk to make it happen."

She frowned. "Every self-help guru would tell me that taking big risks was a good thing, but I'm pretty sure they weren't referring to meeting with cold-blooded killers."

"Jamie . . ."

She sighed. "Fine. Okay. I'll stay here, and if anything goes wrong, I'll call the police and tell them everything. But you seriously have to be careful because I can't be best-friendless. My world just wouldn't be the same."

I spontaneously gave her a hug before straightening. "Here goes nothing."

I stepped out the front door of the museum and walked around to the back side, to the area where Dumpsters lurked, packages were delivered, and priceless pieces of art were first introduced to the building.

My steps faltered for a moment. There was Alexander Cartwright. He leaned against the railing attached to the steps leading to the back door. A cigarette flickered in his hand, but he snubbed it out as I approached.

From the corner of my eyes, I saw two men lingering in the distance: one by the Dumpster, another by a Cadillac.

Instantly, my spine clenched. This could turn ugly.

CHAPTER 26

I'd barely survived last time when strange men had grabbed me. I wasn't sure I had the strength to fight or the capability to win if it happened again.

My gut told me the men wouldn't try anything here.

But, as added insurance, I pulled my phone out and opened my camera app. I put it into selfie mode, turned, and took a picture of myself with Alexander lingering in the background.

Alexander straightened, a wrinkle between his eyes. "What are you doing?"

"Providing myself with a bit of an insurance policy," I told him as I texted the picture to Jamie. "If I disappear, I have proof that you're the last person I was seen with."

He stared at me a moment, and I expected a lecture or outrage. Instead, a smile curled his lip and he shook his head.

"You're quite clever," he said, stepping closer. "I might have to make you my number six."

I blinked in confusion. "Your number six?"

His grin widened. "My sixth wife, of course. Some people say I go through marriages like tissues."

"I don't view marriages as being disposable, among other things. I don't think it would work out." Even when talking to a potential killer, I was being polite. I had to get a grip and tap into some of my meanness. Most people who knew me didn't think I could be mean.

Alexander stood in front of me now, a cocky look in his eyes. He reached toward me, his fingers headed right toward my face.

To choke me?

Panicking, I cringed and backed away. I shouldn't have come out here alone. I knew it. Everyone probably knew it.

One day, my optimism would be the death of me.

Alexander frowned and dropped his hand, sliding it into his pocket. "I was just going to brush your hair out of your eyes."

I reached up, and sure enough, a few strands of hair were plastered against my forehead. I quickly wiped them down.

"Despite what you might think, I'm a pacifist," Alexander explained.

I almost snorted until I saw he wasn't smiling anymore. My grin slipped, and I stared at the man in front of me. "You're serious?"

"Everyone knows I'm against guns—"

His words sounded so ludicrous that my mouth dropped open. "Then what are your men carrying?"

I pointed to one of them in the distance. Something was clearly hidden away beneath his sports jacket. When the wind blew, I could see the metal at his belt.

Alexander raised his eyebrows, as if this conversation were beginning to exhaust him. "Stun guns, and that's just as a safety precaution. They've never used them."

I stared at him, trying to judge his words. He seemed sincere. He didn't laugh or smile, as he might if he was trying to fool me. But I was having a hard time buying it. Men like Alexander Cartwright liked to exude power; guns could convey some of the clout.

"You don't believe me? Look it up. It's online," he insisted.

I just might do that when I had the chance. But for now I

had other more pressing issues to address. "What about the man at your stables who was nearly beaten to death on your property?"

His stare pierced me. "Why would you think that?"

"I was in the stables when it happened. Only inches away, for that matter."

His eyebrows flicked upward in surprise again. "I don't know anything about it."

I placed one hand on my hip. I might be optimistic, but that didn't mean I was naïve—not all the time, at least. "I'm just supposed to believe you? Why? Because you're one of the richest men in the state?"

"In the United States," he corrected. He stared at me, a cold look in his eyes as he shifted his stance. "Look, I don't even have to talk to you right now. I'm doing it to be nice, and I'm not nice very often. I'd hate for you to exploit my kindness."

Really? He was going to turn this back on me, like I was the one who'd done something wrong? How rude.

I needed to get to business, then, because I'd hate to waste the time of such an important person. "From my understanding, there are now two deaths that are associated with you. Explain that."

Something flickered in his eyes. Guilt? I didn't think so. In fact, I thought it was a touch of respect.

"How do I explain them? Easily. I'm innocent of both of them. When you're a man with as many networks as I have, a lot of crimes are somehow connected with you. It doesn't mean you have anything to do with them."

"Or maybe it means that you have plenty of people to blame when things go south."

He stared at me, and I could see the wheels turning in his mind. Then he laughed and waved a finger in the air. "You've got moxie, darling. I like that."

He was trying to change the subject. I wasn't going to let that happen. "I still don't think you're innocent, no matter what diversionary tactics you try to use."

"Is that right?" Alexander smirked again, obviously unaffected by my certainty of his guilt.

I balled my free hand into a fist. I hated it when people underestimated me. "I know you juice your horses!"

His cocky smile faded again. "No, I don't. People just want to explain why I'm successful. Hard work, wisdom, knowledge . . . none of those things are good enough for them. I have to be cheating to be prosperous. If you're rich, it's because you're somehow shortchanging the people underneath you. If you're winning, it's not because you're smart, it's because you're unprincipled. Not everyone likes to see other people succeed."

"What about Aidan Jennings?" I continued, my mind racing. "Was he one of those people who resented you . . . to the point where you had to kill him?"

His eyes narrowed. "He had problems in his life that weren't associated with me. I do employ five hundred people. All their problems can't possibly be my fault."

The man had a point.

"Why are you so concerned? Were you friends with either of these men I supposedly hurt?"

"No, but I have a friend in trouble, and it has something to do with Wyndmyer and horse racing."

Something flickered in his gaze. "If I were you, I'd take a look at Winston Kensington and his wife, Peyton."

Shock rushed through me. "Look at them for what reason?"

"You're concerned about illegal activities in connection with Wyndmyer, right?"

"You could say that."

"That man and his wife have no scruples. They'll do whatever it takes to get ahead. Horse owners and jockeys are threatening to pull out of races there. They claim they're rigged to be in favor of certain horses."

"Do you agree?"

"I recently decided not to race any of my horses there either."

All of that was very interesting, and I'd definitely have to think about it. I licked my lips, more questions simmering in my mind. "What about Hayden Dexter? Was that someone else's fault also?"

He sighed again and looked away. "He was a great worker. I offered a $500,000 reward to anyone who came forward with information. Why would I do that if I were guilty?"

"You did?" I shook my head, realizing I should have done more research.

He nodded and glanced at his watch. "Our time is running out. And, yes, I did. I guess your friend didn't tell you that."

This man was messing with my mind. I couldn't let his suggestions influence my thinking. "Maybe you offered that reward to throw people off your trail."

He said nothing.

"Why did people suspect you?"

Alexander shrugged. "You'll have to ask those people yourself."

"Can you prove any of this?"

He stared at me. "Can you?"

I didn't say anything, because I knew I didn't have a good answer.

He stepped closer again. "I'm many things. But I'm not a killer."

I raised my chin. "You didn't send a van full of men to kill me?"

"I especially don't hurt women, unless you consider divorce hurtful." He offered a smug smile.

"What were you and Chase Dexter arguing about a few days ago?"

He raised his eyebrows. "You saw that? If you must know—and that's up for contemplation—we ran into each other, and he confronted me."

"About?"

"His brother's death."

"Did you kill Chase Dexter's brother?" I knew I was repeating myself, but I needed to know.

His gaze darkened. "No, I didn't. And I have the evidence to prove it."

CHAPTER 27

I sat on the back steps of the museum, needing a moment to unwind. My ruby-colored skirt puffed out around me, a vast contrast to the grungy cement steps. Alexander and his cronies had gone back inside, but I still quaked from our conversation.

As I scooted over to let an employee take the trash out, I closed my eyes, realizing that in many ways I was going back to square one in my unofficial investigation. Alexander Cartwright, by all appearances, was innocent. He was smart enough to cover his bases, to do his research, to anticipate what might happen next.

Just then, Jamie ran around the corner of the building. Her chest heaved like she was out of breath, and her eyes were wide. She stopped abruptly in front of me, confusion showing in the knot between her eyes.

"I saw Alexander come back inside . . ." She drank in a gulp of air. "I thought . . ."

"The worst?" I frowned, realizing I hadn't thought things through. "Sorry. I just needed a moment."

She fanned her face before coming to sit beside me. An overhead light flickered as moths swarmed above us. The stench of one of the Dumpsters drifted our way every time the slightest of breezes grazed the asphalt. Beyond the overhead lights, a few stars peeked through on the cloudless night.

Jamie nodded at the papers in my hands. "What's that?"

192

I pressed my lips together a moment before answering. "Evidence proving Alexander Cartwright had nothing to do with the death of Hayden Dexter."

"What? How can that be possible?"

I stared at all the lines, graphs, and numbers on the sheets in front of me, and replayed my conversation with Alexander. He'd motioned to one of his men, who'd disappeared a moment before returning with an envelope.

"There's no way to definitely prove I didn't hire someone to do my so-called dirty work," Alexander said. "But I do have this."

He handed me a stack of papers with numbers and dollar signs running down it in a list. "What is this?"

"It's my bank records for the three months before and after Hayden Dexter was killed. I was out of town. That's a fact that's been substantiated several times. But this should prove that I didn't hire anyone, either. There are no large sums of cash being distributed, other than my normal transactions."

"How do I know you don't have other accounts?"

He shrugged. "You don't. I'll never convince some people. But for those willing to listen, this is my effort to clear my name."

I relayed the conversation to Jamie.

"He just happened to have the papers with him?" Jamie asked.

"He brought them in case Chase confronted him again."

She was silent a moment, as if processing that news. "Wow. That's pretty forward of him to hand over his bank records. Did Alexander tell Chase any of that?"

I shook my head. "Apparently not. He wants me to."

"But if you tell Chase, then you'll be talking to him, which will mean that you have to turn him in to the—"

I raised my hand. "I know."

I was between a rock and a hard place. Again.

"There's something else," I continued. "This whole time I thought all these crimes were tied in with Alexander Cartwright. But I don't think they are, Jamie."

"Why not?"

"That's just my gut feeling after talking to him. He pointed out that he has more than five hundred employees. Most of them he has no contact with. He's also a pacifist, he said. He doesn't believe in violence. A person who murders usually isn't afraid to lie. I realize that. But I still don't think he's our guy."

Jamie pursed her lips as if skeptical. "But if not Alexander, then who? Who else would want to threaten us?"

I replayed our conversation. "Alexander pointed the finger at Winston Kensington."

"Why?"

"Said he's unscrupulous. Everyone in the horse-racing world knows it, but he's somehow managed to skirt by without getting caught. He thinks Winston was directly involved with the Starting Gate scandal. He's also heard rumor that he's in a heap of financial trouble and that the track is on the verge of shutting down."

"Did you ask him about Aidan Jennings?"

"I did. He said the police are investigating it as part of a crime ring unrelated to horse racing." I shook my head again. "I just have no idea where to go from here."

Jamie sighed. "I really thought when I suggested we come to Louisville that there would be a simple answer. Like maybe Chase was picking out an engagement ring or helping underprivileged children or . . . I don't know! Doing something innocent. I was wrong. Really wrong."

I offered my first smile of the evening. "We're quite the pair, aren't we?"

She put her arm around my shoulders. "As long as we stick together, we'll figure life out . . . one step at a time."

"Or we'll die trying."

***

I reflected on everything as we departed from the art show. Should I investigate Winston or Peyton? If I did, it would seem like I was targeting them because of their connection with Chase. With Winston being out of town, it would be that much more difficult.

Halfway back to Magnolia's, headlights appeared in my rearview mirror. In themselves, they weren't suspicious. But after everything that had happened, I was on edge.

Maybe it was because of everything that had already happened, but sweat sprinkled across my forehead.

Was it the van? Had the men found us again? The ache in my ribs deepened, and my lungs tightened. Flashes of what had happened in the Creeper Van consumed my mind until my hands shook.

"What's wrong? You look like you could pass out," Jamie said.

I glanced in the rearview mirror again. The vehicle was still there. I couldn't tell if it was the van or not. But I definitely felt like we were being followed. "I think we're being tailed, Jamie."

Her eyes widened. "One of Alexander's men?"

I shook my head, my shoulders tight with strain. "I don't know. It could be the Creeper Van."

"We can't lead them back to Magnolia's."

My hands gripped the steering wheel tighter. "I know."

"What are you going to do?"

"Hold on." I jerked the wheel to the left and cut through

195

traffic onto a side street in the busy retail area. Cars honked and swerved to get out of my way. I wanted to close my eyes with fear, but that wasn't an option. I waited for the crunch of metal on metal, but it didn't come.

"What are you doing?" Jamie grabbed the armrest.

"Trying to get away with our lives intact." I veered to miss another car.

"If they don't kill us, you might."

I glanced behind me. The headlights were still there. Still close. And getting closer by the moment.

"They're not backing off, Jamie."

"We've got to lose them somehow."

I swung another quick left, darting right in front of oncoming traffic. The vehicles barely missed us and ratcheted my heartbeat into a dangerously high level. Immediately, I took the next right. A red light stared at me, daring me to keep going.

I was taking a chance. But I had little choice. I sped through it.

As I gunned the engine, Jamie screamed beside me.

I screamed also as I saw my life flash in front of my eyes.

A car skidded to a stop beside us. Then another. And another.

But I kept going.

I glanced in the mirror. A barrier of stopped cars blocked the intersection. Those headlights still stared at us from beyond the barrier, but I'd bought us some time.

I quickly turned into a parking lot, found a spot among the sea of cars, and turned off my headlights.

I prayed they wouldn't find us.

"You think this will work?" Jamie whispered. There was no need to whisper, but I understood the urge.

"I hope so."

We sank lower in our seats.

A moment later, a familiar car drove past. It wasn't the Creeper Van, though.

It was a Jeep with a broken side-view mirror.

Chase's Jeep.

CHAPTER 28

Magnolia didn't have any Frank Sinatra or Peggy Lee, so I settled for Harry Connick Jr. instead. He would work. He crooned "A Wink and a Smile" in the corner of my bedroom. I'd returned to Magnolia's and escaped to my bedroom, where I promptly collapsed on the bed.

Jamie and I had somehow gotten away. I'd been sure the police would track us down. However, I didn't think we'd caused any true accidents, only several skids and sudden stops. Still, I halfway expected law enforcement to show up at the door at any minute.

Why had we seen Chase's Jeep? Obviously, he wasn't behind the wheel . . . right? But if someone had stolen his Jeep and followed us while trying to cast suspicion on Chase, then this was a much more twisted game than I realized.

I sighed, my thoughts heavy and confused. I looked down at my phone. I had to call Ralph. I was supposed to go back to work tomorrow, but I needed one more day.

I hoped he wouldn't answer, that I could leave a message and be done. But, of course, he answered on the first ring.

"Holly? What's going on? I was wondering if I'd hear from you."

"Hey, Ralph. Not much here. I was just calling because I need one more day off. Just one."

He remained silent a moment. "What's really going on,

Holly?"

"What do you mean?" I kept my voice light, though I knew it was futile.

"I'm not stupid, Holly. That cop showed up on Saturday morning saying something about a case he was working on, and I knew there was more to your story. And, for the record, I tried to call and warn you."

I sighed, unable to hide the truth anymore. There was no way I could tell him everything. Not until I had more answers. "Jamie and I are helping a friend out. It's just turned into something bigger than we anticipated. That's the CliffsNotes version."

"I'd ask more questions, but I have a feeling that's all you want to say." He sighed. "Can I do anything?"

"Just pray."

"Done."

I licked my lips. "And Ralph."

"Yes?"

I remembered that oncology bill, and my gut twisted. "Before you go, have you heard from Mom?"

"She's coming home tonight. Why?"

I sucked on my bottom lip, contemplating how much to say. "I was just wondering about her trip."

"I'm sure it was fine. She always has fun with Uncle Paul and Aunt Paula."

I wanted to ask if he knew about her health status, but I didn't. There was no need for him to worry. Not yet. I needed to go straight to Mom first and get answers before I got other people worried.

"All right. See you on Tuesday."

"Be careful. I know how you and Jamie are together. Your love of helping people has gotten you into a pickle more than once."

I couldn't even argue. As soon as I hung up, my phone rang again. I didn't recognize the number, but against my better instincts I answered.

"Holly? It's Chase." Static crackled on the line.

I sat up straight, suddenly at attention. If Chase was calling me now, then something was wrong. "Chase? I can hardly hear you. What's going on?"

"I heard . . ." Static fizzed again. "You can't . . . do you understand?"

I plugged my other ear, trying desperately to understand him. "You're breaking up. What?"

"You . . . can't trust . . ."

"I can't trust you?"

"I just found out . . . you can't trust—" The call broke up again.

"Who can't I trust?" I said it loud, as if that would help.

Before he could respond, the phone went dead.

I sat back.

Chase had called. But what had that meant? Who couldn't be trusted? It sounded like Chase had learned something new, and he was trying to warn me. But I had no idea whom he was talking about. Alexander? Josh?

Another dilemma rolled through my mind. Did I need to call Detective Rollins and let him know I'd talked to Chase? It wasn't like we'd met up. It wasn't as if Chase had told me where he was. Really the conversation would be no help at all.

I put the phone down, the conversation still echoing in my head.

No, I wouldn't call Rollins.

I only hoped I wouldn't regret it.

***

I couldn't sleep that night. My thoughts continually turned over in my head, almost in perfect sync with my tossing and turning. I was so close to answers. I could feel them. What was I missing?

Finally, I threw my covers off and forgot about my need for sleep. Instead, I grabbed my phone and decided to catch up on my e-mails. More than one hundred had piled up in my inbox.

I skimmed through them, realizing I could answer most of them later.

My eyes stopped by one from Chase.

Chase?

I checked the date and saw he'd sent it this morning.

I froze as I clicked on the e-mail, instantly preparing for the worse. So much for being optimistic. What in the world could this be about? Chase wasn't an e-mail type of guy.

I could hardly breathe as the words came across the screen.

Holly,

I'm sorry I have to communicate this way. There are things I haven't been able to tell you. That I haven't wanted to tell you. But I feel I owe it to you to be honest now.

I've done things I'm not proud of. I've gotten into trouble and turned back to my old ways. Alcohol has gripped me. Anger has taken ahold of me. Past relationships have bubbled to the surface. I know you're disappointed, but at least you know the truth.

I killed Aidan Jennings. He started talking
trash about my brother. The two of them
worked together, and Aidan said Hayden
deserved to die. I'm not sure what I was
thinking, but I pulled the trigger and killed him.

My friends helped me to dispose of his
body. At least I thought they did. They turned
against me after they left the body in the
woods. I've been trying to track them down
ever since.

Please forgive me for any heartache I've
caused you.

Love,
Chase

I sat back and shook my head after reading his words. That
couldn't be right. It couldn't be.
I wouldn't believe it.
I read the e-mail again. But who else would send this? Who
would have access to Chase's e-mail account?
Any hacker worth his weight I supposed would be able to.
But . . . what if Chase had sent it?
I shook my head. He didn't.
He would never use e-mail to send a message like this.
But what if someone was still trying to set Chase up? What
if someone still wanted him to look guilty? They'd tried to plant
that gun, driven Chase's Jeep, and now sent this e-mail.
I didn't know. But I seriously needed to think and pray

about all of this.

CHAPTER 29

When I woke up the next morning, I felt more unsettled than ever. After I'd finally gotten to sleep, all I'd dreamed about was that e-mail from Chase, the Jeep that had followed us, and my abduction.

I met Jamie at breakfast and filled her in. Magnolia had already left for work, so we helped ourselves to some toast, for me, and fruit, for Jamie.

"That doesn't even sound like Chase," Jamie said, peeling an orange. "Even if he was guilty, he's smarter than that."

"I agree. Someone's working hard to make him look culpable." I paused, waving a triangle of toast in the air. "I do have an idea."

"Please share."

"I'm going to track down Winston and give him a call."

Her eyebrows shot up. "Are you sure that's a good idea?"

I shrugged. "What do I have to lose?"

"A lot. Your life, to start with."

"I've explored every other avenue I can think of. That leaves Winston and Peyton. At least I can rule out them and their involvement in this."

"More power to you, then."

I leaned closer, brushing away some toast crumbs. "It's like this, Jamie. I don't think this is going to go away. We can go back to Cincinnati, and these men are still going to be out there.

Most likely, they're still going to be terrorizing us. But if not us, then someone else. It's the kind of people they are. I can't rest knowing that I didn't do everything in my power to figure this out."

"You've got some good points."

"Besides, I'm not going to blurt anything about Peyton and Chase," I explained. "I'm going to use the trick that every con artist uses. I'm going to say he won money."

I used Magnolia's laptop to find the number for Winston's mother in Georgia. It hadn't been that hard to find her name and state of residence. A few articles had referenced her, mostly about her status as an aging socialite.

A woman answered on the first ring. "Edna speaking."

"Hi, Edna. I'm trying to reach Winston Kensington."

"Winston? My son?" Her voice lilted with surprise.

"Yes, ma'am." A flutter of nerves played in my stomach. I hated lying. Hated it.

"Well, he's not here. He hasn't lived here for years."

"Do you know when he'll be back?"

"I've been hoping for a visit sometime soon, but my guess is Christmastime. If I'm lucky, maybe Thanksgiving."

I frowned. That didn't fit what I'd been told. "I'm sorry to bother you, but his neighbor said he was down visiting you in Georgia. I had some good news to share with him, so I wanted to reach him as soon as possible."

"No, he's not here visiting. I'm not sure where anyone got that information." She let out a scratchy laugh. "He only visits when he wants something. He got that trait honestly from his father."

"I'm so sorry. I must have misunderstood."

"Who is this anyway?" Her voice changed from humored to curious.

"My name is . . ." I glanced at the banana peel on the table. "Del . . .monica. Delmonica. Winston won a free trip to . . . the Caribbean."

"I see. I'm sorry I can't help you. You're going to have to keep looking for him in Louisville."

I hung up and paused. If Winston wasn't in Georgia, then where was he?

I relayed the conversation to Jamie.

"Call Wyndmyer. See what they say," she encouraged.

I figured I didn't have much to lose. I found the number and called the racetrack. I asked for Winston, and his secretary informed me he was in Georgia visiting his mother.

So he'd told other people that story also. Interesting. Did this have anything to do with what was going on? I didn't know, but I couldn't dismiss the possibility.

At that moment, my cell phone rang. It was Josh. He must have my number from caller ID after I'd called him for help when the Creeper Van men dumped me in the middle of nowhere.

I sat up straighter in the dining room chair. "Josh. Hi. How are you?"

"I'm just calling to check on you. How are you feeling?"

My body ached worse today than yesterday, if that was possible. My jaw hurt, pain radiated from my ribs, and my shoulder and neck muscles were knotted with stress. But I was alive, so I'd take it. "I'm hanging in. Still sore, but it could be much worse."

"Did you go back to Cincinnati?"

"No, I'm actually here still. For another day or two at least."

"I hate to say it, but leaving might be best for you. Nothing good has really come out of you being here."

"I'm not quite done yet, and Holly Anna Paladin has never

been a quitter."

He paused a moment, almost as if contemplating what he had to say next. "Listen, Holly, I contemplated whether or not to tell you this, but I can see you're not going to give up until you get answers."

I waited for him to continue, afraid if I spoke, he might change his mind.

"Look, there's something I want to show you. I was wondering if you could stop by my place sometime today."

My pulse spiked. What could he possibly want to show me? Did he know something about Chase, something that would lead me to some answers? "Sure."

"Great. I'm hoping maybe what I have to show you will help fill in some of the gaps."

My pulse continued to speed. Answers. That was exactly what I needed.

***

When I pulled up to the Belmont Apartments thirty minutes later, I shuddered as I remembered Aidan Jennings. An image of his discarded body in the woods filled my thoughts, and a sick feeling gurgled in my gut. What a nightmare this past month had turned into.

I'd come alone while Jamie researched Winston Kensington and Starting Gate Gate. We figured we could cover more ground if we split, but now I was second-guessing that choice. Thankfully, I hadn't seen anything suspicious on my drive here. No Creeper Vans. I hadn't seen Chase's Jeep either, nor was it in the parking lot now.

Before I even knocked at Josh's apartment, the door opened and Josh stood there with a friendly smile on his face.

"Holly. You made it. You look as lovely as always."

I offered a tight smile. "Thank you."

"Come on in." He extended his hand behind him.

With a touch of nervousness, I stepped inside. Part of me feared Chase would show up. Part of me wasn't comfortable being alone in an apartment with a man I hardly knew.

But it was Josh. The man who'd turned Chase's life around. A pastor.

I had nothing to be worried about.

You can't trust . . .

Chase's words echoed in my mind. Could he have been talking about Josh?

My jitters remained.

They not only remained, they intensified when Josh closed the door and locked it.

There's nothing strange about locking the door behind you. It's just good sense to do it.

I glanced around Josh's apartment, marveling at how well it was decorated considering the man was single. A nice beige couch and loveseat, burgundy curtains, knickknacks in various places pulled the look together. There was even a matching rug underneath an oak coffee table.

"My wife decorated," he explained.

My cheeks flushed. I had no idea he was married. "I see."

"She was killed in an auto accident six years ago."

My hand went over my heart. "I'm so sorry to hear that. I had no idea."

"It's okay." A certain somberness washed over him as he extended his hand to the couch behind him. "Thanks for coming. Why don't you have a seat?"

I laced my hands together in front of me as I walked over to the couch. This was where Chase had been staying. He'd camped out here and obviously felt safe with Josh.

So why was I so antsy? Certainly I would have recognized his voice if he'd been one of the men from the Creeper Van.

"Can I get you something to drink?" Josh asked. "Water? Tea? Coffee?"

I shook my head, just wanting to get this conversation over with. Yet I didn't. I knew the conversation might change my perspective, and while I embraced the truth, it could also be extremely painful at times. What if Josh had evidence that proved Chase really was guilty? "I'm okay. Thank you, though."

Josh's smile faded as he sat on the couch across from me, and I let out the breath I held. "Alexander Cartwright didn't kill Chase's brother," I blurted.

A knot formed between Josh's eyes. "What?"

I explained to him what happened last night, not leaving out many details. I found comfort in wise counsel, and I knew I wasn't seeing any of this objectively. Certainly Chase hadn't been talking about Josh when he'd tried to warn me about someone.

Josh pressed his lips together, a concerned expression across his face. "I'm not sure it was a great idea to meet Alexander by yourself, Holly."

"He said he's a pacifist." My words sounded lame, but that was what Alexander had told me.

He leaned back and squeezed the skin between his eyes. "Alexander may not believe in guns, but he fully engages in being a bully. I don't trust the man."

"You know him?"

"Everyone in this area knows who he is."

I shrugged. I didn't know the man, and I wasn't about to argue the merits of his character. My gut told me Alexander wasn't trustworthy either, nor was he guilty of this crime.

"I know Chase believes Alexander is responsible for his brother's death, but I'm not sure that's true."

"If there's ever a motive to lie, murder is a pretty good one."

"I agree."

Josh shifted, almost as if uncomfortable. "Holly, the truth is, Chase's brother's death has the potential to eat Chase alive. He was obsessed with it for a long time. If there's anything that would bring him back to this area and push him over the edge, it's this."

CHAPTER 30

Josh's proclamation echoed in my head. Over the edge? Was that what Josh really thought had happened to Chase?

My thoughts had gone there before, and I didn't like it. I wouldn't let myself go there again. Not now, especially when so much was on the line.

You can't trust . . .

Chase's words would haunt me until I had some answers.

"I guess until we talk to Chase, we won't know." I rubbed my arms, suddenly feeling chilly.

Josh nodded and stood, motioning for me to follow. "Enough chitchat, right? Come take a look at what I found."

I pushed down my nerves and followed Josh down the hallway. He led me inside the first bedroom we came to. I stepped inside and saw a familiar black suitcase. I smelled Chase's leathery cologne. I spotted his Bible on the nightstand. My heart lurched. I felt so close to Chase, yet so far away.

Josh walked toward the dresser and opened the top drawer. "This is what I found."

Before I even comprehended what he'd pulled out, I stepped back in shock. "You went through his things?"

"Only out of necessity. I don't advocate doing these types of things." Josh held up a stack of photos, a bag with vials inside, and what looked like a map. "Do they make any sense to you?"

I picked up the bag and scanned the labels on the vials

inside. Steroids, I realized. For equines. More facts clicked together in my mind. "I think Chase is investigating Alexander Cartwright, trying to prove he's guilty of being underhanded, in the least, or guilty of murder, at the most," I muttered.

"What?"

"The vials are in a bag—preserving the fingerprints. The photos place the vials at the scene." I shook my head. "I just ruled Alexander out, and now I'm wondering if I shouldn't have."

"Maybe he's not guilty of murder, but something else entirely different."

"You mean two separate crimes?"

Josh shrugged. "Maybe."

I sat down on the edge of the bed and stared at the map. "I have no idea what this is. You?"

He shook his head, sitting across from me. "No idea. The location he marked doesn't look familiar."

The X was in the middle of nowhere. I double-checked, and it wasn't the area where Golden Equestrian was located. Maybe it was another stable? I had no idea. "Can I take a picture of it?"

"Sure."

I pulled my phone out and did just that.

This was evidence. I felt sure of it. Chase was here to try and track down answers, and all of this had something to do with his brother's death.

"The fact that Chase has evidence and now he's disappeared makes me worry," Josh said.

"Disappeared?"

Josh twisted his head in confusion. "I thought you knew. That's why I looked through Chase's things. I haven't seen or heard from him since you were abducted."

My heart panged with concern. "Really?"

Josh nodded. "Really. I've tried calling, but he won't answer his phone."

I leaned back, letting that sink in.

"There's one other thing I thought was worth mentioning. The guys at the station were talking about a crime ring. This one particular group has a long list of charges against them. Robberies. Extortion. Assault and battery. Weapons charges. The whole gamut."

"Okay . . ." What did they have to do with Chase and doping horses and everything else that had happened lately?

He shifted. "There's a black panel van that's been connected with the group."

The color drained from my face. Somehow all of these pieces fit together. I just had no idea how.

***

After I left Josh's place, I picked up Jamie and we started toward Wyndmyer Park, even though we were no longer welcome there. Jamie insisted we needed to go, and I assumed she had a good reason for it.

I didn't see anyone or any creepy black van following us on our way there. I hoped that meant danger was staying away. I hadn't had much luck with that lately, though. I was already jumping at every sound and creak or even the possibility of a sound of creaking occurring.

To say I was tightly wound would be an understatement.

When we arrived, Jamie instructed me to park at the back of the lot, well away from the entrance. When I put the car into park, she turned toward me, finally ready to fill me in.

"Jason Williams is meeting us here," she said.

"Who?" Seriously, of everything she could have told me, I

hadn't expected that announcement.

"Jason Williams. He was the man who talked to us the other day. The one with the crooked teeth who thinks he's a ladies' man."

Yes! How could I forget? "How did you arrange that?"

"Since my online research wasn't getting me very far, I decided to call him. He did give me his number. Long story short, he said he would meet with us."

"Is that such a good idea, especially considering everything that has happened lately?"

"Well, apparently he was fired on Saturday, so he has a bone to pick with Wyndmyer. He seems more than willing to spill the beans."

Just as she finished her sentence, a beat-up truck pulled up beside us. Jason Williams hopped out. He smiled at us, though he didn't preen as much as before. Perhaps being fired had humbled him.

We stepped out of the car. The sky was overcast, and the breeze seemed to promise rain. I hoped it wasn't an omen of how this conversation would turn out.

"I know you two are looking for information." He leaned against his truck. Nope, he still thought he had swagger.

"The well-being of a friend depends on getting the right information," I told him.

He nodded slowly, a smoky, overblown look in his eyes. "I overheard Winston Kensington talking with someone in the stables. Neither of the men knew I was there."

"What did they say?" Jamie pressed, crossing her arms and assessing him with her gaze.

"Winston apparently owes someone a lot of money." Jason enunciated each word carefully and precisely, like he took himself very seriously. "Like, a lot of money. Into the hundreds of thousands of dollars."

"Why?" I asked.

Jason shrugged. "That wasn't clear. I think it was to cover up something, though. That's the impression I had."

I needed something more specific than that. "Any idea what?"

He raised his chin. "I know some suspicious things have been going on here. Some people think the races have been . . . what would you call it? . . . *altered* to favor certain horses. If that's true, Winston could end up in jail. It's enough to make a man desperate."

"You mean like Starting Gate Gate?" I raised my eyebrows.

"You've heard of it?" He nodded, as if impressed. "Winston has been desperate to sweep it under the rug, but word is leaking. I knew it would."

"What do you think about it?"

"I think Winston had someone modify the gates so a few opened more slowly. A couple seconds' disparity can mean the difference in a horse bringing in thousands as winner or lollygagging as loser. Maybe even worse—being sent to the meat factory."

I frowned at the thought of it. "Who came out ahead because of that deal?"

"A couple of horses. People think horse owners paid big-time to let that happen. Those people aren't talking. They'll be stripped of their prize money and titles if it gets out."

And the plot thickens . . .

"We heard Winston Kensington was out of town," I added.

"That's what they say." Jason shrugged, some type of over-the-top attitude encompassing the action. "I think he ran."

"Did you see who he was talking to?"

Jason shook his head. "I have no idea. Didn't recognize the

voice."

"Thank you for sharing that," Jamie added.

"I don't have anything to lose." He paused. "There's one other thing."

"What's that?"

"Winston's wife, Peyton, has been acting strangely," Jason continued. "She trash-talked her ex all the time, and now they're best buddies. That's just weird. Something's up."

"That is strange," I concurred. "Any idea why?"

He opened his truck door and climbed inside. "Who knows? I do know this: Peyton Andrews likes to use people to get what she wants. I wouldn't put that past her now, either. I just don't know what her angle is."

His words haunted me after he said good-bye and pulled away.

"Okay, hear me out," I started, a new theory forming in my head. "What if Peyton called Chase in her hour of need? He feels guilty about the way things ended between them, and feels obligated to help. I know his failed marriage haunts him."

Jamie nodded, the action growing in intensity with each bob of her head. "Then he hears that Alexander Cartwright is involved, and that gives him even more motivation to step in. He's never liked the man, and this could give him the opportunity to get some dirt on the man he thinks killed his brother."

The scenarios continued to play in my head like a reel of black-and-white film from days of old.

"Maybe this was never about getting back with Peyton— although being together could have stirred up old feelings." I shook my head, unsure about the last part. "I still don't want to believe it. Peyton is married."

"I don't believe it. But suddenly everything is starting to

make more sense, yes? From the start this has been about an investigation that ties in with Chase's past. There's still a lot we don't know, but we're getting closer."

"I agree." I decided to push that last thought to the back of my mind. "Let me check that Friend Finder app and see where Chase is now."

Against my better instincts, I pulled up the app and waited for it to load. When it finally did, I frowned.

This couldn't be right.

The pit in my stomach grew deeper.

"Anything?" Jamie asked.

I continued to stare at the screen. "Something's wrong, Jamie. He's not showing up anywhere."

"Maybe he turned it off?"

I bit down, my thoughts heavier than hers. "Maybe. Or maybe something happened to him."

CHAPTER 31

When I walked inside Wyndmyer Park, I spotted Peyton sitting in the stands alone. Crowds lingered by TVs inside, cheering and rooting for their favorite horses as they watched simulcast races.

I stood on the deck in the background and lingered behind a column, watching Peyton. She looked beautiful but troubled, striking me as the type of woman who had no girlfriends and didn't care. Was Jason right? Was she a manipulator? It was pretty bold to bring your ex around the racetrack owned by your husband.

Every once in a while, she pulled out her phone and stared at the screen. Then she would frown and put it away before staring blankly at the racetrack in front of her. Was she waiting for a call? From Chase or Winston, maybe?

"What do you think she's doing?" Jamie whispered.

"I have no earthly idea," I finally whispered. "But I'm tired of hiding. I need to confront Peyton and ask her a few questions."

"Confront? Is that a good—?"

Before Jamie could talk me out of it, I charged forward. I marched down the aisle and plopped myself into the empty seat beside Peyton. She glanced up from her phone, which she'd pulled out again, and her eyes widened when she recognized me.

"You're that photographer." She narrowed her eyes. "I hope

you have permission if you're taking pictures or interviewing any of our employees."

And here went nothing . . . "No. I mean, yes. That's what I said. But I'm not."

Peyton angled her shoulders to get a better look at me. Peyton was no shrinking violet—she obviously liked to confront issues head-on. "What do you want? Do I need to call security?"

I needed to be equally direct. "I'm worried about Chase Dexter, and I hoped you might have some answers for me."

"Who are you?" Her eyes narrowed even more. She was like the snobby girls in high school, I realized. The kind that Chase had dated. The kind who liked to gloat when they found out I had a crush on a boy who was out of my league.

I considered what to say and decided not to hold back. I really had so little to lose at this point. "I'm Holly."

She blinked but continued to stare at me. I could almost see the wheels turning in her head. "His girlfriend?"

I did a double take this time, unsure about how to respond. I didn't expect her to say that. Maybe I'd expected her to say *The poor sap who's in love with Chase.* Thankfully she hadn't.

"I don't know what we are anymore," I admitted. "But I'm worried about him. I do know that."

She stared at the track again, resting her elbows on her legs and appearing generally burdened. "You're all he talks about."

I was all he talked about to his ex-wife whom he was getting back together with? I couldn't imagine how those conversations went. "Well, that sounds awkward."

She pulled her chin back and stared at me like I'd just claimed I was Etta James reincarnated. "Why would that be awkward?"

This conversation was not going as I planned. There were obviously a lot of misunderstandings between Peyton and me.

"Aren't you back together with Chase?"

Her jaw went slack and she shook her head. "No. Why would you think that?"

"Why wouldn't I think that?" My voice rose, though I wished it hadn't. But my thoughts weren't that absurd. I'd seen the two of them interacting with my own eyes.

Peyton opened her mouth, then closed it again. She glanced down at her phone once more before letting out a sigh. "This is really a bad time to talk about this."

"So I've heard." I sat there silently for a moment, patiently waiting to hear what she said next.

"Chase is missing," Peyton finally said.

I jerked my head toward her, her melancholy voice jolting me more than any amount of panic would. "You mean even you don't know where he is?"

She nodded. "That's right. He was supposed to meet me tonight, but he never showed. I don't know what happened."

I pushed down my resentment about the secrets between them. There were bigger issues at hand. "Any idea where he might be?"

"No, but I think he's in trouble and that it's my fault."

My heart sped for a moment as possibilities raced through my mind. Trouble? Missing? Maybe this was worse than I thought. "What do you mean?"

Peyton glanced around, her eyes big and perceptive as she looked at the crowd. Finally, her gaze zeroed in on me again.

"I can't talk about it here," she whispered. "There's a restaurant called Callie's on Wayward and Fifth. Meet me there in an hour, and I'll explain everything."

***

I sat across from Peyton an hour later at a trendy little restaurant that apparently specialized in every kind of slider imaginable—patty melts, sloppy joes, buffalo chicken, veggie burgers, and even chili dog on a bun. Though the waitress insisted I should try one, I'd declined and opted instead for some sweet tea. I needed the caffeine to keep me alert.

Peyton, on the other hand, had ordered some kind of mixed drink. She didn't bother to keep it on the table, but instead she'd held it since we'd arrived, sipping from the tiny stirrer nearly as often as she breathed.

Jamie lingered by the door, keeping a lookout in case the men from the van came back. We had to be careful because one slipup and we could both be dead.

In the background, various sporting events played on the overhead TVs, the patrons murmured, and silverware clinked. The smell of fried foods and spicy wings filled the air.

"Someone abducted my husband, Winston," Peyton said, finishing her drink and clanking the glass on the table. "They're demanding a ransom, and I asked Chase for his help. These guys said I couldn't bring the police into this or Winston would die."

"Come again?" I was trying to process what she said, but it was a lot. And nothing that I expected.

Peyton glanced around again, the action making me wonder if she was being followed also. She lowered her voice and said, "You heard me correctly. My husband is gone. Someone grabbed him, and I haven't seen him since."

Suddenly, some of the facts started to make sense. "That's why you're telling everyone he's visiting his mother in Georgia."

She narrowed her eyes, as if my snooping offended her. Apparently, she'd expected me to come in here totally clueless and without having done any research. Had she underestimated me? Most likely, but I hoped to use that to my advantage.

"Correct," Peyton said. "He was snatched out of our front yard on his way to work last Sunday. The men who grabbed him left a ransom note and warned me not to call the police or Winston would die. I didn't know what to do. That's when I called Chase."

"Why Chase?"

"I knew if anyone could find him, it was Chase." She shrugged. "What can I say? I was desperate enough to call the man who'd broken my heart. And now I'm afraid I may have gotten him killed."

CHAPTER 32

I played with my straw, which I still hadn't put in my tea yet. Instead, I pushed the paper wrapper into an accordion, needing something to occupy my hands and, in essence, my thoughts.

Winston had been abducted. On one hand, things were making more sense. But, on the other hand, I had a lot more questions.

I locked gazes with Peyton across the table. Her eyes were striking. But were they also calculating? "Why do you think you got Chase killed?"

"He's disappeared. I haven't heard from him in two days. I'm afraid he's done something foolish."

"Why would you think that?"

"Because there's no other reason for him not to contact me!" Her voice rose in pitch.

I leaned back, trying to keep a cool head. "Why couldn't Chase tell me any of this? Why was it a secret that he was meeting you?"

Something flashed in her gaze. "I asked him not to tell anyone. Anyone! My husband's life was on the line, and I knew there were only a few people I could trust. I didn't want to take any chances. I wouldn't give Chase any more information until he agreed."

"I see." I supposed that made sense. It was a sensitive situation, and Chase probably felt compelled to keep his promise.

She leaned across the table, licking her lips as she assessed me. "So how did you find out? Did he tell you after all? Because I was certain I could trust him."

I frowned as I remembered the crazy path that had led me to this point. It wasn't a path I was proud of, but what was done was done. "To be honest, I thought Chase was drinking again. I came here for . . . for an intervention, for lack of a better word. I got more than I bargained for."

"An intervention?" A slight smile played on Peyton's lips.

I was glad she found this amusing. My defenses started to rise. "I was worried."

Her smile slipped, and she laced and unlaced her fingers on the table. "That's good. He needs someone who has his back. But I assure you that he hasn't been drinking. I tried to tell him just one or two couldn't do any harm."

"For an alcoholic? You have no idea what you're saying."

Her face morphed into a scowl.

"What about his gambling?"

Her scowl deepened. "He didn't gamble. But he did make some wagers for me. He told me not to do it. That it was a bad idea. But I needed the money, so I wanted to take the risk."

"Why didn't you do it yourself?"

"Code of ethics. I can't place bets at the racetrack I own."

I nodded. "Makes sense."

"Anyway, back to the subject at hand. I thought everything was on track. We were collecting the ransom money and trying to track down the people responsible—"

"Which were you going to do? Give them money or try to find them?" It wasn't very usual that I didn't care if I played nice or not. But the fact that Peyton had tried to get him to drink again really irked me. Chase had been an alcoholic! What kind of person did that?

Peyton scowled and glanced around. Was she paranoid, or did she think someone was watching her?

"If we didn't first find the men who snatched Winston, then I was going to give them the money," she whispered, her voice coming out as a hiss. "You've got to understand that I was going to do whatever it took to get my husband back in one piece. I won't apologize for that."

I wasn't about to apologize either. She was playing a dangerous game, not only with her husband's life but with Chase's as well. "These people who snatched him . . . did they drive a black van? Three guys?"

Her eyes widened with surprise. "Yes. Exactly. How did you know?"

The memories came back like a slap. My body literally shuddered at the thought of what had happened. I was lucky to be alive. "Because they snatched me also."

Her eyes got even wider than before. "You got away?"

I shrugged, finally pulling the paper off my straw and jamming the plastic cylinder into my drink. "I don't think they ever really wanted me. They wanted to know how I was involved in all of this. When they found out I was the scorned girlfriend, they suddenly didn't seem to care anymore."

Peyton leaned back in the booth and seemed to process that for a moment. "That's good for you. Because these guys are no joke. I wouldn't put it past them to kill you."

"You have any idea who they are?"

"No, we were never able to pinpoint any identification. Chase told me he had a lead. That was the last time I heard from him."

My heart panged. I hoped that Chase was okay. I prayed he hadn't stumbled into some information that led to him being hurt . . . or worse.

"Did these men kill Aidan Jennings?"

"You really do your research, don't you?" Peyton grabbed my straw wrapper and was now trying to straighten it with nervous, frantic motions with her fingers. "We think so. And they tried to frame Chase for his death. When these men found out Chase was involved, they wanted to get rid of him."

"Why?"

"Because he had a great track record as a detective. And he's determined. Before he started drinking, he was the most focused person I knew. Then he injured his knee and his brother died. Everything changed after that."

Right—he'd lost his money, and therefore Peyton had lost interest in him. I was sure it was more complicated than that. Relationships always were. But that did seem to be what it boiled down to.

"I know what you're thinking," Peyton said, studying my face.

I blinked. I hoped she didn't know what I was thinking, because the thoughts weren't that flattering on her end. "Do you?"

"I used to be materialistic. I liked the life Chase and I had together. But it was more than him losing his money that caused us to break up. I didn't even know him anymore. He was obsessed with his brother's death, and, when he couldn't find answers, he started drinking. That was difficult on our marriage."

"I can imagine."

"As you can see, we've both moved on. We're both doing well, despite our history."

"As much as I appreciate you sharing that, right now I'm much more concerned with his future than I am his history. Is

226

there anything else you can tell me that might help me figure out where Chase is?"

She let out a sigh, the air ruffling her hair. "I don't know."

Okay, then I would ask some leading questions. "Did Chase think Alexander Cartwright was connected with all of this?"

"Alexander. Of course! Chase did suspect he was involved."

Peyton was getting testy, so I needed to proceed carefully. "Do you have proof your husband is still alive?"

She pulled out her phone, hit several buttons, and scrolled up for a moment before showing me a picture. "This."

I stared at the photo. He had blood drizzling from his lip, but he was alive. The date at the bottom said it was taken yesterday.

The words "Only two days" were scrawled at the bottom of the message.

I frowned. I had more answers now, yet those answers had led to more questions. I still had no good idea what to do or how to solve this problem in my life.

I leaned closer to Peyton. "Peyton, I'm sorry about your husband. I'd love to help find him. But first, I have to ask, do you have any idea where Chase is?"

"If I knew, I would tell you. Last time we talked, he was investigating Alexander down at the stables. He hasn't been in touch since then. I've been beside myself."

"Did you think about calling the police?"

"Only if I wanted both Winston and Chase to die." She halted her words and shook her head. "Sorry. I'm not trying to bite your head off. I'm just worried. Chase was my only hope, and now that he's out of the picture . . . I don't even know what to do. The kidnappers want the money in two days. I'm a few thousand dollars short, but I want to attempt it anyway."

"Where are you meeting them?"

"They're supposed to call with the information."

I nodded and stood. "Thank you for sharing."

"Holly, you can't go to the police with this either. My husband will die if you do."

"I understand."

"And Holly?"

I stayed where I was.

"Chase really does care about you. I think it's really sweet that you would go out of your way like this to help him. For what it's worth."

CHAPTER 33

As I reflected on my conversation with Peyton, there was only one thing I knew to do. Jamie agreed, and we'd piled into my car to take a little drive.

I slowed the car as I passed an old farmhouse nestled into the Kentucky hillside. Jamie and I stared at it a moment. The one-story building was old and not well tended. If a strong wind came up, the whole structure might fall down.

The grass was a little too tall all around the house, and there were no cars parked outside, at least not that were visible to my eye. The mailbox overflowed with flyers and envelopes and other items that had been stuffed inside.

A barn, far larger than the house but equally old, lurked at the back of the property.

"Where are we?" Jamie asked.

The house looked like something from a modern-day horror story. Or the kind of place where the police discovered someone had been held captive for a decade and no one noticed. But that was aside from the point.

I shrugged. "That's what I need to find out. It was important enough that Chase marked it on a map. It has to be significant somehow."

"Are you sure you want to do this?"

I dragged in a deep breath, trying to gather my courage. "I guess. I mean, I don't know. How else are we supposed to get answers?"

I didn't sound very confident, but that was only because I didn't feel very confident. This was no time to be fake. I needed all the courage I could get to go forward with this.

"The hunter becomes the hunted," Jamie said in a deep, dramatic voice.

"That does not make me feel better."

"It wasn't supposed to. This could be dangerous. You've got to keep that in the back of your mind."

I continued down the street until I found a little dirt road through the woods where we could conceal the car. There was a stretch of probably a quarter mile of woods that I'd have to trudge through in order to get to the house. But I'd rather walk through the woods than announce my arrival on the property.

The tension was thick in the air as Jamie and I sat there for a moment. We were near the last leg of this investigation. I could feel it. I only hoped everything turned out . . . well, turned out happy.

"I'm going to walk with you," Jamie announced.

"But who's going to be my backup in case something goes wrong?"

"I'll still be your backup. I won't go near the house, and I'll stay at a distance. But I just feel like I need to be closer in case something happens."

I had to admit I felt relief at her words. "Okay. That sounds good."

We set off on foot toward the house. I had no idea what I was expecting to discover. A black van, maybe? A voice changer, ransom letters, pictures of Chase with a dart through his nose?

The possibilities were endless.

I knew this could be fruitless, but I had to try something.

With the right evidence, we could turn all of this over to the police and our hands would be clean . . . for the most part, at least.

Jamie and I trudged through the woods. At times, the trees were close and the underbrush thick. Other places, the oaks and maples were spaced out and the landscape was rocky. We tried to stay hidden, to remain quiet, to do nothing that would give away our presence.

With each step, my anxiety grew. The fear of the unknown—of not knowing how all of this would play out—kept haunting me. I knew all too well that the future wasn't promised to me. My life here on this earth could end in the blink of an eye.

When I learned the doctors had gotten my diagnosis wrong and I discovered I had more than a year to live, I felt like I had a new lease on life. But the grim reality remained that all of that could change in a heartbeat. God offered us a lot of promises, but "no suffering" was not one of them.

Finally we reached the edge of the woods. The sunlight streamed through the open canopy of sky in the distance. We'd arrived at the X that had marked the spot.

Jamie and I crouched down beneath a hedge of shrubs and low-lying trees at the edge of the property. We were just here to observe. Not to take action. We'd call the police for that.

I was in no state to fight or fend off the bad guys. My ribs were still killing me. My face was tender. My energy was running on fumes.

I stared at the house, which looked worse up close than it did from the road. The clapboard siding was both moldy and falling off. Trash had collected around the edges. I couldn't imagine anyone living here.

There was no sign of movement. Even from this side view, I didn't see any cars or anything else that would indicate someone was home. Nor did I see Chase. But this place was important to him.

Jamie began creeping down the edge of the woods toward a dilapidated barn at the back of the property. As she got closer to the structure, she waved me over.

"Check it out," Jamie said.

I followed her and peered behind the building. The Creeper Van! It was barely visible, but it was there. I did a little celebratory dance in my mind. Score! We had at least one answer.

Josh had said the van was connected to a crime ring. Somehow, all of this tied together.

"Isn't that already enough evidence?" Jamie asked. "We can go now and call the police."

"Except someone's coming from the other side of the house," I whispered.

I quickly dropped to the ground, fearing we'd been spotted. The man had a hat pulled down low over his face, concealing his features, and he wore a generic sweatshirt and jeans. I couldn't get a good look at his features.

Instead of going toward the van, the man opened the doors to the barn. A sedan was inside, along with boxes of other things. I couldn't tell what; I just knew it wasn't your typical barn fare.

Just then, my phone buzzed. I glanced down at the screen and saw that Josh had texted me.

There's an arrest warrant out for Chase.

What? Someone was determined to frame Chase. Someone had sent me that e-mail. The gun had been planted by his Jeep. All their hard work had paid off, and now Chase's good name was on the line.

I remained where I was, trying my best to remain unseen. I didn't want to make any sudden motions. The man paused at the door and glanced around, almost as if his spidey senses were tingling. Did he know Jamie and I were out here? Did he sense he was being watched?

I held my breath.

Finally, he took off down the road. I released my breath, realizing just how close that had been.

"Did you recognize him?" Jamie whispered.

I shook my head. "No. Not really. I couldn't get a good enough look at him."

"Do you think it's safe to go check out the barn?" Jamie said.

"Maybe. But first . . ." I needed to text Josh.

Josh, we're at the place
Chase marked on the map.

He quickly replied.

That's a bad idea. I'm checking
out another lead for you. Will let you
know when I hear back. Should be
anytime.

"I just want to get this over with." I held up my phone. "I'm going to start by getting some pictures of that van and sending them to Josh. I consider that a little insurance in case something happens. But you stay here. You're my other insurance policy."

I stayed at the edge of the woods as I made my way toward the building. With one last glance down the lane and no sign of anyone, I bypassed the front of the barn and walked toward the Creeper Van. I paused by the double doors at the back of the vehicle. I remembered the fear I'd felt when I'd been pushed inside. I remembered wondering if I'd live or die. My entire body tensed with each memory.

Push through, Holly. Push through.

I snapped photos of the license plate. As I walked around the edge of the vehicle, I tugged on the back door. To my surprise, it opened. Inside, there were more boxes of . . . items. All kinds of things. Antique-looking figurines and jewelry boxes and electronics.

What? How did all these things tie in with the abduction of Peyton's husband? It just didn't make sense.

"What are you doing here, Holly?"

I twirled around at the deep voice, fearing the worst. I raised my fists, ready to fight, ready to defend myself.

Chase stood there with hands on his hips and a look of disapproval in his eyes.

"Chase?"

He gingerly lowered my fists and gave me a "really?" look. I shrugged and straightened like I really was tougher than he knew.

"Did you follow me?"

"You're asking me that?" His eyebrows shot up.

I started to defend myself but stopped and frowned instead. "You're okay."

"Of course I'm okay."

"No one's heard from you for two days."

"No one?" He shook his head, as if giving up even trying to figure that out. "I've been investigating something. I dropped my phone and it died."

"Oh."

He glanced behind him, his jaw rigid and his shoulders tight. "What are you doing here?"

My frown deepened. "We found your map. I wondered if you'd come here."

"So you came here to find me, bringing nothing but your . . . your fists of doom . . . to defend yourself with?"

I shrugged, my emotions swerving wildly all over the place. Relief at seeing Chase. Agitation with his assessments. Fear over the truth in his words. "I just needed to know that you were okay. Or, if there was anything I could do to help, I wanted to do it. I didn't want to leave any stone unturned."

"You're not Liam Neeson, Holly. You're not a trained professional who's equipped for these things. You're going to get yourself killed." He grabbed my arm and led me back toward the woods. "You need to go home. Now. I appreciate your concern, but you're only making this worse."

I jerked away from him, fire igniting in my eyes. "You are not the only one in danger. These men have been chasing me as well. I've got a stake in this now, like it or not."

He pressed his lips together, but his eyes softened. "You should have stayed in Cincinnati. I was trying to shield you, Holly. I should have known . . ."

My phone buzzed. I glanced down at the screen and saw that Josh had texted me back.

> If Victor Rollins tries to contact you, don't trust him. He's not really a cop again.

My blood went cold.

"I'd say you're all too late for any of this," a new voice said. Chase and I both turned toward the sound.

Victor stood there, holding a gun to Peyton's head.

CHAPTER 34

Peyton's eyes were wide with fear, her limbs trembled, and sweat beaded across her forehead.

Where had the two of them come from? How had Victor grabbed Peyton and gotten back here so quickly? It didn't make sense.

"I got the call saying I had to meet or Winston would die. Victor brought me here," Peyton said, her voice trembling. "He's going to kill us all."

I forced myself not to look toward the woods and give away Jamie's presence. She should still be there. She should be calling the police.

I prayed that she didn't get caught.

"Victor, let Peyton go," Chase pleaded, suddenly bristling with adrenaline.

"I knew it was only a matter of time before you put it together that I was behind all of this. I can't let you ruin me again." Victor stepped closer, still pulling Peyton along beside him. She whimpered as he manhandled her.

Chase subtly pushed me behind him. "Why? Why are you doing this, Victor? What are you trying to prove?"

Victor sneered. "You turned on me and ruined my life. My wife left me. I lost my job. No one would hire me. You destroyed my life, Chase Dexter."

"I had no choice but to report you for stealing those drugs,

Victor. You should have thought about that before going into the evidence locker like that."

Victor was the other officer who lost his job at the same time Chase had. Josh had mentioned him to me in our first conversation. Victor obviously blamed Chase for what happened, and now he'd gone out of his way to ensure Chase paid for turning on him.

"Need I remind you that I lost my wife? I lost my job. I didn't breeze through life either." Chase held his arm up, urging me back. "I made mistakes that I also paid for."

Victor shook his head, the gun remaining at Peyton's head but teetering with every movement. The man was so unstable that he could accidentally pull the trigger at any time.

"I can't feel sorry for you," he muttered. "You were always the golden boy. You fell, but you rose from the pit of despair and remade yourself. You got a new job. You got another pretty girlfriend. It's like everything you touch turns to gold."

"That's not true, Victor. I've had a lot of struggles. I've just tried to make the most of them."

"You sound so self-righteous. Meanwhile, men like me toil away with no fame or glory or reward. But all of that is going to change."

"Listen, why don't we talk about this like two rational human beings? Like two former colleagues? Let everyone else go. Peyton and Holly have nothing to do with what happened between the two of us. Let's not make a bad situation worse."

Victor sneered again. "I can't do that. They've seen my face. They know who I am and what I'm doing. I don't want to go to jail."

"Why are you doing this? Why turn to a life of crime?" Chase asked, changing tactics. "You've been impersonating a police officer. Abducting people. Probably murder."

"Crime pays. All that stuff in grade school that they told us? It wasn't true. I've found theft, murder, and extortion to be very profitable."

"Why did you kill Aidan Jennings?" I asked. At least my question would buy time and keep him talking. Maybe it would give Jamie a chance to call the police and give them time to arrive.

"Aidan was friends with Linwood—"

"Who's Linwood?" Chase asked.

"He was a security guard at Wyndmyer. Linwood ran his mouth to Aidan about our little side business here, and then Aidan threatened to turn us in if we didn't let him be a part of it all. We had to take care of him. We couldn't take that risk."

"So you dumped his body and planted the weapon near me?" Chase asked. "Why did you even bother to show up before I could be implicated?"

"Because those fools that I work with forgot to wipe it down for prints. I saw you outside before I could grab it, and I knew I had to take action."

"You've been trying to set Chase up for Aidan's murder," I muttered. "You sent me that e-mail that was supposedly from Chase, confessing the crime. And I'd bet the only reason you showed up at Magnolia's was to see what Jamie and I knew and to plant more suspicions in my mind about Chase. You hoped I would report him myself."

"Chase needs to take some of the blame!" Victor was a man on the edge of losing it. Anyone could see it in the way his eyes bulged, his voice rose, and his muscles trembled. "He's the reason I had to turn to this life."

Chase shook his head and jabbed a finger into his own chest. "I took the blame for what I did. I've faced my consequences. You have to take responsibility for yourself."

Victor's nostrils flared. "You need to pay for your role in all of this. But my plans kept getting thwarted, thanks to her." Victor pointed his gun at me. "I thought at least that she would lead me to you, but she didn't even do that."

But there was one thing I didn't understand. Victor obviously saw an opportunity and tried to set Chase up. But how had he known Chase was going to be here in Louisville? He'd threatened Peyton and Winston with his extortion plot. He couldn't have guessed Peyton would call Chase. Yet every detail seemed so carefully planned.

Something gnawed at the back of my mind as I tried to fit the pieces together.

"Chase, help me!" Tears glimmered in Peyton's doe-like eyes.

I still hadn't put all of this together, but the picture was becoming clearer. There was a lot of manipulation involved. Greed. Revenge.

It had all of the makings of a great story—if we survived.

Victor's grip on Peyton remained firm. All he had to do was flip the gun toward her, and he could take her out. It was too risky for her to run or for Chase to charge at them.

"Let her go," Chase urged. "Please. She's already been through enough."

Some of the crazy left Victor's face, replaced with a smirk. "Fine, I'll trade you. You come here, Chase, and I'll let Peyton go."

"Chase, don't do it!" I whispered.

He turned his head slightly toward me but never took his eyes off Victor. "I'm sorry, Holly. You know I can't have anyone get hurt. Not if I can help it."

Tears glimmered in my eyes. I wasn't sure what was going on between Chase and me. I knew I still cared for him, though, and I didn't want to see him hurt . . . or worse. But I had no doubt in my mind that he would trade his life for Peyton's. He wouldn't let someone else suffer in his place.

"Fine. We'll make this between you and me."

"I know you have a gun on you," Victor said. "Put it on the ground."

Chase frowned and pulled out his Glock. He placed it on the gravel and stepped forward. "Just let her go."

I stared at his gun. Could I grab it? Would I be fast enough? Or would Victor shoot me as I tried?

I rubbed my lips together.

Victor gave me a little "Ah ah ah" like a dad might do when a toddler veered close to a hot stove. He must have seen me eyeballing the weapon.

"Kick it toward me," he said.

Too many lives were on the line for me to act impulsively. With regret, I did as he said, watching as the weapon skimmed across the gravel.

As soon as Chase moved close enough, Victor grabbed him and held his gun to his temple. His grip on Peyton slipped, and she scrambled away.

I expected her to join me, to find safety in numbers like normal people did. Instead, she grabbed Chase's gun.

I held my breath, waiting to see how things would play out.

Would she shoot Victor? Would Chase get away?

Or would Victor react first?

A tremble rushed through me.

I sucked in a deep breath when, instead of raising the weapon to Victor, she pointed it at me. What was going on?

"You should have never gotten yourself involved in this, Holly," she muttered. "You weren't a part of the plan."

CHAPTER 35

"Peyton? You're a part of this?" Hurt dripped in Chase's voice. He'd had no idea.

I'd had no idea.

How had this slipped past everyone? Maybe everyone except Jason. He'd warned us that Peyton was a manipulator. I just had no idea she would take it this far.

"I'm sorry, Chase." Peyton kept the gun on me. Her voice lacked sincerity, despite her so-called apology. "I didn't want to do any of this. But I didn't have much choice."

"You always have a choice, Peyton." Chase shook his head, the hurt in his eyes proving that this betrayal had cut deep. "That whole thing about Winston—you made it up, didn't you?"

"No, I didn't. He is in trouble. Financial trouble." She grabbed my arm and kept the gun on me.

"Why?" Chase asked. The hurt in his eyes had turned to anger—pure anger. "Why would you do this, Peyton? Why get me involved in your problems?"

She straightened, suddenly as cool as a cucumber. The sweat across her forehead, her cowering stance, the fear in her voice—it had all been an act. She was exactly the kind of person I despised.

"Thanks to Linwood, Victor found some information on Winston and how he'd messed with the starting gate," Peyton said. "Victor threatened to go public with what he knew. "

That must be whom Jason overheard Winston talking to that day.

"Victor tried to blackmail us, which was a problem since we're on the verge of bankruptcy," Peyton explained. "Victor made a deal with me. If I helped to frame Chase, he'd stay quiet."

"So you used me."

"You've got to understand, Chase—Winston would have gone to jail, and we would have lost everything we'd worked so hard for."

"Again, you think you're the most important person in the world," Chase said, bitterness creeping into his words. "I should have known better than to think you'd changed, Peyton. I couldn't have been more wrong."

"I didn't know everything that Victor had planned. I thought it was just blackmail. I had no idea about the rest."

Chase stared at her, shooting daggers with his eyes. Whoever had coined that expression had been spot on. But I had more important things to think about at the moment. Like buying time. And what better way to buy time than to try and connect some of these puzzle pieces?

"Where's your husband now, Peyton?" I asked. "He's not visiting a sick mom in Georgia."

She snorted. "No, of course not. He's hiding out in the Caribbean until all of this blows over. We just needed an excuse so people wouldn't ask questions."

"How could you, Peyton? I never thought you would stoop this low," Chase said. "I might have expected something like this from Victor."

"Enough talking. Both of you. Inside. Now." Victor pointed toward the house.

Begrudgingly, I drug my feet toward the house. Both Peyton

and Victor had guns, so I didn't see any heroic moments coming when we could slap their weapons away. It was too dangerous.

They pushed us inside, through the dilapidated house, and down the stairs into the basement. I nearly took a tumble, but I grabbed the railing just in time and stopped myself from cracking any more ribs.

Just as I righted myself and Chase's hands circled my waist to steady me even more, I heard a click behind me.

They'd locked us down in this dungeon-like pit.

***

I glanced around the room and shivered. It was dark down here. Really dark. It smelled dank, and I imagined creepy crawlies every time I closed my eyes. Footsteps faded upstairs.

They'd left us here, I realized.

Thoughts of starving to death threatened to overtake me.

No, I had to keep a cool head. There was one window, but it was up high and it was narrow. I didn't even think I could fit through it. But maybe there was another way out.

Chase climbed the steps and rattled the door, to no avail. He stomped back down and stood in front of me, his hands on his hips and a look of intense concentration on his face. Even in the darkness, I could see it, thanks to the one small window.

"I can boost you up to the window," Chase said.

"It's worth a try."

We walked to the wall, and my throat went dry as I spotted the cobwebs there. I could do this. I had to put aside my inside-girl persona for the moment.

Chase boosted me up, and I reached the sill. Balancing precariously in his hands, I tried to nudge the window open. "It's no use. It's stuck."

244

"I figured as much," Chase said.

He moved his hands, and I dropped down into his arm with a little gasp. The start of a smile tugged at his lips, but it quickly disappeared. He set me on my feet and began pacing again.

"Jamie is in the woods. She'll call the police."

He nodded. "That would be nice."

"I also texted Josh earlier. He can probably track us down."

His eyebrows quirked up. "You know Josh?"

I shrugged. "I do now."

"What else do you know?"

"I've discovered quite a bit. But the important thing right now is that there's an arrest warrant out for you."

He let out a long breath and ran a hand over his face. "I didn't know Victor hated me this much."

"Why does he hate you so much?"

"I was the one who caught him stealing those drugs, as you probably heard earlier. He begged me not to turn him in, but I did it anyway. He lost his job. I lost my job maybe a month later because I was searching for Hayden's killer off books."

"Did you know his hatred of you ran this deep?"

"No. Maybe I should have. I mean, he trash-talked me every chance he had. But I thought by now he would have gotten over it. Apparently, it's been building up all these years."

"It sounds like he blames you for everything."

"I wanted him to get help, Holly. I really did. I told him he should turn himself in, and maybe they would be lenient with him."

"People have to face up to the consequences of their decisions," I told him.

Chase paused in front of me, studying my face until I flushed. I wanted to look away, but I didn't let myself. I had to face up to the consequences of my decisions, as well.

"What were you thinking coming here to Louisville, Holly?"

I pointed to myself. "Me? It sounds like you weren't doing much thinking either when you came here."

He shook his head and continued pacing. "Peyton was in trouble."

"And you couldn't stop yourself from helping a damsel in distress?" I wanted to smack myself as soon as the words left my lips. I hated being reactionary, but that's exactly what I was being.

"Holly, you've got this all wrong. This was never about wanting to get back together with Peyton."

"Then why couldn't you tell me?"

"Because I promised Peyton I wouldn't. I've already failed Peyton miserably in the past, Holly. I've told you before that I was a terrible husband. I want to make things right. I want to make it up to her that I wasn't there, that I didn't fight harder for our marriage. I couldn't say no."

"I see." I'd surmised that much, that Peyton might have played on Chase's guilt.

"My question is: Why would you ever think that I'd gotten back with her? I thought you knew me better than that."

I frowned. "I didn't want to believe it. Then I saw the two of you hugging at the horse track. It looked . . . intimate. It sealed the deal for me."

He shook his head. "Peyton had to whisper something to me. She thought the men who supposedly abducted Winston were there at the races watching her. The hug wasn't what it looked like. It was just a private conversation."

I felt foolish. If I'd only stuck to my optimistic side, none of this would have happened. But it was too late to undo the past.

"How does what happened at the stables fit in with all of this?" At least if I died, I'd die with some answers.

"I was hoping to find something to get Alexander on. I felt certain he was behind the abduction of Winston. That's what Peyton had led me to believe, but obviously none of it was real. She knew if she mentioned Alexander, I wouldn't be able to say no. I don't know how I could have been so stupid."

"Peyton is the villain in this situation, Chase. She's . . . well, selfish, to put it nicely."

He ran a hand over his face. "I don't want to think about her right now. I've wasted too much of my life with her shenanigans. About the stables. I originally went to look for Winston. I thought if Alexander abducted him, that maybe I'd find some evidence there. I didn't find him, but I did find some vials that proved someone had been doping his horses. I went back to try and take pictures and get some evidence. I figured if we could frame Alexander for doping his horses, maybe he'd fess up about Winston and Hayden. That's when I saw you."

"That man who got beaten up, who was he?"

"One of the vets. He was giving anabolic steroids to the horses for a hefty paycheck. He claims Alexander doesn't know, but that his horse trainer was behind it."

"Is the vet okay?"

Chase nodded. "I tracked him down. He's fine, but he'll be losing his license."

"I'm glad he's okay, at least."

Chase let out a long breath. "You shouldn't have come, Holly. I'm not sure I can protect you from all of this."

"I never asked you to protect me."

"I love you. How could I not want to keep you safe?"

"You . . . you love me? Still?" My voice held so much vulnerability that my cheeks warmed. But I'd been certain that I messed everything up, beyond the point of repair.

His face softened. "Of course I do. Do you know how hard

this was to keep from you? Do you know how hard it was when I saw the hurt look in your eyes when I told you I was going somewhere?"

I sighed. "I can imagine."

He sat down on the steps. His entire frame looked burdened, like he had chains dragging him down, preventing him from moving. He shook his head. "I can't believe Peyton was involved in this."

I sat down beside him. "She's beautiful. I can see why you fell for her."

He turned toward me and gently brushed the backs of his fingers against my cheek. "Beauty has to be more than skin-deep, though. That's why I fell for you so quickly. You've got both."

"Oh, Chase." My head fell against his shoulder, regret pressing on me. "I'm so sorry. I really messed things up."

His arm, heavy and strong, stretched across my back as he pulled me closer. "No, I'm sorry. I should have handled things differently. I was trying to protect everyone, and I ended up protecting no one."

"You couldn't have known."

"I just want to take the wrongs in my life and make them right."

"It's an admirable quality."

We sat silently for a moment.

"I'm kind of surprised that Jamie isn't here yet," he finally said.

At his words, fear rippled through me. What if something had happened to her? What if Victor had found Jamie and done something horrible?

Please, Lord, no . . .

"I just can't figure out what they're planning from here."

Chase stared at the floor and shook his head. "This isn't the end of it."

Another chill rushed up my spine. "They could leave us here to die."

"That wouldn't be poetic enough. This whole time, Victor's wanted to ruin my reputation. I have a feeling that's still his endgame."

I knew what that meant: the worst was yet to come.

CHAPTER 36

An hour later, I realized that Jamie wasn't coming. Apparently, the police weren't either. Both of those facts left me unsettled.

Chase had been pacing. He checked the door again and even tried to boost me up to the window a second time. I managed to reach the sill, but the window itself was nailed shut, and I couldn't make it budge for the life of me.

Frustration, agitation, and anxiety all felt material in the room, like we could actually touch them.

Finally, I heard something outside. A car door slammed. Someone was here.

Could it be Jamie? The police?

My heart raced.

I glanced at Chase. He'd heard it also.

A moment later, footsteps stomped across the floor above us. More than one set. Then the door opened.

I blinked against the light.

And, in that instant, my heart sank. It wasn't Jamie or the police.

It was Victor.

"I hope you're both enjoying your stay here," he muttered as he lumbered down the stairs with a gun in his hand.

His gaze was set on Chase, and a hunger filled his eyes. Hunger for vengeance, I realized.

Had he come alone? What about that other set of footsteps I'd heard?

As soon as the thought entered my mind, another shadow crossed over the doorway at the top of the stairs.

It was Peyton. And she had Jamie with her, a gun to her head.

I gasped. No. Not Jamie . . .

"We found your friend snooping in the woods," Victor said. "We caught her right before she was able to call the police. Lucky us."

"Please don't hurt her. She has nothing to do with this." My voice trembled.

"She didn't—until she inserted herself." Victor stopped in front of us, a smug look in his eyes.

He thought he was going to get away with all of this, I realized. He thought he was smarter than Chase and me, and that he held too much leverage over us. His arrogance only flamed my fire more. I had to figure out a way to beat him at this game he was playing.

"People have to learn there are consequences for their actions," Victor continued. "I certainly had to learn that."

"What do you want from us, Victor?" Chase had ensured that he was between Victor and me. He had a habit of doing that, and I loved him for it.

Victor smirked. "I'm glad you asked. Because I do have something you can do. If you complete your mission, I'll let you all go. If you don't, your friend will die. Any questions?"

Chase scowled. "Yeah, I have a lot of questions, starting with: What exactly is this mission?"

Victor smirked again. "It's fairly simple. You just have to break into Alexander Cartwright's house, steal a few prized possessions, and get out without being caught. Sounds easy enough, doesn't it?"

My stomach plunged. Certainly I hadn't heard the man right. But one look at his cold, cocky expression, and I knew I had.

Break into Alexander Cartwright's home? Steal? This was getting worse and worse.

"Just how are we supposed to do that?" Chase asked.

"Oh, I have a plan all figured out for you. All you have to do is follow my instructions."

Chase shook his head. "You're trying to get us killed, aren't you?"

Victor's smile was all the answer we needed.

I had no idea how we were going to get out of this. Because I faced the death of my friend on one side and being charged with a home invasion on the other.

***

Two hours later, nighttime had fallen. Peyton had given both Chase and me dark clothes to wear, and Victor had spent the last ninety minutes running through the plan to get inside Alexander's place. This plan included bypassing a security guard, eluding an alarm system, and studying the blueprint of the man's home so we could determine exactly where his horseshoe collection was located.

No one had to say anything for me to realize there was no way out of this. If Chase and I managed to go through this without being shot and killed, Victor and Peyton would take the money and escape before they were caught. Meanwhile, Chase and I would be charged with the crime. Who knew where that would leave Jamie?

And none of this would have ever happened if I hadn't

checked that Friend Finder app on my phone. If I had minded my own business. If I had stayed out of things.

Meanwhile, Chase had been seen making threats toward Alexander. He'd been on his property. A dead body had been located near the apartment where he was staying.

I had to hand it to Victor and Peyton: they'd meticulously planned this down to the last detail. It would look exactly like Chase was behind this and doing it for revenge.

"Let's roll." Victor stood and put his gun in his waistband. "We need to get on the road. Time's a-wasting."

I felt sick as I climbed into the van. Peyton drove. Victor sat in the back with Chase and me, but Jamie was beside him. His gun pressed into her rib cage. With every bump of the road, my anxiety built. It was like there was a ticking time bomb in the background.

I'm sorry, Jamie mouthed.

My heart broke. She should have never been involved in this. All of this was my fault. Again. If I'd just minded my own business . . .

Chase sat beside me, crouched like a tiger waiting to strike. His eyes stayed on Victor's gun, and I could tell he wanted to lunge but he knew better. I leaned against the carpeted wall, trying not to let the familiar yet putrid smell of the van's interior make me sick.

I wasn't a criminal. I liked to help people overcome their problems, and somehow I'd found myself helping Victor overcome how to get caught doing a crime instead.

"Where are your cronies?" I asked.

"They're preparing things for our departure. As soon as we have these horseshoes, we're out of here. There's no market for them here. We're going to the foreign market."

The Creeper Van pulled up at the edge of Alexander's

property. I stole a glance at Chase. He looked just as preoccupied as I did as his gaze remained focused on Victor's gun. I was certain he was trying to formulate a plan right now. When we had a moment alone, maybe he'd share it with me.

Please, God, let it be a good one.

"Here you go," Victor said, raising his gun and reminding us of all that was at stake. "Have fun. And remember—mess up and your friend dies."

"There's got to be another way," I pleaded. There was so much room for error. The pressure started to get to me.

"There's no other way. You've got an hour. You know what items to look for. Now, you better get a move on."

I crouched in the van and waited as Chase slid the door open. As soon as we hopped out, the van sped away.

Chase took my hand and led me toward the metal fence. Crickets chirped around us. Somewhere in the distance a dog barked. Normally, those sounds would be soothing, but right now my soul felt numb.

"Holly . . ."

I looked up at Chase. Just as I did so, he pulled me to a stop and pressed his lips into mine.

"I don't know how this is going to turn out," he whispered as he stepped back.

"Let's find out," I said, my voice lackluster.

I pulled my black mask over my face, and Chase did the same. I wished I'd wake up and find this was all a dream. But I knew that wasn't the case.

We scaled the fence surrounding the property. My feet landed hard on the grass on the other side, the impact reminding me of my earlier injuries.

With no time to dwell on that now, we darted toward the house. Victor had instructed us to hide behind the shrubs at the front of the house. Victor would call the security guard inside, posing as the police, and tell the guard that someone suspicious had been seen lurking outside the home.

When the guard came outside, Chase and I would slip inside. We'd grab the horseshoes and then get out.

Hopefully, without being caught.

We waited until we heard the front door open. Chase kept watch. As soon as the man stepped out of the house and paced toward the front of the property, we slipped inside.

"We've got to go to the master bedroom." Chase grabbed my hand and pulled me through the house. He'd studied the blueprints and must have been able to focus more than I had. He knew exactly where the horseshoe collection was.

We slipped into a dark room and closed the door. Chase wasted no time hurrying to the window and peering out.

"He's still by the street," Chase whispered. He rushed toward the dresser.

"What are you doing?"

"Grabbing this." He reached between the mattresses and pulled out . . . a gun?

"How'd you know it was there?" I felt a bit speechless, as if Chase knew something I didn't.

"A man like Alexander Cartwright? He wants to keep a weapon close in case there's ever a home invasion. He has no kids, so between his mattresses is the most logical place. Rich, powerful people are always a target. Always."

"Smart thinking."

"Victor thinks he's smarter than he is." He tucked the gun into his waistband. "It's in case we need it when we see Victor again."

I nodded and swallowed hard. "Now, where are those horseshoes?"

Chase peered out the window again. "But the guard is headed back this way."

"What are we going to do?"

"Proceed quietly."

The front door opened and footsteps sounded inside. I couldn't take the pressure of doing this much longer. Scenarios continued to play out in my head—scenarios where we got shot by the guard, where Chase and I ended up spending our lives in jail, or where Jamie died because of my actions.

"Look at this, Chase." I stepped toward a bookcase. On display there were all kinds of horseshoes. Some were made into paperweights and others into tchotchke horses and cowboys and other animals. These were at least part of the collection.

"Those should work. At least for long enough that we can get Jamie and go. However, I think the more expensive ones are in his office." Chase turned me toward him. "Holly, whatever we do, it's going to require risk."

I forced myself to nod. "Okay. Let's do it."

He stared at me another moment before nodding. "Okay."

He grabbed the bag and began slipping the horseshoes inside.

I found a piece of paper in the nightstand and a pen, and I began scribbling a note.

"What are you doing?" Chase whispered.

"I'm writing an apology and promising we'll return these as soon as we can." I looked up, already knowing what his expression would be. Stupefied. I was right. "Look, it makes me feel better. I'm not a thief."

A slow smile spread across his face. "You always surprise me, Holly."

I finished writing the note and decided not to sign my name.

Instead, I put the paper on the bookcase where the horseshoes had stood. Since I was wearing gloves, there shouldn't be identifying markers that we'd been here. I preferred that things played out on this in my time, but I probably wouldn't be that lucky.

Chase grasped the bag. "I've got the horseshoes. Now we have to figure out how to get out of here."

I glanced at the clock on the nightstand. "Our hour is almost up."

"We're going to have to climb out of the window and make a run for it."

Please, Lord, help our plan work!

It would only be by God's grace and mercy that all of this worked out. I certainly couldn't do it on my own.

I walked toward the door and peered out. The guard walked down the hallway, chatting on his phone with someone. He stepped inside a doorway across the hall.

Into the bathroom.

Now was our time to go.

"Now," I muttered.

"As soon as I open this window, the alarm is going to go off. We're going to have to move fast. Understand?"

I nodded, wishing I was more athletic and that I'd trained more for endurance. Really, all the experience I had lately was in running for my life.

"Here goes," Chase muttered.

He shoved the window up, and immediately, a siren began wailing overhead. Chase knocked the screen out and grabbed my hand, and we climbed from the window.

We ran as fast as possible toward the front. If we could just get over the fence, I'd feel better.

Shouting sounded behind us. I didn't dare look back, but I

could easily imagine the guard standing there. Would he have a gun? Would he use it?

As if to answer my question, a blast cut through the air.

The guard was firing.

CHAPTER 37

Just as I cleared the fence, a bullet struck the post beside me. The sound was loud and clinking. The smell of hot metal filled the air.

That was close. Too close.

Chase heaved himself over the iron fence, and we dashed away. The van squealed to the side of the road, the back door opened, and we hopped inside. Peyton zoomed away before the door was even closed.

My chest heaved with exertion. Sweat had scattered across my forehead. My heartbeat pounded out of control.

I glanced at Jamie. She sat against the wall of the van, Victor's gun still pressed into her side. She looked stoic—and my friend never looked stoic. If Peyton hit a bump, it could all be over for Jamie.

"Did you get the goods?" Victor asked. His eyes were wide with hunger and lust. I was surprised he didn't have drool coming out of his mouth.

Chase nodded. "We did. Now you can let Jamie go. Holly too. This was never about them."

"It's not quite that easy." Victor reached his free hand out. "Now, let me see."

"Put the gun down." Chase's voice sounded hard and unyielding.

"You're not the one calling the shots here," Victor said

through clenched teeth. His grip on Jamie must have tightened, because she let out a small gasp. "Need I remind you? Now, you have until the count of three or I pull the trigger. She's no loss to me."

Anger surged inside me. How dare he talk about my friend like that? My fingers dug into the gritty carpet beneath me.

He was going to kill us all, wasn't he? Or, at least Jamie and me. Then he'd let Chase take the blame for everything. He'd probably arranged everything to make Chase look guilty. The e-mail. The stolen Jeep. The erratic behavior. He even had motive: everyone would think Chase wanted revenge for his brother's death.

I couldn't let that happen.

"One . . ." Victor started.

"Just give him the horseshoes," Peyton yelled from the front seat. "Don't make this more complicated than it has to be, Chase."

"I'd venture to say you were the one making things complicated here, Peyton," Chase said. "You manipulated me for your own gain. I don't know how you live with yourself."

"It's easier when I have money. Lots of money."

"Two . . ." Victor continued.

"Okay. I'll give you proof." Chase's gaze softened, probably in an effort to defuse the situation.

I held my breath.

Instead of a horseshoe, his gun appeared.

This was my opening. If I was going to do something, it was now.

I lunged toward Peyton, throwing her off guard.

The van swerved toward the ditch alongside the road as she fought against me.

"What are you doing?" she screeched.

"Trying to let justice prevail," I muttered, still fighting for control of the vehicle.

Behind me, Victor and Chase struggled. Their bodies flew from one side of the van to the other. Jamie had backed into a corner, trying to stay out of the way.

I had to concentrate on Peyton right now, though. As she elbowed me, I stumbled into the back of the van again. My gaze swept the floor and I saw . . . Victor's gun. He must have dropped it during his struggle.

As I grabbed the gun, what felt like an earthquake rattled the sides of the van as Chase and Victor went at each other.

"Stop the van," I ordered Peyton, raising the gun to her head.

She kept going. I really—really—didn't want to have to use this gun. Instead of making another empty threat, I drew my fist back and punched Peyton in the nose.

When she gasped, I jumped into the front seat and shoved her out of the way. Sliding into the driver's seat, I grabbed the steering wheel and threw on brakes right before we careened into a ditch.

It wasn't pretty, but I'd done it. As the van screeched to a halt, I raised the gun to Peyton before she could scramble away. "I wouldn't do that," I muttered.

I glanced back. Chase had Victor's gun now, and he aimed it at Victor.

"You weren't ever going to get away with this," Chase said.

"My plan was perfect," Victor growled as his wiped blood from his mouth.

"You never counted on Holly Anna Paladin sweeping onto the scene," Chase said.

"Girlfriend, you were tough," Jamie muttered from the other side of the van. "Remind me not to make you mad."

Just then, sirens sounded around us.

Police cars.

Lots of police cars. They surrounded us from every direction.

"Come out. Your hands in the air!" an officer shouted.

Peyton climbed out first. "I don't know what happened, Officer. These people jumped into our van and demanded that we do what they said. I was so scared. I'm so glad you found us."

My stomach turned with disgust. How could this woman live with herself?

"You've been obsessed with your brother's death," Victor mumbled. "You have no idea the things he was involved with."

Chase's eyes lit. "What do you know?"

"I know he had it coming for him. He tangled with the wrong man. If Hugo hadn't killed him, someone else would have."

"Who's Hugo?"

A spark ignited in Victor's eyes. "Wouldn't you like to know?"

Before he could say anything else, he grabbed Chase's gun and pulled the trigger. I screamed and turned away as blood splattered throughout the van.

He was dead.

***

It wasn't until the next morning that Chase, Jamie, and I were finally cleared of any crimes that were committed. Josh had gotten my texts and had gone to one of his friends in the police department with what he knew. He'd arrived at Victor's just as we were leaving and had called the police before following the van to Alexander's.

Peyton hadn't owned up to her part in anything, but the police had enough evidence to put her away. The rest of Victor's gang had also been rounded up before they left the country, and they'd been arrested.

Winston Kensington had been found in the Caribbean, and a team was on their way there now to pick him up. He was being brought back here, and he faced a number of charges. It also appeared that Wyndmyer Park would be closing. It was too soon to tell, but that was the talk around the police station. There were too many financial troubles and too many scandals for it to stay open.

Alexander Cartwright had been informed about my apology letter, and he wasn't pressing charges, especially when he heard the details about what had happened. In fact, my letter was apparently the talk of the police precinct. All the officers had a good chuckle over it.

Jamie seemed to have gotten over her trauma. Now she was basking in the limelight and giving an interview. The more she talked, the more animated her voice became. Magnolia, of course, had gotten first dibs on all the details.

Josh had even shown up and checked on all of us, and we'd agreed to go for dinner together sometime. Jamie wanted to come too, and she couldn't stop fanning her face behind Josh's back.

My mom had also called. I couldn't wait until I got home to ask her about the doctor's bill. She'd admitted that she'd had a precancerous skin spot removed, but that it was no big deal. My shoulders drooped with relief. It was one less worry I had to deal with. For the moment, my family was safe and healthy, and I was thankful for that.

Finally, it was time for me to go home. Chase's Jeep hadn't

been recovered yet, so he was driving Mom's Lexus. Jamie had somehow convinced Magnolia to give her a ride home. I had a sneaking suspicion it had something to do with the article Magnolia was writing. Maybe Jamie had agreed to give more quotes. Mostly, Jamie had probably realized that Chase and I needed to talk.

And now that everything else had settled down, Chase and I did need to talk. We'd only been on the road for thirty minutes when we pulled over—in what else but a parking lot?—and we sat in silence for a moment.

My gut churned. Where would this conversation go?

"I'm sorry about what Victor said, Chase," I started. "I know it was hard hearing that about your brother. Hard to know that Victor had the answers and wouldn't give them to you before he killed himself."

Something clouded his gaze. "It's not the way I wanted to get more information, that's for sure."

"Who's Hugo?"

He shook his head. "I have no idea."

I swallowed hard. "Are you going to keep investigating?"

He stared off into the distance, and I gave him time to gather his thoughts. "I'm afraid investigating it will consume my life."

"I know it's hard not having the answers." I squeezed his hand. "But you'll figure out the right choice. I know you will."

He squeezed my hand back, and we sat in silence for a few more minutes.

"You were brave back there, Holly," Chase started, snapping out of his lethargy and turning toward me.

I remembered all my actions and frowned. I didn't feel brave. I only knew I had to fight for my life. "More like desperate."

"You kept your head in all of it. That's more than I can say for most people."

I nibbled on my lip for a moment. There were so many other things we needed to say. I started by blurting, "Chase, I'm sorry for the trouble I caused."

His fingers caressed mine. "Holly, you proved one thing."

His steady caresses calmed my racing heart. "What's that?" And did I really want to know?

"You'll do everything in your power to help someone you love."

More of the tension left my shoulders. "I will. I believe in fighting for people. I'd want someone to fight for me."

"That stubborn determination will, no doubt, drive me insane and feel like an extreme invasion of privacy at times—"

The tension returned.

His lips curled in a smile. "But it's good to have someone looking out for me."

I released my breath. "I'll always have your back, even when you don't want me to."

He chuckled, the sound deep and soothing. But it faded. "I guess all of this has brought to light one other fact, Holly. We have some trust issues."

I licked my lips, wanting to deny it, but knowing I couldn't.

"I wouldn't call it trust issues," I told him. "I believed the best—at least, I tried to—for a long time. Then I jumped to conclusions. I couldn't have imagined what was going on. Who could? Even after what happened to us back when my sister got married, I never thought we'd have another situation that tested our faith in each other so much."

He glanced at his lap, and when he lifted his head, I saw the agony in his eyes. I reached for him, my hand cradling his jaw, his cheek. I wanted to wipe away his pain, but I knew that wasn't in my power.

"I'm afraid there will always be demons lurking inside me, Holly. There's a part of me that gets eaten alive whenever I think about my brother and his death. There's a part of me that wants another drink sometimes. That craves the attention I received as a football player."

"We've all got parts of us that are less than pleasant. As long as we don't feed those desires—"

His hand covered mine as he shook his head. "They don't always go away, Holly. No matter how much I pray. No matter how I try to turn it around and into something good. Sometimes the shadows feel like they're a part of me."

I could sense his inner struggle. I liked providing answers, but this was a complex situation. What I wouldn't do to have a magic wand.

"Every day we make choices, Chase," I told him gently. "And every day you have to make the choice to stay on the straight and narrow versus giving in to addictions and vengeance and anger. It's what we all do to an extent."

He smiled at me, almost sadly, before pulling my hand to his lips and kissing it. "I love that optimistic side of you."

"What are you trying to say, Chase?"

He wiped the hair out of my eyes, his gaze still torn, tortured. "You being with me scares me sometimes."

"I didn't think you got scared of anything." I tried to add humor, but it fell flat.

He lowered his head again. "Yeah, I do. I get scared of hurting the people I love."

"I get that."

He took my hand in both of his, and when he looked up, his gaze was earnest, pleading. "I don't want to lose you, Holly. You make me a better person. But I'm not sure you can say the same."

"Chase." I gently turned his chin until he faced me. I wasn't used to seeing his insecurities. "You make me feel safe and protected and like I can face giants. I'd say that makes me a better person."

He lowered his forehead until it touched mine. "You're one of a kind, Holly."

"You keep talking sweet, and you might get a thank-you note. It's the polite thing to do, after all."

"I'll take this as a thank-you note." His lips touched mine.

And for a moment, and just a moment, all our problems disappeared.

###

RANDOM ACTS OF MALICE

Coming soon: *Random Acts of Scrooge*, a Christmas novella!

If you enjoyed this book, you may also enjoy these other Holly Anna Paladin Mysteries:

Random Acts of Murder (Book 1)
When Holly Anna Paladin is given a year to live, she embraces her final days doing what she loves most—random acts of kindness. But one of her extreme good deeds goes horribly wrong, implicating her in a string of murders. Holly is suddenly thrust into a different kind of fight for her life. Could it also be random that the detective assigned to the case is her old high school crush and present-day nemesis? Will Holly find the killer before he ruins what is left of her life? Or will she spend her final days alone and behind bars?

Random Acts of Deceit (Book 2)
"Break up with Chase Dexter, or I'll kill him." Holly Anna Paladin never expected such a gut-wrenching ultimatum. With home invasions, hidden cameras, and bomb threats, Holly must make some serious choices. Whatever she decides, the consequences will either break her heart or break her soul. She tries to match wits with the Shadow Man, but the more she fights, the deeper she's drawn into the perilous situation. With her sister's wedding problems and the riots in the city, Holly has nearly reached breaking point. She must stop this mystery man before someone she loves dies. But the deceit is threatening to pull her under . . . six feet under.

Squeaky Clean Mysteries:

Hazardous Duty (Book 1)

On her way to completing a degree in forensic science, Gabby St. Claire drops out of school and starts her own crime-scene cleaning business. When a routine cleaning job uncovers a murder weapon the police overlooked, she realizes that the wrong person is in jail. But the owner of the weapon is a powerful foe . . . and willing to do anything to keep Gabby quiet. With the help of her new neighbor, Riley Thomas, a man whose life and faith fascinate her, Gabby seeks to find the killer before another murder occurs.

Suspicious Minds (Book 2)

In this smart and suspenseful sequel to *Hazardous Duty*, crime-scene cleaner Gabby St. Claire finds herself stuck doing mold remediation to pay the bills. Her first day on the job, she uncovers a surprise in the crawlspace of a dilapidated home: Elvis, dead as a doornail and still wearing his blue-suede shoes. How could she possibly keep her nose out of a case like this?

It Came Upon a Midnight Crime (Book 2.5, a Novella)

Someone is intent on destroying the true meaning of Christmas—at least, destroying anything that hints of it. All around crime-scene cleaner Gabby St. Claire's hometown, anything pointing to Jesus as "the reason for the season" is being sabotaged. The crimes become more twisted as dismembered body parts are found at the vandalisms. Someone is determined to destroy Christmas . . . but Gabby is just as determined to find the Grinch and let peace on earth and goodwill prevail.

Organized Grime (Book 3)

Gabby St. Claire knows her best friend, Sierra, isn't guilty of killing three people in what appears to be an eco-terrorist attack. But Sierra has disappeared, her only contact a frantic phone call to Gabby proclaiming she's being hunted. Gabby is determined to prove her friend is innocent and to keep Sierra alive. While trying to track down the real perpetrator, Gabby notices a disturbing trend at the crime scenes she's cleaning, one that ties random crimes together—and points to Sierra as the guilty party. Just what has her friend gotten herself involved in?

Dirty Deeds (Book 4)
"Promise me one thing. No snooping. Just for one week." Gabby St. Claire knows that her fiancé's request is a simple one she should be able to honor. After all, Riley's law school reunion and attorneys' conference at a posh resort is a chance for them to get away from the mysteries Gabby often finds herself involved in as a crime-scene cleaner. Then an old friend of Riley's goes missing. Gabby suspects one of Riley's buddies might be behind the disappearance. When the missing woman's mom asks Gabby for help, how can she say no?

The Scum of All Fears (Book 5)
Gabby St. Claire is back to crime-scene cleaning and needs help after a weekend killing spree fills her work docket. A serial killer her fiancé put behind bars has escaped. His last words to Riley were: *I'll get out, and I'll get even.* Pictures of Gabby are found in the man's prison cell, messages are left for Gabby at crime scenes, someone keeps slipping in and out of her apartment, and her temporary assistant disappears. The search for answers becomes darker when Gabby realizes she's dealing with a criminal who is truly the scum of the earth. He will do anything to make Gabby and Riley's lives a living nightmare.

To Love, Honor, and Perish (Book 6)
Just when Gabby St. Claire's life is on the right track, the unthinkable happens. Her fiancé, Riley Thomas, is shot and in life-threatening condition only a week before their wedding. Gabby is determined to figure out who pulled the trigger, even if investigating puts her own life at risk. As she digs deeper into

the case, she discovers secrets better left alone. Doubts arise in her mind, and the one man with answers lies on death's doorstep. Then an old foe returns and tests everything Gabby is made of—physically, mentally, and spiritually. Will all she's worked for be destroyed?

Mucky Streak (Book 7)
Gabby St. Claire feels her life is smeared with the stain of tragedy. She takes a short-term gig as a private investigator—a cold case that's eluded detectives for ten years. The mass murder of a wealthy family seems impossible to solve, but Gabby brings more clues to light. Add to the mix a flirtatious client, travels to an exciting new city, and some quirky—albeit temporary—new sidekicks, and things get complicated. With every new development, Gabby prays that her "mucky streak" will end and the future will become clear. Yet every answer she uncovers leads her closer to danger—both for her life and for her heart.

Foul Play (Book 8)
Gabby St. Claire is crying "foul play" in every sense of the phrase. When the crime-scene cleaner agrees to go undercover at a local community theater, she discovers more than backstage bickering, atrocious acting, and rotten writing. The female lead is dead, and an old classmate who's staked everything on the musical production's success is about to go under. In her dual role of investigator and star of the show, Gabby finds the stakes rising faster than the opening-night curtain. She must face her past and make monumental decisions, not just about the play but also concerning her future relationships and career. Will Gabby find the killer before the curtain goes down—not only on the play, but also on life as she knows it?

Broom and Gloom (Book 9)
Gabby St. Claire is determined to get back in the saddle again. While in Oklahoma for a forensic conference, she meets her

soon-to-be stepbrother, Trace Ryan, an up-and-coming country singer. A woman he was dating has disappeared, and he suspects a crazy fan may be behind it. Gabby agrees to investigate, as she tries to juggle her conference, navigate being alone in a new place, and locate a woman who may not want to be found. She discovers that sometimes taking life by the horns means staring danger in the face, no matter the consequences.

Dust and Obey (Book 10)
When Gabby St. Claire's ex-fiancé, Riley Thomas, asks for her help in investigating a possible murder at a couples retreat, she knows she should say no. She knows she should run far, far away from the danger of both being around Riley and the crime. But her nosy instincts and determination take precedence over her logic. Gabby and Riley must work together to find the killer. In the process, they have to confront demons from their past and deal with their present relationship.

While You Were Sweeping, a Riley Thomas Novella
Riley Thomas is trying to come to terms with life after a traumatic brain injury turned his world upside down. Away from everything familiar—including his crime-scene-cleaning former fiancée and his career as a social-rights attorney—he's determined to prove himself and regain his old life. But when he claims he witnessed his neighbor shoot and kill someone, everyone thinks he's crazy. When all evidence of the crime disappears, even Riley has to wonder if he's losing his mind.

Note: *While You Were Sweeping* is a spin-off mystery written in conjunction with the Squeaky Clean series featuring crime-scene cleaner Gabby St. Claire.

The Sierra Files

Pounced (Book 1)
Animal-rights activist Sierra Nakamura never expected to stumble upon the dead body of a coworker while filming a project nor get involved in the investigation. But when someone threatens to kill her cats unless she hands over the "information," she becomes more bristly than an angry feline. Making matters worse is the fact that her cats—and the investigation—are driving a wedge between her and her boyfriend, Chad. With every answer she uncovers, old hurts rise to the surface and test her beliefs. Saving her cats might mean ruining everything else in her life. In the fight for survival, one thing is certain: Either pounce or be pounced.

Hunted (Book 2)
Who knew a stray dog could cause so much trouble? Newlywed animal-rights activist Sierra Nakamura Davis must face her worst nightmare: breaking the news she eloped to her ultra-opinionated tiger mom. Her perfectionist parents have planned a vow-renewal ceremony at Sierra's lush childhood home, but a neighborhood dog ruins the rehearsal dinner when he shows up toting what appears to be a fresh human bone. While dealing with the dog, a nosy neighbor, and an old flame turning up at the wrong times, Sierra hunts for answers. Her journey of discovery leads to more than just who committed the crime.

Pranced (Book 2.5, a Christmas novella)
Sierra Nakamura Davis thinks spending Christmas with her husband's relatives will be a real Yuletide treat. But when the animal-rights activist learns his family has a reindeer farm, she begins to feel more like the Grinch. Even worse, when Sierra arrives, she discovers the reindeer are missing. Sierra fears the animals might be suffering a worse fate than being used for entertainment purposes. Can Sierra set aside her dogmatic opinions to help get the reindeer home in time for the holidays?

Or will secrets tear the family apart and ruin Sierra's dream of the perfect Christmas?

Carolina Moon Series

Home Before Dark (Book 1)
Nothing good ever happens after dark. Country singer
Daleigh McDermott's father often repeated those words.
Now, her father is dead. As she's about to flee back to
Nashville, she finds his hidden journal with hints that
his death was no accident. Mechanic Ryan Shields is the
only one who seems to believe Daleigh. Her father
trusted the man, but her attraction to Ryan scares her.
She knows her life and career are back in Nashville and
her time in the sleepy North Carolina town is only
temporary. As Daleigh and Ryan work to unravel the
mystery, it becomes obvious that someone wants them
dead. They must rely on each other—and on God—if
they hope to make it home before the darkness
swallows them.

Gone By Dark (Book 2)
Charity White can't forget what happened ten years
earlier when she and her best friend, Andrea, cut
through the woods on their way home from school. A
man abducted Andrea, who hasn't been seen since.
Charity has tried to outrun the memories and guilt.
What if they hadn't taken that shortcut? Why wasn't
Charity kidnapped instead of Andrea? And why weren't
the police able to track down the bad guy? When
Charity receives a mysterious letter that promises
answers, she returns to North Carolina in search of
closure and the peace that has eluded her. With the help
of her new neighbor, Police Officer Joshua Haven,
Charity begins to track down mysterious clues. They
soon discover that they must work together or both of
them will be swallowed by the looming darkness.

Other Books by Christy Barritt:

Dubiosity

Savannah Harris vowed to leave behind her old life as an investigative reporter. But when two migrant workers go missing, her curiosity spikes. As more eerie incidents begin afflicting the area, each works to draw Savannah out of her seclusion and raise the stakes—for her and the surrounding community. Even as Savannah's new boarder, Clive Miller, makes her feel things she thought long forgotten, she suspects he's hiding something too, and he's not the only one. As secrets emerge and danger closes in, Savannah must choose between faith and uncertainty. One wrong decision might spell the end . . . not just for her but for everyone around her. Will she unravel the mystery in time, or will doubt get the best of her?

The Good Girl

Tara Lancaster can sing "Amazing Grace" in three harmonies, two languages, and interpret it for the hearing impaired. She can list the Bible canon backward, forward, and alphabetized. The only time she ever missed church was when she had pneumonia and her mom made her stay home. Then her life shatters and her reputation is left in ruins. She flees halfway across the country to dog-sit, but the quiet anonymity she needs isn't waiting at her sister's house. Instead, she finds a knife with a threatening message, a fame-hungry friend, a too-hunky neighbor, and evidence of . . . a ghost? Following all the rules has gotten her nowhere. And nothing she learned in Sunday school can tell her where to go from there.

Death of the Couch Potato's Wife (Suburban Sleuth Mysteries)

You haven't seen desperate until you've met Laura Berry, a career-oriented city slicker turned suburbanite housewife. Well-trained in the big-city commandment, "Mind your own business," Laura is persuaded by her spunky seventy-year-old neighbor, Babe, to check on another neighbor who hasn't been seen in days. She finds Candace Flynn, wife of the infamous "Couch King," dead, and at last has a reason to get up in the morning. Someone is determined to stop her from digging deeper into the death of her neighbor, but Laura is just as determined to figure out who is behind the death-by-poisoned-pork-rinds.

The Trouble with Perfect
Since the death of her fiancé two years ago, novelist Morgan Blake's life has been in a holding pattern. She has a major case of writer's block, and a book signing in the mountain town of Perfect sounds as perfect as its name. Her trip takes a wrong turn when she's involved in a hit-and-run: She hit a man, and he ran from the scene. Before fleeing, he mouthed the word "Help." First she must find him. In Perfect, she finds a small town that offers all she ever wanted. But is something sinister going on behind its cheery exterior? Was she invited as a guest of honor simply to do a book signing? Or was she lured to town for another purpose—a deadly purpose?

The Gabby St. Claire Diaries (a tween mystery series)

The Curtain Call Caper (Book 1)
Is a ghost haunting the Oceanside Middle School auditorium? What else could explain the disasters surrounding the play—everything from missing scripts to a falling spotlight and damaged props? Seventh-grader Gabby St. Claire has dreamed about being part of her school's musical, but a series of unfortunate events threatens to shut down the production. While trying to uncover the culprit and save her fifteen minutes of fame, she also has to manage impossible teachers, cliques, her dysfunctional family, and a secret she can't tell even her best friend. Will Gabby figure out who or what is sabotaging the show . . . or will it be curtains for her and the rest of the cast?

The Disappearing Dog Dilemma (Book 2)
Why are dogs disappearing around town? When two friends ask seventh-grader Gabby St. Claire for her help in finding their missing canines, Gabby decides to unleash her sleuthing skills to sniff out whoever is behind the act. But time management and relationships get tricky as worrisome weather, a part-time job, and a new crush interfere with Gabby's investigation. Will her determination crack the case? Or will shadowy villains, a penchant for overcommitting, and even her own heart put her in the doghouse?

The Bungled Bike Burglaries (Book 3)
Stolen bikes and a long-forgotten time capsule leave one amateur sleuth baffled and busy. Seventh-grader Gabby St. Claire is determined to bring a bike burglar to justice—and not just because mean girl Donabell Bullock is strong-arming her. But each new clue brings its own set of trouble. As if that's not enough, Gabby finds evidence of a decades-old murder within

the contents of the time capsule, but no one seems to take her seriously. As her investigation heats up, will Gabby's knack for being in the wrong place at the wrong time with the wrong people crack the case?

About the Author:

USA Today has called Christy Barritt's books "scary, funny, passionate, and quirky."
Christy writes both mystery and romantic suspense novels that are clean with underlying messages of faith. Her books have won the Daphne du Maurier Award for Excellence in Suspense and Mystery, have been twice nominated for the Romantic Times Reviewers' Choice Award, and have finaled for both a Carol Award and *Foreword Magazine*'s Book of the Year.

Christy is married to her Prince Charming, a man who thinks she's hilarious—but only when she's not trying to be. She is a self-proclaimed klutz, an avid music lover who's known for spontaneously bursting into song, and a road-trip aficionado.

When she's not working or spending time with her family, she enjoys singing, playing the guitar, and exploring small, unsuspecting towns where people have no idea how accident-prone she is.

Find Christy online at:
www.christybarritt.com
www.facebook.com/christybarritt
www.twitter.com/cbarritt

Sign up for Christy's newsletter to get information on all of her latest releases here: www.christybarritt.com/newsletter-sign-up/

If you enjoyed this book, please consider leaving a revlew.

26805230R00179